THE GENTLEMAN SPY

THE GENTLEMAN SPY

GEORGINA NORTH

PEPPERBERRY PRESS

Library of Congress Cataloging-in-Publication Data

Names: North, Georgina, author.
Title: The Gentleman Spy: A Novel / Georgina North.
Description: First U.S. edition | San Diego: Pepperberry Press, 2024.

Identifiers: LCCN 2024909975 (print)
ISBN 978-1-959794-06-6 (paperback)
ISBN 978-1-959794-07-3 (hardcover)
ISBN 978-1-959794-09-7 (ebook)

Cover design by Jennifer Therieau

For writers I return to time and again
Austen, Heyer, Li-Young Lee & Louise Glück

---

*B*eauden Calverleigh's gloved hand flexed on the reins. The gnawing creak of leather scraped against the soft sounds of the Kentish countryside: the distant rush of constant water, a cold wind with just enough power to rustle leaves loosened and fallen to the ground, the airy grunt of an impatient horse. Astride his mount, Beau took in the moody grey sky, the damp verdant knolls, the sprawling honeyed structure at their seam—the place that held duty, responsibility, and little else. He pulled in a long, solemn breath, tasting the faint smoky aroma of winter on his tongue.

The last long stretch of road leading to Oakmoss Manor was edged in by old, deeply rooted oaks, timeworn and gnarled, like the one in black ink that snaked up his forearm, spreading its long limbs around his bicep and shoulder. Beyond the oaks, a Palladian bridge yawned wide across the lake. At sunset on a clear day, the golden stone would catch fire, sending long, blinding rays shimmering across the water below. After the bridge, home—although it had never quite felt that way. Not as a child. Not once it became his to protect, or wreck, or ravage.

In the breast pocket of his overcoat sat two letters. The first was from the Home Office. His most recent mission should have been an easy one—a *tête-à-tête* with the mistress of a high-ranking diplomat posted in Antwerp who'd been suspected of copying and disseminating classified documents, forgery, and the murder of a foreign contact. History had proved time and again that men confided all sorts of things when tangled in bedclothes smelling of sweat and cheap perfume. Still, the exchange had nearly cost Beau his life.

The second letter, oppressive and unwieldy like a stone hung from his neck, announced his father's death and had come edged in black above four years ago already—the address penned in a hand he had not recognised.

Mr Calverleigh,

I am sorry to be the bearer of news which must give you pain, particularly when you are far from this country. Your father has passed on. May it provide you some little solace to know his spirit did not linger. Your mother and sister would benefit from your presence, and, as you are aware, you are now master of Oakmoss Manor. Mr Sims will no doubt write you as well.

God bless you,
Miss Doubleday

Beau had doubled over and put a hand to the wall of his room in Vienna to keep from crumbling entirely. When he'd been able to unfold himself, he'd swayed a little. His head had shaken back and forth of its own accord in a vain attempt to deny the truth of the words blurring on the paper clutched in his hand. Threaded between his shock and grief, confusion. He had been so caught out by the message, he'd overlooked the name of the sender. Even as he'd run a shaking thumb over her signature, he hadn't been able to conjure up more than a hazy vision of a slip of a girl with dark, wild hair—and certainly not a reason why she'd dispatched the news rather than his mother, steward, or solicitor.

There was a gulf between himself and his father's ward—in age, disposition, and experience. Rather, *his* ward, unfortunately, with his father dead and gone. His brow furrowed as he struggled to recall even a single exchange between himself and Miss Doubleday. He was ten years her senior, and if he thought of her at all, it was because that young lady had been the source of a great row between him and his father during one of their last rides. The late Lord Avon had been teaching Miss Doubleday how to manage a great estate, lending her books, discussing such matters as what to grow in the hothouse and which crops to turn over.

'Why should she be interested in these matters at all?' Beau had questioned. 'Men don't care about such things in a wife.'

'Foolish men don't. I won't see that girl married to a fool.' When Beau had made no reply, his father had added, 'She shows more interest than you do.'

Beau had scoffed. He'd spent every summer and school break between the ages of twelve and twenty at home, learning to run the grand pile that would one day be his.

'I've been a constant by your side, always have done what you've asked of me.'

'And very little else. You seem to feel your talents—if that's what you choose to call them—are better spent in town or at house parties or doing who knows what else.'

Beau forced himself to unclench his teeth as pain emanated from his jaw. It had been impossible to reveal his true self and equally unbearable to live with the burden of his father's disappointment.

As a child, he'd spent much of his time playing by himself —climbing trees, slipping in and out of rooms through long-forgotten passageways, listening to conversations never meant for his ears. So often he'd spent the hours after his lessons spying on the steward and imagining that man an informant for some nefarious foreign government. Beau could never have imagined how closely his life would imitate his childhood fancies.

The offer he'd received had been for more than just a job. It'd been a chance to establish an identity outside of being Lord Avon's son, an opportunity to do something for Crown and country beyond hosting house parties and siring children. His father had had the estate and his good health. Beau would have his work—something meaningful, something all his own.

Yet there he was; he could slip from one assumed identity to the next, but he'd never be able to outrun who he was in blood and bone.

Beau's horse dipped his head, no doubt frustrated with how long they'd been standing still while Beau glared down at the distant golden brick of Oakmoss. He urged Arion forward, moving towards his future as his history faded, catching on a gust of wind and carried off as if it were never a part of him to begin with.

As he entered the sweeping great court, a groom came to greet him and take his horse.

'M'lord!' exclaimed William, once he was close enough to recognise Beau.

'Not a word,' Beau said, handing over the reins before skipping up the dozen steps to the front door almost four times his own height. Inside, he was assailed by the rich, sweet scent of roses. All at once, he felt certain he could recall every time he'd come through that door. His mother always kept a large vase filled with several dozen stems on a table near the entry. When he looked over to his right, his gaze landed on blooms of vibrant pink, cultivated in Oakmoss's large hothouse.

His Hessians echoed on the black and white marble floor of the great hall as he came to its centre, where he paused to look up and up and up, some sixty feet to the ceiling. Above him, painted in gauzy whites and heavenly blues, the first Earl of Avon loomed large, surrounded by the Muses and receiving a laurel wreath. Along the walls were arches and columns done by master carvers, an ormolu clock that had ticked away the minutes of his secret missions as a child, and an inscription in Latin above each of the two archways set at the back of the hall, the words as familiar to him as his own name.

'Sir!'

It was the first and only time Beau had ever heard the butler gasp, and his own pensive expression was replaced by a closed-lip smile as he turned.

'How did you know it was me, Buddle?'

'The hair. The set of your shoulders. From the back you are equal parts your mother and your father,' he replied, a look of fondness or pain or remembrance clouding his features before he added, 'My lord,' with a slight bow.

My lord. The words rang in Beau's ears. How different they sounded, resonant and echoing in the yawning halls of this house.

'Might you tell me if my mother and sister are at home?'

'You will find the ladies in the blue drawing room, sir.'

'No one could ever accuse you of loose lips, Buddle, but if

5

you wouldn't mind keeping my presence to yourself, just for a time? I rather enjoyed giving you a start.' Beau moved towards the wide stairwell that split the grand entry hall in two but bent his steps to the right of it, pausing beneath the words *fortitudo, patientia, prosperitas*. Bravery, patience, success. 'Oh, and Buddle, Saunders is following with the luggage. Have him unpack my trunks in *my* room.'

'Understood, sir, and if I may add, welcome home.'

Beau nodded once in acknowledgement, but grimaced as he began the long walk down the quiet corridor.

The drawing room door was a little ajar, and a laugh like tinkling sleigh bells floated through the air, bringing him to a halt. His eyes closed and, for a moment, he imagined his mother and sister side by side, smiling over a letter, a shared memory, a humorous passage in a book. For the first time, he considered just how long he'd been away. In his mind, they were exactly how he'd left them, but standing there, he wondered if his mother's smooth skin had begun to wrinkle and how grown up Louisa must look.

When he pushed in, the conversation ground to an abrupt end as three sets of eyes turned his way, all widening in droll unity. There were concurrent cries of 'Brother!' and 'Beau!' and two of the three ladies rushed forward to claim his embrace. A young lady he didn't recognise remained seated, a book open in her hands. His mind worked to place her—a cousin, a friend, a neighbour?—but there was no memory, no woman he'd ever met, who compared with the one quiet on the settee.

Over his mother's head, and impervious to his sister's exclamations, he studied her. She was one of the loveliest creatures he'd ever seen. A tiny mole just above the right corner of her mouth drew all his attention to her bow-shaped lips, and he licked his own as an afterthought. Beau watched with interest as the surprise on the woman's face slipped into something much more like dismay.

Looking at her lap, she closed the book, balling a hand into a fist after she did so. Her shoulders had gone rigid, and he wondered at the tension tugging the edges of her pretty features. A quick scan of her person told him she was slender, tallish, and well off, but hadn't purchased her dress in London. Kid leather boots instead of slippers indicated she walked often, outside as well as in. And the book—he glimpsed the title as he set his mother and sister at arm's length from him —*The Mysteries of Udolpho*.

'Beau, come, sit. I just rang for tea and cakes. You can refresh yourself after accounting for your presence,' his mother instructed, taking his arm and leading him to an empty chair.

'You'll excuse me, ma'am,' the young lady said, rising from her seat and making for the door as she spoke. 'I've some pressing correspondence which can be put off no longer.' She looked to him then, her countenance frigid, her eyes sharp, insolent, so dark they devoured the light. Heat flooded his body. His lungs filled to bursting. Something inside him, intangible and transcendent, ignited like he'd swallowed a lightning bolt.

In calculated silence, she brushed past him with movements so elegant of dismissal he was as impressed as he was bewildered.

'Charming house guest,' he said to his mother as the thud of a door closing sounded around them. 'It's the first time my presence has offended a woman instead of pleasing her. Tell me, is her stay coming to an end?'

'Doubtful,' remarked the dowager, looking a little bewildered. 'But since she is your ward, I suppose the decision is yours.'

Beau sent the tide of desire that had rushed in back out to sea. As her guardian, he had the power to control every aspect of her life, from determining which books she read to selecting whom she married. Honour forbade him from abusing his position by using it to pursue her. He sighed and ignored the tightening in his chest—the sudden awareness of his own heartbeat as it thudded in his ears.

There was nothing more damnable about being home than discovering the woman he was most drawn to was the only one he couldn't have.

2

---

*E*merald felt the bones in her body loosen as soon as she closed the door between Beau and herself, but the breath she'd been holding wasn't expelled in one relieved exhale. It came out in short, uneven huffs as she tried to steady her panicked heartbeat. For years, that man had moved through Oakmoss like a ghost. Lady Avon would reference some joke he'd made. Lord Avon had so often sung his son's praises, Emerald felt as though she knew the tune by heart. Louisa shared memories of a doting older brother, one who would tease and spoil and take tea with her in the schoolroom whenever he was home. Even in her mind, he was only ever 'Beau', the son and brother who moved in and out of other people's lives but not her own. She would catch the sound of foreign boots on the marble as they faded around a corner or detect a movement—swift, dark, elusive—at the edge of her vision. Then he'd disappear completely.

When Beau had come striding into the drawing room, moving with the innate grace and certainty that came from being born to his position, it'd been as if Emerald were a girl in the schoolroom all over again.

She could remember exactly how hot and clammy her hands had felt, feverish almost, when she'd last seen him nearly five years ago. At the time, she'd said a silent prayer the book she'd been holding wouldn't slip from her grasp and had licked her suddenly dry lips as she'd waited for him to notice how grown up she'd become. When his crystalline blue eyes had eventually flicked her way, the look had been so quick, so cold, a chill had rolled down her stiff spine. Then he'd turned away, left the drawing room with his father, and she hadn't been sure he'd even seen her at all.

Emerald shook her head to clear away the memory as she gained the safety of her own rooms. She slumped against the heavy door at her back, feeling foolish for her reaction to his return. It was not as if she were desperate to have his smile turned upon her or wished for some sign that distance had softened his rough edges and hard feelings.

At her hairline, beads of sweat gathered. She raised her hand to wipe away the moisture, noticing as she did so that she was trembling. Emerald stared, detached, curious, almost as if her hands belonged to another person. Her skin prickled with gooseflesh, and Emerald worked to pull in more air as her vision narrowed at an alarming speed. Her role within Oakmoss Manor suddenly felt uncertain, her future skidding along a wave, waiting for it to break.

There were several months after the passing of the previous Lord Avon during which the dowager couldn't bring herself to leave her bed, and with Beau far from home, the natural hierarchy of the house had fallen apart. In the end, it was Emerald to whom the staff had turned: the steward with a question about an irrigation technique Lord Avon had wished to implement; the housekeeper with an appeal to increase a charitable donation; even the butler, reluctant at first, with requests to replace a footman or order more wine.

With Beau home, she no longer had utility, a purpose, something to tether her to the estate.

Dropping to the floor, she tucked her head between her knees, trying to focus on her breathing. When a knock on the door startled her a few minutes later, Emerald could at least rise and answer with an imitation of composure.

Louisa's fair, knowing face peered through the wide crack. 'You would *never* tend to correspondence or do anything which might whisk you from a room when sweets are present.'

Emerald tipped her head in acknowledgement and opened the door further so the girl she'd long thought of as a sister could enter.

'You looked peaked,' Louisa said, smoothing the back of her dress before taking a seat in one of the two chairs uphol-stered in plush cream velvet and set a comfortable distance from the low fire burning in the grate. 'His arrival is a shock to us all. After you left, Mama asked why he didn't write.'

'And?' Emerald barked the word and immediately chas-tised herself. Lou was not the cause or target of the ire stirring inside her.

Louisa pinched her lips before responding, a tell-tale sign she was displeased. 'He changed the subject.'

'Of course he did.' Beauden Calverleigh thought of one person and one person only. Not that Emerald would have said so aloud, not to his sister anyhow. Instead she settled on an ambiguous 'Hmm' and sunk into the other chair.

'You need not be closed with me, Em.'

'He's a veritable stranger to me, but he's your brother.' A stranger whose beautiful face had haunted her dreams before

11

she even understood what attraction was. All those years ago, the only thing she'd known with any certainty was that his face would echo in her mind for as long as she lived.

'Yes,' the younger girl replied, reaching across the space to Emerald and giving her hand a reassuring squeeze. 'But I also consider you as much of a sister as I'll ever have.'

'What about when he marries?' teased Emerald. 'His future wife may wish to have some say in your sentiments.'

'She'll be some diamond—a superlative beauty with connections and a dowry to make one's eyes water, no doubt— but who could ever usurp you in our shared experience if not also in affection?'

A little laugh escaped Emerald's lips, even as her eyes fell to her hands, her fingers fiddling with one another in her lap. An odd sadness settled in the pit of her stomach. She didn't wish to think about the upsetting things they'd been through together or about the woman Beau would one day marry. Emerald crossed her arms, running a hand up and down the soft velvet sleeve of her dress although she wasn't cold.

'I wish I were surprised by his lack of consideration, but I am not and cannot pretend to be.'

'No,' Louisa said after a thoughtful pause. 'Nor am I. I'm sure Mama isn't either.'

'Nevertheless, you must be pleased to have him home.'

Louisa shrugged. 'We've got on all right without him. I quite like our little life. I wasn't sure I'd ever feel that way again after Papa.'

'Yes, well, I daresay much will remain unchanged,' Emerald lied through a small smile of commiseration.

Louisa cocked her head a little to one side and lifted her brows.

'What?' asked Emerald. 'Why do you give me such a look?'

'Because you don't believe that and cannot convince me to either.'

Staring across at the younger girl, Emerald considered her next words carefully. Unlike Louisa, Emerald had not been born to this life, nor had she chosen it through marriage like the dowager. Coming to Oakmoss hadn't been Emerald's decision; neither had running the estate. After Beau failed to return following his father's death, and weeks had turned to months, and months to years, Emerald had begun to feel as if her role as caretaker of the estate was immutable. She'd let go of the grand visions she'd built up of an exhilarating London season, beautiful gowns, dance after dance with charming partners. The one dream she'd kept closest to her heart—finding a husband and having a family of her own—had seemed to slip further and further from her grasp. She'd let it all go without comment, without protest, and it had always been for nothing. Oakmoss wasn't hers and could never be, but as long as Beau had remained away, she'd been able to focus on the work and not on the truth.

'You are right, of course. Change is inevitable. Your brother was bound to take up the reins here at some time or other.'

'Only we all went on as if he'd never do such a thing, and now—'

'And now…' repeated Emerald on a gusty exhale.

Together, they were quiet for a long moment.

'Oh, is that the time? Goodness. I'm late for a lesson with the music master.' Louisa flung herself from her chair and out of the room without another word, leaving Emerald in an oppressive silence that threatened to crowd all the air from her lungs and make it impossible to fill them back up.

It was true Emerald didn't have any correspondence so demanding it necessitated her fleeing Beau's presence, but there was one letter on her writing desk she'd been avoiding which did indeed require a reply.

After staring at the closed door a moment or two, she walked over to the solid mahogany writing table. Her fingers glided over several lines of the diamond box pattern in the polished wood veneer with a kind of careful reverence. With its crossbanding around the edges and brass oak leaves inlaid in each corner, it was one of the most beautiful pieces of furniture Emerald had ever seen. It had been a gift from Lord and Lady Avon not long after she arrived. A private place to write her family or collect her thoughts.

Emerald took a seat and picked up the letter from her stepmother. She sighed, or perhaps it was simply the air releasing around her skirts when she sat. She couldn't tell.

The letter was very much the same as all the others she received. Rose, the elder of her two half-sisters, excelled on the pianoforte, while Agatha showed an interest in watercolours. Mrs Doubleday went to Mrs Jenkinson's for tea, Mrs Cotterel's for a card party, and she had received a visit from Mrs Standage. Emerald reread the few lines discussing her sisters' accomplishments, rubbing away the soreness in her heart that came on every time she thought of them.

The date at the top of the page may change, but the content of the letters never varied. There was never an invite to visit or inquiries into Emerald's interests and her life at Oakmoss. Mrs Doubleday was unaware Emerald had thrown herself into music after her father died and by now had the entirety of Haydn's, Beethoven's, and Pleyel's catalogues committed to memory and was well on her way to knowing several others by heart. Nor did the woman have any idea Emerald veritably managed Oakmoss, that she'd developed insomnia after the death of her father, or that she hadn't had her favourite white cake with strawberry rhubarb compote for her birthday since before she left her childhood home.

The letters had always been impersonal and infrequent. In the beginning, Emerald had hoped, if not for a wish that she might return, perhaps for words full of a mother's concern: Was Emerald eating well? Keeping up with her French and Italian lessons? Making herself useful to the family? But no, her stepmother wrote without any real interest—all obligation. Still, Emerald always replied.

She smoothed out the folded page before her—it had been sitting for more than a sennight already—scanned it once more, and opened one of the frieze drawers, withdrawing a fresh sheet of elegant, hot-pressed notepaper. If Beau's arrival was good for anything, it was forcing her to finally pen a reply.

When her own missive was finished, signed, and sealed, rather than retreat to the study to review the ledgers or to the music room to practise, she climbed upon her bed. She didn't sleep, or even close her eyes. She lay there, ankles crossed, hands folded right where her ribs began to sew together, her eyes open, and her mind focused on everything and nothing all at once.

---

3

*B*eau woke early, as was his habit. His limbs were loose and heavy, given over to the comfort of a place long-familiar after only one night. Dawn had just begun to break, and he dragged the thick brocade curtains apart, letting in what little light there was as the sun slowly rolled over from the other side of the world. Beyond his window, the dirt paths wending through the Italian garden were sodden from overnight rain.

He took up the book of poetry from the desk near the window and flipped until the little hollow in the middle was exposed. There were hidden compartments in most of his clothing and many of his belongings—the soles of his shoes, the brim and crown of his hat, his snuff box, and other sundry items, including books, his walking stick, and his pocket watch.

From the empty space between the pages, he plucked the letter from the Home Office and reread it.

In light of the incident which took place at the Viennese ball hosted by the Archduke Rainer and the subsequent injuries to your person resulting from human error—Beau winced at the words; he still had no idea where the ladybird had hidden the knife or how she'd so quickly been able to access it—*the office requests your immediate return to England with the strong recommendation to remain at your ancestral estate for the duration of your recovery, where invigorating fresh air and quiet may aid in the restoration of your health. In due course, you may be permitted to return to work. A letter will follow with additional details. Do nothing which may otherwise jeopardise your hardiness until further advised.*

The word *nothing* was underlined twice. Between the lines he was being punished for bungling the mission. Antwerp was a rare, unwelcome blemish on his pristine record. He would have died had Saunders not followed him from the ballroom to the parlour. Perhaps such a fate would have been the better alternative to being reprimanded by his esteemed commandant, Lord Duffy, and sent to the place he'd actively avoided for years.

Beau refolded the letter and placed it back inside the book. Once a fire was lit in his grate, he would burn it. After ringing for his valet, he sat patiently while Saunders executed a perfect close shave, then descended to the breakfast room several minutes before ten. Within, he found his mother and his ward, the latter dressed in a rich green woollen riding habit and filling a plate with generous portions of ham, eggs, toast, and plum jam.

'Have you tried a Mirabelle plum, Miss Doubleday?' he asked, coming to a stop at her side before reaching for the bacon. 'They feature a more delicate sweetness and contain no pit.' Then, more to himself than the other occupants of the room, he added, 'I'll talk to Walker about growing a few trees in the hothouse. Pineapple too.'

'Walker is no longer with us,' chimed his mother from her seat at the table.

Beau whipped his head around. The dowager's focus remained on the bread she was buttering. He was on the verge of demanding to know why no one had informed him the head gardener had expired, when a low, silvery voice said, 'Pensioned off, is what your mama means.'

'Yes,' the dowager confirmed, cutting the air around her with a casual wave of her small knife. 'That.'

Beau ignored his mother and turned towards his ward. Her black eyes caught him in their unfathomable depths and his thought broke in two. She blinked, and he recovered himself. 'Walker cannot be more than five-and-fifty.'

The young lady lifted her chin, and her mouth pursed with impatience before she answered, 'Fifty-seven, and with the arthritic hands of a man decades older.'

The plate each was holding forced them apart. At the edge of awareness, Beau heard the shrill whine of bone china biting bone china as he leaned into their discussion. 'Who replaced him? How long past? No one thought to seek out my opinion or at least inform me of such a change within my household?'

Miss Doubleday's features tightened just enough for his keen eye to discern the change. He'd been observing and reading people for so long; it was a skill turned habit turned instinct.

When it became clear neither his mother nor his ward would respond to his questions, he stepped back and moved towards the table. 'Allow me,' he said, pulling out a chair for Miss Doubleday.

'Oh, you mistake my intentions,' said she, backing towards the doorway. 'I'm already returned and wouldn't dream of leaving dirt on the chairs.'

There was not a speck of mud or grime to be seen on her riding habit, and he wondered how she managed to look so pristine after a damp morning ride. When she left, he watched her go, pretending not to notice how the thick fabric swayed about her hips.

'You need not have come down on my account,' said Beau to his mother, although his attention was still on the empty doorway.

'I didn't. I stopped taking a tray in my room several months after your father passed.'

He said nothing but moved to take the seat at her right.

'Your correct place is there now,' replied his mother, with a nod to where his father used to sit at the head of the table.

'Yes, but so much further from you. Have we not enjoyed enough distance between us?' Distance he'd created by choosing work over duty, work his mother knew nothing about.

The dowager flicked her eyes in his direction before setting down her toast and picking up *The Morning Post*.

'Is Louisa still abed?'

'No. She rode out with Emerald. I suspect half of what was on her plate will get eaten by your sister. Very likely Louisa has already changed for some lesson or other.'

Beau looked at the small silver clock on the mantel across the room. 'Rather early for a ride, is it not? I don't recall Lou having any partiality for the morning hours.'

'It took some encouragement from Emerald, but I daresay Louisa has learned to enjoy being up with the sun. She's certainly benefited from both the exercise and the education.'

Beau paused mid-chew before swallowing the bite of eggs in his mouth. 'Education?'

The dowager tipped the top half of the paper down,

looking directly at Beau as she spoke. 'This morning I believe they were inspecting some work being done on a new bridge to replace the rickety old one washed away after the last big storm.'

A muscle twitched in his jaw. 'If the steward is no longer able to do his job, perhaps he ought to be replaced with a man more competent and capable.'

His mother snapped the paper back up, saying from behind her printed wall, 'I wouldn't wonder that Mr Sims went with them, as is typical.'

'This is a regular occurrence then?'

Behind the fine black print he could hear his mother sniff, take a sip of tea, and replace the cup on its saucer.

'Louisa is sixteen, and Miss Doubleday—'

'Your sister is seventeen, and there's no need for you to finish your thought.'

Beau set his fork to the side of his plate. 'There's no need for *me*, is what you really mean.'

'Beauden.' The paper came down once more, his mother's countenance displaying not a trace of emotion. 'What would you have me say?'

'I would be pleased to have an honest conversation.' So much of his work was half-truths, secrets, disguise.

'You do not get to turn up without warning, years late and spent doing who knows what—certainly nothing I care to imagine—and disrupt my breakfast with your demands for a conversation I've no interest in having with my tea and toast. You may take yourself off somewhere conducive to sorting out the ills that plague you and leave me in peace.'

A hard pang of frustration grabbed at Beau's jaw as he stared at the paper dividing the space between him and his mother. His mouth opened, but no retort was forthcoming.

Instead, he pushed back from the table, turned on his heel, and left the breakfast parlour behind him in three long strides. He intended to return to his room, but with a hand on the smooth mahogany stair rail, he changed course, stopping a footman he passed on the way to his study and requesting a fresh pot of coffee be brought round before slipping into the dim room.

It was an odd sensation, closing the door behind him but not seeing his father awaiting his arrival in the tufted chair behind the grand desk dominating the space in front of two tall windows.

The room remained just as Beau remembered—all cherry-wood and rich worn leather that groaned when sat in. He drew in a slow, deep inhale. The scent of tobacco and berg-amot he associated with his father had faded to nearly nothing. In its place was something sweet but citrusy. On the wall across from the desk hung the painting of his grandfather. As a youth, it had been nothing more than another silly portrait of an old man with his horse and dogs. As the master of Oakmoss, he wondered how his father had been able to work with his own looking down on him.

The shelves were crammed full of books, much as they always had been. He brushed his fingers over their spines, their varied titles proof of the breadth of knowledge his father had possessed in economics, poetry, and history. There were back issues of the *Annals of Agriculture*, and some titles unfamiliar to him—books on herbal remedies, kitchen gardens, cultivating different types of apples.

He turned away from the long wall. Facing the desk were the same two chairs that had been a staple of the room since Beau was a child. The left was more worn than the right from all the time Beau had spent ensconced there.

Sitting in that chair, Beau had laid out his life for his father to understand—what kind of work he did, the pleasure he derived from it, the feeling of satisfaction from having found something to call his own. The row following Beau's revelation had been terrific. What he saw as opportunity, his father had seen as negligence and dereliction of duty to the family name. If something happened to Beau, the Calverleigh family line would end. The interminable and at times onerous efforts of nine generations would be for naught. The estate would go to a second cousin, and his mother's life as well as his sister's would be upended.

'It's been years,' Beau had defended himself, 'and nothing has happened to me, as you can see for yourself.' So long as he'd kept the scars on his body covered.

'Yet. Nothing has happened to you *yet*. It's only a matter of time. All it takes is one person, one mistake, one ill-judged choice…' His father's voice had tremored with bridled emotion, but Beau's anger had been too strong then for him to question why. He'd accused his father of being selfish—and worse, jealous—because Beau was bold enough to find meaning in life beyond what had been foisted upon him while his father had been anchored to Oakmoss, forced to accept a legacy not of his choosing.

Standing behind the chair, Beau rested his hands on its high back and pushed the ugly memory from his mind. The leather creaked under the pressure of his fingers as they squeezed. With a determined nod, he made his way to the desk.

On its corner, the odd little figurine that Beau had loved as a boy—a snail with a shell made of silver and pearl and a small rider perched on its back holding a bow and arrow. He picked it up to feel the weight of it in his hand, the cold of the silver against his bare skin, and noticed for the first time the papers in front of him organised into neat little stacks. Setting the sculpture down, he picked up the top sheet—a receipt of sale for cow's milk. Next to it was a list of purchases to be reviewed, and atop that, a note to inspect the linens. He picked up the paper and stroked his thumb along Miss Doubleday's decisive, elegant handwriting. It would be impossible to forget her script when he had reread the letter announcing his father's death so many times it was thinning at the creases. On a sigh, he released the page, watching it nest among the others as the implications of her presence in the room settled over him.

4

'*A*m I interrupting?'

The words said with cutting self-possession caused poor Mr Sims to pale till he was as white as the lace trimming Emerald's dress. She looked over the steward's shoulder to the owner of the voice. She knew Beau had been in the room the day prior, riffling through her carefully organized papers, and was displeased but unsurprised to find him leaning against the doorframe, arms crossed, his face the perfect mask of haughty indifference. She had always thought his eyes were cold, two beautiful cubes of ice with the same chilling effect, and as they raked her down, she fought against the inevitable shiver.

'Not at all. In fact, we just concluded our business. Thank you, Mr Sims. You may go.'

The man rose to leave but was not quick enough to make his escape.

'Stay.' Beau stepped into the room, pinning the steward between them. 'Beg pardon, Miss Doubleday. It sounded to my aged ears like you said *our* business, but I feel certain you meant *my* business.'

A quick, low groan escaped Mr Sims, who looked as if he were doing his best to melt into the floor.

Emerald's eyelids fluttered, betraying her surprise and indignation. The man had been home mere days. If he wished for a hostile takeover, hostile she could be.

'Business is synonymous with responsibility, is it not? Perhaps you can clarify—are you referring to the business that kept you from home for so many years, or the responsibilities here at Oakmoss from which you abdicated to the extent your name, title, and sex allowed?'

Mr Sims blotted his forehead with a handkerchief and uttered a distressed 'Oh, my,' but Emerald kept her eyes on Beau, watching his hard face for any indication he was humbled by her set-down. To her frustration she noticed nothing, not even the tick of a jaw muscle. Then, the unthinkable: He smiled, lopsided, wry, wolfish.

'How kind of you to give me credit for the work I've accomplished abroad.'

'Is that what you call it on the continent? Forgive my ignorance. Here in England I've only ever heard it referred to as gambling, partying, whoring.'

Mr Sims choked on a harsh cough and dropped back into one of the chairs. Both Emerald and Beau glanced at his red face, but neither was willing to call a truce.

'I'd prefer you moderate your language to that which is more fitting for a young woman of genteel birth. You are not a slattern in a pub,' said Beau, seating himself in the open chair next to the steward.

'I'd prefer we not have this conversation at all. The words I choose to employ ought not even factor into your concerns.'

Beau brought his hands up in front of his chest and steepled his fingers. 'You, Miss Doubleday, are one of my foremost concerns. Young ladies of your age and station should not be doing estate work.'

She rose from her seat and took several steps, finally coming out from around the desk dividing them. Beau dropped his hands and pushed up from the chair, taking one step to her three and stopping when he stood with his boot tip kissing her own.

His sudden nearness forced Emerald to tilt her head up to meet his stare. A faint scar sliced through the corner of his left brow. She spared a moment to wonder how it came to be there before saying, '*Have no right* is what you mean to say, is it not?'

A muscle in his jaw flexed, and she refrained from smiling in perverse satisfaction.

'I say what I mean, Miss Doubleday. You are my concern.' His countenance was serious and he spoke with quiet emphasis, letting the words come to rest in the tension stretching between them. 'You ought to be going for rides in a little phaeton, organising picnics, attending assemblies, considering your future.'

'An impossible task when one must spend her days surveying storm damage, settling tenant disputes, delivering charity baskets, paying calls, balancing the ledgers, discussing sick cattle—the list does run on.'

'These responsibilities, as you pointed out, are mine, and I am happy to relieve you of them.'

'You plan to remain then? The country has never kept you for long. There is not much in the way of…' She paused, put her finger to her chin as she pretended to think, and finally added, '…*entertainments* here.'

'Good girl.'

Mr Sims sucked in a loud breath through his teeth. Emerald's skin caught fire, fury burning her from the inside out. And Beau grinned, a small, derisive, devastating thing. All at once, he was too close, too tall, too beautiful. In the folds of her skirt, she clenched her hands into fists, the edges of her nails biting into the tender flesh of her palms.

'Is it my running the estate that sets your back up, or my doing it so well?'

Beau studied her, his head cocked, his face unreadable. Emerald forced her muscles to remain still under the heavy weight of his gaze. His eyes dropped to her lips. The insolent man had the nerve to let his attention linger. She imagined him studying the shape of her mouth, wondering if she'd ever been kissed, and heat spread its unseemly fingers over her chest.

Finally, he spoke. 'How long have you resented me?'

'How long have I lived here?'

'What a wit you've become.'

Mr Sims made to rise once more. 'I really ought to—'

'Sit,' they said in unison, neither relinquishing the stare of the other.

She shifted her weight from one foot to another. 'I don't resent you. I detest you: your apathy, your total want of duty, your complete disregard for what you owe your name, your lack of respect for those who depend on you, your decision to avoid your responsibilities at the expense of others. Most of all, your ability to do so.'

They stood across from each other in charged silence. Emerald's chest was heaving. Beau removed his snuff box from a pocket and took a pinch. The enigmatic look he gave her made her stomach clench hard, forcing a soft puff of breath from between her parted lips.

He leaned forward, a hand on the desk at either side of her

—his face, his lips, so close to her own. 'Were you afforded some measure of relief, Miss Doubleday, in venting your spleen?'

Against her will, she flushed. The display was beneath her. Her outburst was hoydenish and poorly done at best, cruel at worst. For almost nine years she had lived in this house—*his* house—and he'd never before taken notice of her. His audacity to do so now, and in such a way, infuriated her. 'The only thing which could provide me any relief is your absence.'

'I'm afraid you're stuck with me, dear girl, either until I die or you marry. Shall I throw myself from my mount?'

Emerald's dark eyes formed two narrow slits. 'I begin to understand the appeal of a biddable husband.'

He raised an eyebrow as he withdrew a little, and she felt the immediate rush of cool air filling the space where his body had been.

'Biddable? An unusual choice for a young lady. Have we done with handsome, rich, titled? By the by, should you find one matching your singular criteria, you may send him along at your leisure.'

'To whom am I sending him? Your mother would not deny my happiness, and I am not *so* far from my majority. I'll be one-and-twenty in little more than three months.'

'I had not meant to suggest otherwise.' Beau was the picture of equanimity, but Emerald couldn't shake the sudden foreboding looming over her. 'But she cannot approve of your marriage as she is not your guardian. I am.'

5

'*Y*ou never had Father's will read.'

Beau had trailed Emerald out of the study when she'd brushed past him, mouth agape, eyes wild, but he hadn't followed her as she'd stormed down the corridor. He'd turned up the stairs and sought out his mother in her private sitting room, where she was poring over a pile of correspondence. The dowager glanced up, her expression bemused.

'Of what are you speaking, Beauden?'

'Father's will. Did Anders read it to you?' he asked, referencing the family's long-time solicitor.

The dowager would never do something so unladylike as shrug, but the slight lift of her delicate shoulder came close. 'There hardly seemed a reason to do so.'

'I'm shocked he didn't force the issue. He certainly should have.'

'Oh, let poor Mr Anders be. He tried,' replied his mother in sulky tones. 'You know how men are. They come all undone at the seams when faced with a lady's tears.'

Beau levelled a stern stare at his mother. 'However true that may be, I suspect there is an exception when dealing with one's mama.' A peevish expression flitted across her face, which he ignored. 'Miss Doubleday appeared to have no notion of my guardianship over her.'

'Well, to whom else would such a responsibility fall?'

'You cannot expect young ladies who have never been out in the world to have a mind for such things. I suspect Miss Doubleday had greater concerns.' Because of his protracted absence, but his mother was not guiltless in allowing his ward to take on so much of the estate management and so wisely said nothing to condemn him or herself.

'She'll be of age soon enough. Who bears that title on paper can hardly matter. It hasn't for years.'

'It seems to matter a great deal to her. While I have sole guardianship of Miss Doubleday, you share that responsibility with me where Lou is concerned, of course. Although I have charge of her property and funds, as well as Miss Doubleday's small dowry, and it is my approval each will require for marriage.'

His mother pretended to examine her finely manicured nails. 'You say that as if you care who Miss Doubleday selects as a husband.'

'I do, insofar as he's not a rake, scoundrel, gambler, drunk, bumpkin, blackguard, flat, fop, blood, buck, Corinthian, rattlepate, hellhound, or wastrel of any other sort. Father desired a good match for her. I will do my part to uphold his wishes.'

A derogatory little murmur was as close to a rebuke as his mother was capable of. 'You are several of those yourself, are you not?'

With a smile neither open nor encouraging, Beau replied,

'My attention is all yours, if you care to enlighten me.' He stared at his mother for another full minute. 'No?'

With a graceful lift of her chin, the dowager stared down her nose. 'It was my intention to invite you to attend the assembly in Ramsgate this evening with me and Emerald, although I won't if you're going to be uncivil.'

He glanced at his watch fob. 'It's half past three. When were you to share your plans?'

'When the opportunity presented itself, and here we are.'

Beau was standing just inside the open doorway and heard Miss Doubleday's forceful exhale before he caught sight of her pale blue morning dress. The garment had come under his notice earlier in the study, the way it flattered her figure, the colour like the sky on a winter's morning.

'Miss Doubleday.'

'No.'

'No?'

'No,' she repeated once more with finality. 'There is some mistake, a misunderstanding.'

'Your father left nothing to chance when planning your care until you came of age. When he passed on, my father became your guardian. When my father departed this earth, _I_ became your guardian. I grant you, your father very likely never imagined the latter as a real possibility.'

'You haven't even been here,' she cried.

'All the same. Had you never wondered whose responsibility you became when my father died? It's an assumed thing, you know, for guardianship to pass from father to son in cases such as these.'

Her mouth opened and closed as if she were forming words but had decided to eat them rather than speak them. 'You haven't even been here,' she repeated in a whisper. He could see her working through the implications and attempting to suppress her irritation. 'There is no recourse.' It was a question but came out more like a statement.

'You could petition the courts and more likely than not bring them round to the idea of my mother as your guardian. However, as you are neither titled nor richer than Croesus, it would be some time before they heard your case, and by then your majority would be a thing many months past. Take heart, Miss Doubleday. Your birthday is not so very far off. You said so yourself.'

'Any length of time is an eternity when one cannot do what one pleases.'

'You have done me an unfair turn if you believe I have any intention of interfering with those things which bring you pleasure.'

Her eyes were as dark as a moonless night, but a faint blush swept across the apples of her high cheekbones. He watched with rapt attention, warmth spreading in his core. She nodded, said not another word, and retreated down the corridor and out of view.

BEAU DIDN'T SEE his ward again until he handed her into the carriage bound for the Ramsgate assembly rooms. In the dark, her face was inscrutable, and although she carried on easy conversation with his mother during the ride, she said almost nothing to him. When they alighted in front of the Albion Hotel, he offered one arm to his mother and the other to Miss Doubleday, who cast a sidelong glance at him before placing her hand on his bicep in such a delicate way he wasn't certain whether she was touching him at all or merely hovering her hand where it ought to rest.

As he helped her remove her cloak in the antechamber, he inquired whether she would permit him to lead her out for the first.

'That pleasure is already afforded to Mr Lyon.'

'Charles Lyon?'

'He's the one, yes. You know him a little. Or perhaps, as my guardian, you will forbid me from dancing with any partner not personally selected by yourself.'

Her face wore a wide-open, innocent expression. He was not deceived and did not think she expected him to be so. The Lyon family lived in the North, but Charles Lyon and his sister, Miss Esther Lyon, spent a considerable amount of time with an aunt who lived less than ten miles from Oakmoss. Given the young man was closer to Miss Doubleday's age than Beau's own, he had very few memories to draw upon when Lyon was mentioned and only remembered him as a slightly awkward youth with troublesome skin and a weak jaw.

'I already promised not to suspend any pleasure of yours. To that end, is he still a gangly thing at war with his body for control of his limbs?'

Miss Doubleday nodded towards the open doors of the ballroom. 'He comes this way now. You may judge for yourself.'

Beau turned, and although he knew his features remained neutral, he bit his tongue in dismay. Awkward Charles Lyon needed no padding to fill out the shoulders of his coat and had surpassed Beau in height. A handsome young man was nothing to Beau. A handsome young man upon whom his ward bestowed her most winning smile was an altogether different matter. He pulled his quizzing glass to inspect Mr Lyon, savouring the young man's quick flinch and fluster as he did so, before inclining his head and greeting him as Beau knew he must.

'Welcome home, Lord Avon. Your return must be an endless source of joy to your family.'

Lyon was sincere in his sentiments, but Beau struggled against a natural urge to dislike him.

'The musicians have finished tuning their instruments. You are here to lead my ward out for the first, are you not? Do you always plan your dances so well in advance?'

'Only when Miss Doubleday is concerned. She is the most elegant dancer in all of Kent and well beyond, if I may be permitted to say, as you will see for yourself.'

Beau watched the pair join three others for the opening cotillion. Mr Lyon wasn't wrong. Miss Doubleday's steps were light, her movements graceful. Her face soon pinked with exertion, and she radiated unaffected delight that drew him to the edge of the dance floor. To give his attention to anything other than his ward would have been impossible. The King himself could walk in and Beau's eyes would remain steadfast on her person, transfixed by her bright, happy smile, the warmth and amusement shining through her dark eyes, the way Mr Lyon clasped her hand, and the roiling knot of jealousy surging hard and sudden through him.

He had been powerless to ignore the jolt of attraction he'd felt when he first saw her—the fleeting moment of cosmic magic which put in front of him a face so striking he could never have imagined and now could never replace. But an urge to flick the four-inch blade out from his black patent opera shoe and retrieve his ward from the side of Mr Lyon at any cost necessary was annoying, inconvenient, and not something on which he cared to linger.

Beau stood motionless, hands clasped behind his back, and ignored the feeble, hesitant, and ridiculous attempts of those trying to capture his attention until his mother came to his side and said, 'Really, Beauden, I ought to have left you home. Who do you think you are? That Mr Darcy fellow?'

'My ward is dancing. It's my responsibility to ensure her partner does not attempt anything untoward.' At the odd choking sound his mother made, he turned to look at her. 'Did you just scoff at me?'

'It wouldn't matter a jot to you if I did.'

In a steady, even tone, Beau replied, 'You think me incapable of doing what is right.'

'Yes, that's what I was thinking,' said his mother in a tone suggesting otherwise. 'I see Mrs Skeffington.' With those words, she flitted away, leaving Beau to count down the minutes left in the set.

No sooner had Mr Lyon led Miss Doubleday back to Beau than the small group was swarmed with other gentlemen begging the pleasure of her hand for a dance—any dance.

'The young lady has honoured me with her second. You will excuse us,' Beau stated with icy hauteur as he folded her hand into his own and ignored her look of burning reproach.

'How dare you?' she gritted through a smile as he turned them back to the dance floor. Her fingers were long, delicate, strong, and she crushed his own to illustrate her displeasure.

'As your guardian, I dare as much as I choose.' Inside his gloves, his palm burned where it pressed against hers, and he could detect a faint pulse as it beat a fast, agitated rhythm. 'You may add that to my list of crimes if it pleases you.'

'I've no room left on your sheet.'

They took their places across from one another and waited as other couples completed the set.

'I see why young Lyon was so eager to secure your first.'

The music began. When they slipped past each other to turn with the other couple, wisps of her sweet, fresh scent filled his chest on a breath.

Miss Doubleday glided to his side. She had just enough time to raise a brow in amused contempt and say, 'Ah, so that's what this is about,' before the steps parted them once more.

'Indeed.' Beau was captivated by the exquisite way she wielded her scorn. When she chasséd back to him, he held her hand in his, more firmly than any dance required.

'Had you only been home to make your own request sooner.' She held a stiff smile, turning to face him for a promenade, and kept her body as far apart from his as the steps and his hungry grasp would allow.

'If you wished for my presence at Oakmoss, you only had to say so,' said Beau when they were once more side by side as the couples around them took their turn. Even in the crowded room, he could hear her sharp inhale.

'Beg your pardon? You're suggesting I should have *asked* you home?' she hissed between clenched teeth and upturned lips. 'You needed to be reminded of the responsibilities you continued to shirk with your extended absence? No, you knew what needed to be done and didn't wish to do it. I suffer under no misapprehension that anything I could have written would have made a difference to the date you deigned to walk through the doors of Oakmoss once more. You could have returned home at any time and *chose* not to.'

His icy eyes landed on an unknown young lady across from him whose face wore an open, curious expression. When she discovered herself caught in his gaze, she went red as a ripe cherry and shifted her own to one of the dancers moving between them. Miss Doubleday was right, of course, and he was torn between admiration of her forthcoming speech and irritation with her indictment of his character.

'You know nothing of me nor of my *extended* absence. Although had I any notion my ward was so popular, perhaps I would have returned sooner to oversee your education and better audit the company you keep.'

She turned her head to fully look at him, and the fire in her eyes set him ablaze. 'Your concern with my dance partners fascinates me.'

Beau swallowed the growl rising in his throat. 'You've impressed upon me the full effect of my absence, Miss Doubleday. Until you come of age, you have the singular distinction of being the object of my solicitude. May you find the honour both pleasurable and gratifying.'

He watched gooseflesh prickle the skin of her long, graceful neck despite the heat of the room. At his side, his fingers twitched with wanting. The dance ended, and her chest heaved with a full breath, as if startled back to life. With defiant focus on everything around her but him, she applauded the musicians before turning away and melting into the crowd under his acute, inscrutable stare.

6

The morning after the assembly, Beau spent the first hour of the day pacing the length of his room, wondering what had possessed him to declare himself Miss Doubleday's shadow and knowing himself to be in foreign territory where she was concerned.

At one-and-thirty and having lived several lives already, Beau was a man in possession of himself. She would not be his undoing. No matter how many men clamoured for her attention. No matter how he yearned to feel the soft skin beneath her glove. No matter the authority and elegance she had exuded standing behind his desk.

He had lingered in the doorway of the study longer than she'd realised with her head bowed over the ledger and a scatter of papers. Her intelligence, and her unwillingness to hide it, was as surprising as it was attractive. Anyone of middling intellect could be taught the fundamental elements of running an estate and keep it afloat with a bit of application. But Miss Doubleday was sharp. Since returning, he'd begun an exhaustive review of the estate's books, including her observations on changes she'd implemented and her ideas for future projects, some nascent, some more fully formed with diagrams and data. If he hadn't already established a firm opinion on her acuity, the careful praise doled out by both Mr Sims and the housekeeper, Mrs Marshall, would have done away with any indecision.

She was no threat to him where Oakmoss was concerned. He had absolute power over the estate. For more than a decade, he'd also believed himself to have absolute power over his feelings. Every moment he'd spent in her company forewarned him to set a strong guard over his emotions, so rather than seek out her company as he wished to do, he removed himself from Oakmoss, and his ward, for the better part of the morning.

He was overdue to have his elbow examined, particularly after a long period of travel, and took himself off to Broadstairs, where he visited the home of a physician prized for being discreet. The gentleman, after a brief inspection and a few probing questions, sent Beau on to the apothecary with a prescription for something to help with the lingering inflammation and occasional pain. One of the required medicines necessitated half an hour to prepare, and so Beau wandered in and out of the other shops on the high street, not having visited the village in years and more than willing to find things to distract himself from wondering what Miss Doubleday was doing at the very same moment.

Drawn to a small bookshop, he was standing in the alcove of its entry about to walk in when a man came out of the Silver Swan at the end of the lane. Beau could only see the man's profile at a distance, but something stirred in his memory. The look of the well-dressed gentleman was at odds with the shabby inn, a known haunt for smugglers. Such operations,

Beau knew, were alive and well in this part of the county. Tea and brandy, perhaps cigars, leather, and silk, all hauled in for dispatch to London and further afield. Most often, large smuggling cutters would drop barrels into the water and men would take smaller fishing boats out to retrieve them.

Lingering for a moment, Beau watched as another man, short, stocky, and rough around the edges, ran out, caught the gentleman by the arm, and shifted his weight from one foot to the other while speaking. There was no chance he could make out what was being said, but the coarse man's face was exposed. Beau committed it to memory as best he could and pushed into the bookshop.

He'd selected several interesting texts and was returning to the counter at the front of the store to complete his purchase when the bell over the door dinged and the gentleman from down the lane came in, pausing on the threshold when he discovered Beau within.

'Your lordship.' The man bowed.

Up close, Beau recognised the man, having met him several times, although it had been many years since. Knowing the questionable reputation of the establishment from which the gentleman had just come, Beau planned to use this encounter to glean information. He tipped his head to acknowledge the greeting, but said with false confusion, 'I'm afraid you've got the advantage, Mr—'

'Babin, Samuel Babin, of Ivy Hall near Tideford. It's no Oakmoss, to be sure.'

'Ah, right,' Beau said, holding up a staying hand. There was a subtle thread of offence, or perhaps bitterness, woven through Babin's words. 'A fine estate.'

Quite fine if it afforded the cut and quality of clothes the man was wearing—a touch above for a country squire.

'How does it go on? Ivy Hall produces wool, I think.' He knew. 'And…' Beau paused, pretending to consider what other crops or goods might be cultivated in the area, then added, aware he was wrong, '…straw?'

Babin did an admirable job withholding the smirk tugging at the corner of his mouth but seemed to stand a little taller. 'Permanent pasture for the livestock.'

'Of course. I'm afraid I've left my estate duties with the steward for too long.' A half-truth, or a whole lie if using a half-truth to conceal one's depth of knowledge could be considered prevarication.

'Yes, what a charming life you lead. My understanding is you've been on the continent a considerable while.'

Beau cocked an eyebrow. 'There is a world beyond England, although some would disagree.'

'Perhaps one day I'll be fortunate enough to travel further than the metropolis. Ivy Hall, for its modest size, demands a significant portion of my attention.'

The dig wasn't subtle.

'You have my sympathy, Babin. It's always a shame when the previous generation leaves the property worse off for the next.' Beau was beginning to suspect how Babin's father had supported a family when the man had been an indolent owner at best. 'My condolences, too, on your father's passing. Despite anticipating our parents predeceasing us, we are never truly ready for the void opened by their absence.'

In front of him, Beau noticed colour flare in the younger Mr Babin's cheeks. Tension gathered around the man's mouth, and his eyes narrowed and shifted—tiny little movements side to side—as if puzzling something out.

'How kind of you to say so.'

There was something sinister under the false gratitude Mr Babin employed in his response.

'Not at all. You'll excuse me,' replied Beau, holding up the books still in his hand for which he had not yet paid. Babin tipped his head and retreated further into the shop as Beau turned towards the counter. When he left, he hid himself away to be sure Babin went in a direction other than towards the apothecary. After waiting above half an hour, the man had not yet reappeared.

Beau re-entered the bookshop. When the man at the counter looked up, surprise plain on his face, Beau said, 'I seem to have misplaced my snuff box,' and wandered to the shelves under the pretence of searching for the missing item.

The shop was small, only one room with shelves lining the wall, the counter, a door at the back labelled *Office*, and not a soul besides Beau and the proprietor inside.

'No luck,' he said with a sigh. 'Should it turn up, you may enjoy its contents with my compliments.'

Beau left and walked towards the apothecary, his demeanour composed, his face settled into its natural state of haughty indifference, and nothing to betray the disturbing implications of the scene that had just unfolded.

7

*'Y*ou were missed at the assembly, Esther,' remarked Emerald, watching a little greenfinch hop down the quiet country lane. The day was particularly fine for January and she was glad to be out of doors once more, the weak winter sun shining on her face.

'Monthly courses administer no mercy, as I'm sure you know,' Esther Lyon said with an exasperated little laugh, bumping Emerald's shoulder as they walked. 'Tell me what I missed. Leave out no detail!'

'Goodness, where to start?' said Emerald, kicking a little pebble. Her exchange with Beau had haunted her since that night; the possessive way he'd claimed her hand, the intensity with which he'd studied her, the way his glowing eyes had looked into her darkest corners. Instead of exposing herself, Emerald shared all the gossip she'd heard as she passed through the rooms.

'The new baron was certain to display his humility.' The former Mr Bowmar had received the title only two months prior for his part in sussing out a small smuggling operation in the cove near his home. 'And Miss Crenshaw seemed to advance her campaign for the role of baroness.'

Miss Lyon rolled her eyes to the sky. 'If she wishes to take on a tedious bore of five-and-forty with children grown enough to see through her ploys, she is welcome to him. I will own to being as shocked to hear it was he who helped the authorities as I was to learn smugglers are active here. I'd just assumed, the war with France being over, the *profession*, if we can call it such, hadn't remained lucrative enough for men to risk life and limb.'

'No, nor I. I find the whole idea rather unsettling, to say nothing of the unscrupulous men who seek to line their pockets through criminal means.'

The two friends strolled without a word between them for several minutes, a pall cast over their easy conversation.

'This will never do,' announced Emerald. 'It's too nice a day to spend it sullen and fretful.'

Esther heaved a sigh of relief. 'Oh, yes, please. Let us go back to speaking of the assembly. Surely there's more I missed.'

After a moment's consideration, Emerald brightened. 'Mr Lambert trod upon Miss Dagmar's dress and tore the bottom flounce clean off. The chill between the Misses Abram was palpable to anyone standing within a foot of them. It appears the younger has not forgiven the elder for driving away her "suitor," if we are being generous with the term. And I was accosted not once, not twice, but thrice by Mr Bosworth, who seemed to think me capable of divining information about your whereabouts as the night wore on.'

'Goodness me.'

'His crestfallen countenance made me feel quite sorry for him.'

'No doubt,' Miss Lyon said with a touch of asperity. 'How a man can see interest where not even encouragement exists is beyond my comprehension. I feel I'd much rather have him come to the point so I may reject his suit and be done with the business. He's making a cake of himself.'

Emerald squeezed her friend's arm but made no reply.

'Curious you, as of yet, have made no mention of Lord Avon's return. Charles mentioned seeing him at the assembly.'

'Yes, your brother had the dubious pleasure of his company before our dance.'

'Is his lordship as handsome as he ever was?' The tail of her question pitched up as Miss Lyon's breath caught.

'If you find dereliction of duty attractive.'

Miss Lyon let out a bark of laughter. 'I understand your frustration with the man. I do, truly, as much as I am able. But even *you* cannot deny what's so obvious.' Miss Lyon laughed again, smaller, self-effacing, and shook her head. 'You know, I still recall the day I first met him. I must've been seventeen. It was at one of my first assemblies with Aunt Margaret. Up until then I'd only ever heard of him. He'd become rather mythical, always away at school or in London or wherever else it is men of his station go. When he asked me to dance, I almost swooned.'

There should have been no surprise in Miss Lyon dancing with Beau; the young lady was several years older than Emerald and therefore had been out much longer, but curiosity welled within her nonetheless, and she hoped her friend would say more as she would not ask the questions multiplying rapidly in her brain.

'Of course, he was not interested in me, no matter how much I may have wished it. One only has to pick up a paper, or so it was before he went abroad, to see him linked to some fair-haired angelic beauty. Besides, I was hardly out of the schoolroom and couldn't string two coherent thoughts together as we danced. Poor man. He was quite patient and kind when I think on it.'

Emerald felt her eyebrows rise of their own accord and consciously lowered them before her friend noticed. In the distance, two riders approached.

'My brother and Mr Babin, I think. They rode out earlier to do who knows what.'

'You say so even knowing your brother is about as capable of causing mischief as a new kitten.'

'He'll be flattered to hear you say so,' replied Miss Lyon with a grin.

Mr Lyon's kindness to Emerald bordered on interest, and even on occasion flirtation, but at five-and-twenty he was young yet and showed no interest in settling down. Perhaps because he would inherit his aunt's estate, and the hardy woman showed no signs of springing from her mortal coil.

'What think you of Mr Babin?' Emerald asked.

Her friend made a little humming noise. 'Even features, well-distributed proportions. I prefer light eyes and honey-coloured hair, which Mr Babin displays to fine advantage. The friendship between him and Charles is quite new, and I can't say he has ever paid us much attention the many winters or summers before when we've visited this part of the country. You know him better.'

She didn't. Emerald knew a little of the family as they resided in a neighbouring county. The mother was widowed, there were two girls married off in the last few years, and Mr Babin, when she saw him at the rare assembly he attended, was polite but had never asked her to dance.

The riders were almost upon them and slowed their horses as they approached.

'A lucky thing for us to come upon such fine company. Never say we are trespassing on a cosy *tête-à-tête* and must take ourselves away forthwith,' Mr Lyon called out.

His sister replied, 'We were just discussing the assembly last night and everything I missed.'

'Then we have no reason to apologise for our interruption, I hope,' said Mr Babin, with unwarranted solemnity. His serious countenance appeared almost grim when contrasted to Mr Lyon's happy, open one. There was nothing wanting in his face or figure, but his complexion was as pale as the first flakes of fresh snowfall, and Emerald found herself wondering if he spent much of his time sequestered indoors.

Miss Lyon waved away the gallantry. 'Not at all. In fact, you've rescued me from making any more embarrassing confessions about my girlhood *tendres*.'

'And you, Miss Doubleday? Have you escaped sharing such mortifying intelligence, or do we arrive just in time?' teased Mr Lyon as he wiggled his eyebrows in her direction.

Emerald dipped her head on a light laugh to give the pretence she enjoyed the joke as much as they did, but there wasn't a soul who walked the earth in whom she'd confide the extent of her youthful admiration of Beau during his last visit at Oakmoss. When she first was sent to live with the Calverleighs, she'd been too young still to see him as more than some man, the kind of man she'd known mamas everywhere wished their daughters to marry, but with enough years between them that his getting married and hers had seemed to be two events which could not possibly take place even in the same decade.

But then he'd come and gone, come and gone, and in the

meantime, Emerald had shed her girlhood. The last time he'd returned home before his father died was the first time Emerald had ever experienced the jolt of attraction—instant, sweeping, painful even. He'd been exquisite to look upon, yes, but confident, composed, like a man who said what he meant and kept the promises he made. He had also been cold, aloof, and dismissive, and if he looked in Emerald's direction, it was only to see something beyond her. What a fool she had been at sixteen, to think herself so grown, to think a man like him would pay her any special attention. What a bigger fool she was now to still wish it.

'Won't you join us?' asked Esther while Emerald continued to chew on her thoughts.

Mr Babin hesitated. 'You are certain we are not treading upon your confidences or interrupting some errand of great importance?'

'Not at all. There is no destination in mind, merely the desire to catch what we can of winter's sunshine and to do so in good company,' replied Emerald.

As the men dismounted from their horses, Mr Babin said, 'How flattered I am to be included.'

There was no pretence in his manner, maybe a little shyness, Emerald thought, as she studied the man and the countenance her friend found so pleasing. He was fine looking, a touch shorter than herself, and dressed well without showing an inclination to dandyism. Without any wish to, she pictured Beau and the intricate embroidery of his waistcoats, the careful and plentiful knots of his cravat, the fine tailoring of every outfit. She might wish to label him a dandy, and she supposed to some extent he was. Still, Emerald couldn't think of his raiment as anything other than exquisite. He was almost more handsome than any gentleman had the right to be. Why shouldn't he wear the clothing to match?

The conversation had continued to ebb and flow around her. Mr Lyon shared some anecdotes from the assembly, as Mr Babin also had not been in attendance.

'The more time I spend out, the more I prefer country assemblies to engagements of a similar nature in town,' said Esther. 'It puts me at ease to feel as though I know many of the people present and to not always be concerned some bit of gossip will get away if I miss a step or say the wrong thing. But alas, in her last letter, Mama wrote to request our presence in London before the first of February. 'Tis very likely the next assembly will be our last, depending on how fair the weather remains and when we depart. Will you come to London for the season, Em?'

Emerald had never been to London, despite all the promises made to her. First by her father when he'd tried to ease her pain at being sent away: *Lord Avon will give you a season, likely as many as you wish for, the finest dresses, perhaps even a pretty trinket or two.* Then by Lord Avon himself. But timing proved a troublesome thing. She had been too young to come out when Beau's father was still alive, and after he passed, she hadn't felt right leaving the estate for such a protracted period of time—nor had the dowager offered, and Emerald couldn't bring herself to make the request, although she was certain it would be granted.

She looked ahead rather than at anyone in particular when she finally answered her friend. 'The thought had not crossed my mind.' It was an honest response and the best she could give without revealing too much.

'It occurred to me perhaps with his lordship home…' Miss Lyon let her thought trail off.

Nearly everyone knew the responsibilities of managing Oakmoss had fallen to Emerald with Beau far from home, but still people were reluctant to say so outright, to indict the lord of the land, no matter how well deserved. She swallowed her bitterness. Her feelings were complicated, and although she was willing to censure him, to do so in a public way also felt like censuring the family, the dowager, and she could never, would never.

Mr Lyon broke the silence Emerald wasn't sure how to fill. 'How about you, Babin? I don't recall meeting you in town years past. Do you not often visit the metropolis?'

'I do, although my time there has been inconsistent and at the whim of my work here. I went when each of my sisters made her come-out. The younger chose not to marry her first season, and for the following two years we went to Bath. Like Miss Lyon, she prefers closer company. Bath gave her a change of scenery from her home county and the company of some cousins to lean on.'

Emerald said the first thing that came to her mind. 'You sound like a fine brother, Mr Babin.'

'Thank you, but I was only doing my duty by them.'

She couldn't figure out the look he pinned on her when he spoke, but she didn't think his choice of words an accident and felt the heat of a faint flush creep up her neck.

'If only my own sister would take a note from yours,' Mr Lyon said with a teasing smile while dodging a playful swat from Esther.

'Miss Doubleday,' Mr Babin began, turning to face her and almost entirely excluding the Lyon siblings from the conversation. 'I had the pleasure of meeting your guardian in Broadstairs yesterday.'

'Whatever was he doing there?' she blurted out before thinking the better of it, but she couldn't fathom what would take him to the smaller village when Ramsgate was closer to the estate.

'I couldn't say. It's frequented by smugglers, but I daresay his lordship would never be involved in something so lawless as that,' he replied with a chuckle, and Emerald found herself offering a weak smile in return. 'The bookshop is small, but the proprietor is an old friend of my father's, and he often has unusual volumes in his possession. Perhaps that was the draw.'

'Indeed. My guardian very much enjoys losing himself in a good book.' Emerald didn't know if such a statement was true, but she said it with quiet confidence, hoping to cover the real doubt and confusion she felt.

'Oh! Look at the crocus!' exclaimed Miss Lyon, her attention on the bright purple blooms set a few feet back from the road; the radiant buds against the feathery green grass a tease of spring still months away. 'I wish to pick some for pressing, but everyone need not wait for me.'

'We certainly cannot allow you to remain back by yourself,' replied Mr Babin gallantly.

'Perhaps you will lend me the use of your hands then, sir?'

Mr Babin laughed and acquiesced with a courtly bow.

'Come, the sun is warm, but we don't want to linger in the cool air if we don't have to,' said Mr Lyon, taking Emerald's hand and looping it through his arm as he steered her down the lane. Behind them, the other two promised to catch up in only a minute or two.

'Truthfully, I'm glad for this moment alone. I do not wish to overstep my bounds, but it did not appear to me you were entirely pleased with Lord Avon at the assembly. If you are unhappy, if he has made you so, I hope you know I remain a steadfast friend in your corner.'

Emerald wondered at his speech and knew not what to make of it. The three of them—Mr Lyon, his sister, and herself —had become fast friends when first introduced six or seven years ago. Before Emerald was out, she was allowed to visit with the pair, shop with Esther, and ramble about the country-side. Despite his mild flirtation, Mr Lyon had never declared himself to her, nor did she wish him to. If he had, she wouldn't have known how to respond. They weren't in love with one another, and love in a marriage was something Emerald was desperate for. The sentiment had been missing between her father and stepmother, and she hadn't known it was some-thing she could wish for, hope for, until she came to live with the Calverleighs. They had more of everything, including affection between husband and wife, parents and children, and between the children themselves. Emerald craved that feeling —to love and be loved without conditions, without obligation.

Some reply was necessary, and Emerald was careful in her answer. 'Thank you, sir. Your friendship has always been a source of pleasure and comfort, but you need not worry. There is, naturally, a period of adjustment. He's been home hardly a sennight. Already we rub along better than before.' Not quite a lie. They were speaking at least, even if their exchanges were fierce, unrestrained, and at fault for the violent storm of want and rage thrashing within her. 'In very little time, he and I will be as easy between ourselves as he and Louisa, as brother and sister.' A definite lie. The words felt funny in her mouth. She could live a dozen more years in his house. It mattered not. There was no world in which she could imagine looking at Beauden Calverleigh as a brother.

---

8

*E*merald couldn't sleep, but she often stared wide-eyed into the canopy of her bed until the first faint rays of dawn peeked through the heavy brocade curtains. After her father died, grief had refused to let sleep claim her. Even as grief dulled to a constant ache, and the ache faded to an abstract sense of loss, sleep remained elusive. Some nights, she'd float through the halls like a spectre, stopping in the long gallery to speak to the portrait of the previous Lord Avon, or she'd bring a candle to the orangery. There was a magical quality to the moonlight streaming through the pitched glass roof, and the tangy scent of citrus transported her far away.

In the lambent light of the candle, she could see the small hand on the clock pushing towards the one; the long hand following close behind.

Her eyes traced the gold embroidery on the deep blue fabric above her, the looping vines, the pointed leaves bent this way and that, the flowers so tiny they looked more like stars scattered among the night sky. She was still reeling from

Beau's sudden return—the way he'd reappeared without word or warning to upend her life once more—from the way he'd spoken to her at the assembly, and the meaning she wished to read into his words. Worse still was the staggering realisation her feelings of the past weren't a thing of the past at all.

Despite him having been hundreds of miles and countries away, he had remained a fixture in her mind. Every morning when she rode out with the steward to look at something broken or breaking. Every time a tenant's chicken coop was burgled by a fox. Every year when she held her breath until assured of the yield from the harvest. Every dispute she resolved, every sick child to whom she delivered pork jelly. Every letter from him the dowager read aloud over breakfast in which he wrote of dinners and balls and hunting parties and theatre and opera and art on the continent. Every moment she'd carried the full weight of his responsibilities.

She had never, not even for a day, stopped thinking about him, where he was, what he was doing, with whom. Emerald tried to keep her anger close. It was the only thing protecting her traitorous heart, which pounded an unsteady beat whenever he drew near. But living in her upset became a greater challenge the longer he was home. She relished the way he challenged her, appreciated the way he spoke to her as an equal, and craved his notice.

With the kind of sigh that could sweep every leaf from a tree, Emerald climbed out of bed and tied a delicate dressing gown over her nightdress. She plucked the lit candle from her bedside table and then made for the study. Work didn't soothe her the way playing the pianoforte did, but it could at least provide some distraction.

A soft light emanated from the open door, and she wondered if one of the footmen had forgotten to put ash on the fire. Her soft steps came to an abrupt halt in the doorway, the candleholder wavering precariously in her hand. Beau sat behind the big masculine desk, head bent, shirtsleeves rolled to his elbows, a glass of brandy within easy reach. Even with some distance between them, she could see black lines snaking up his left forearm and found herself leaning forward, desperate for a closer look.

'A little late to be up and about, is it not?'

She jumped at his voice. Her eyes flew from his bare arm, but he wasn't looking up. 'The same could be said of you.'

He gave her his attention then, and whether it was just a trick of the shadows in the room she couldn't say, but it seemed his eyes grew darker and more intense as they roamed over her. A chill ran down her neck despite a healthy fire burning, and her free hand clutched the bodice of her dressing gown; she was painfully aware of how dressed down they both were.

'I'm glad for a few moments alone with you, Miss Doubleday. I've been going through the ledgers and have some questions you might be able to answer.'

Emerald lingered on the threshold, hesitant to step into the room. He unsettled her, always had, but there was something both vulnerable and powerful about him in this informal state. Something she wasn't sure she could trust herself to be around.

'All right.' She took one uncertain step and then another till she was standing in front of the desk.

'Here, the haberdasher'—he pointed to a line in the book— 'and a little ways back the tailor. I believe you settled and closed the accounts given my absence and my father's passing?'

She couldn't read the ledger from her vantage point, but

she had paid off the bills after his father's death and so nodded in agreement.

'There is a new line, beginning two years ago in December.' He flipped about halfway through the volume. 'And some writing here I cannot make out. It's not so elegant as yours, but I trust you've been able to make sense of it?'

Emerald inhaled a wobbly breath—he'd noticed her handwriting, thought it elegant—as she went round the desk to stand at his side, letting her eyes fall to where the tip of his finger rested.

'The writing is Gwen's, my lady's maid.'

He lifted his head, a brow raised in inquiry, but she couldn't see past his sculpted jaw, his full lips. Her fingers went to the thin gold chain round her neck, fiddling with the delicate cross hanging from it for a moment as she recovered her thoughts.

'There was a brief period of time where she completed the entries for me.'

'Because?'

She wet her lips, her hesitation evident in the prolonged intermission between his question and her forthcoming answer.

'Because I fell off the ladder in the library. I broke my wrist and experienced a mild concussion as well.'

'No one thought to make mention of the incident? To inform me my ward had injured herself?' His tone was razor sharp, but two lines of concern drew his brows together.

''Twas nothing, really. Very likely, no one thought it worth the postage.'

'I do.'

Emerald's breath swelled in her chest. 'The headaches

lasted only a few days, and my wrist would have been healed by the time you received the missive.' She worried she might crumble under the scrutiny of his close, keen stare, and allowed her own gaze to settle once more on the mesmerising ink winding up and around his taut skin. Under the black, hard planes of muscle, the soft, rolling ridges of veins.

Some books in the library included mentions of tattoos, but she'd never seen one in real life. Until such a moment, she had always thought them reserved for sailors or pirates. He was speaking again, but she couldn't pull her attention from the oak tree wrapping up his arm. It looked just like the ones lining the drive. Its narrow, stable base sat just above his wrist, sure to be hidden by the cuff of his shirt. From the trunk grew several sturdy branches, but several more disappeared under white cotton. Her eyes burned with effort to see through the fabric.

Beau turned his face up to her. 'Miss Doubleday?'

'Did it hurt?'

'Did what hurt?'

She nodded at his arm.

His eyes followed hers. 'Yes, but often we feel pain and gain strength in equal measure.'

At her side, her fingers stretched, desperate to trail along the long limbs reaching out over the corded muscle of his forearm.

Quiet filled the room. She knew it was her chance to ask what he'd been doing in Broadstairs the other day, but she was spellbound by the privacy of their exchange. Her mouth refused to form words that would do nothing but wreck whatever alchemy was holding the moment together.

'When?'

'Three years ago.'

After his father died. She gave a bewildered little shake of her head, her mind unable to make sense of the man in front of her. 'But you stayed away.'

He leaned back in the chair, taking one arm with him but leaving the other on full display. 'Love and hate are most easily distinguished in their simplest forms, but the truth is the parameters of each are as fragile as gossamer. Passion cares nothing for your resentments; disdain can be overcome with understanding. We are capable of feeling both at once and in equal measure.'

Emerald was too plagued by a chaotic surge of emotion to speak, and she was spared the necessity to do so when Beau looked from the ledger in front of him to the room at large and then to her, his eyes never giving anything away. 'Would you care to play a game?'

'A game?'

Beau tipped his head towards the chessboard sitting on a table in the corner of the room. She hadn't touched the pieces since before the previous Lord Avon died.

She wandered over and picked up a knight, running her thumb over the cool marble mane as the piece sat heavy in her hand.

'That's a yes, then?'

Emerald sucked in a sharp inhale, surprised at how close and how low his voice was as the deep timbre rolled over the bare flesh of her neck. She agreed, stepping away from him to take her place in one of the two chairs. When he sat, he stretched his long legs to one side of the table. His stockinged feet were mere inches from the tip of her slipper. She stared, trying to recall if she'd ever even seen a man without his shoes. How easy it would be for her to close the distance, to touch her toes to his. Instead, she turned the board so the white pieces sat in front of him.

He opened the game, and she responded with the Sicilian Defence. They had both learned from the same man, so it was no surprise each countered the other's moves with intelligence and strategy, or that after dozens of turns, the match was still even.

She surprised herself when she said, after having a quiet moment to study him, 'When I first came here, I thought you looked just like your mother, in features if not so much colouring, but the longer I sit here with you, the more impossible it becomes to see her rather than your papa. Or perhaps it is due to the way you play.'

He glanced at her with casual interest. 'And which of your parents do you most resemble?'

Emerald drew circles over the top of a pawn she'd taken as she studied the board. 'My mother, I suppose, although I've no way to be sure. My father had fair colouring, not unlike the dowager. There were no pictures of my mama at Whichwood, and my father rarely spoke of her. She died the same day I arrived in the world.'

'You know nothing of her?'

She gave her head a little shake. 'Very little. They were happy, I think. Sometimes, he'd get this faraway look, and a little smile would grace his serious face. I always knew it was because he was thinking of her. But when I asked questions, it seemed a subject too painful for him to speak on. I thought perhaps when I was older, when more time had passed, but then…' But then he'd gotten sick and sent her to Oakmoss and she never saw him again. She forced herself to swallow the sorrow in her throat.

'Why didn't he wish you to remain with his wife when he

passed? Surely some male relation could have acted as a testamentary guardian.'

Surprise at his question quickly ceded to pique. 'If you're hoping to pass me off—'

'Swallow your rebuke, Miss Doubleday. My question is borne of genuine curiosity, and as your guardian, can we agree I've a right to know how I became so?'

Emerald pulled in a slow breath, filling her lungs completely and using the moment to recover her equanimity. 'The second or third cousin who inherited through the entail has six children of his own to provide for. It is doubtful he wished for any more responsibility, nor were he and my father particularly close. With regards to your first question...' Her sentence tapered off, but she began again once she completed her turn. 'My father's wife was never unkind to me, but I always felt like a guest who had overstayed their welcome. Her concern was with herself, with giving my father an heir, and eventually with my two half-sisters many years younger. Your father, I suppose, was the only one who wanted me. That you became my guardian is a misfortune shared between us.'

They drifted into silence. Her attention was on the board, but she could feel him staring at her, studying her.

'Have you ever looked at me other than to find fault? Have you ever looked at me before at all?' The question came out soft around its edges, as did his answer.

'No one looking at you, Miss Doubleday, could ever find fault.'

Her eyes lifted swiftly to his and dropped just as quickly as she felt colour rush into her cheeks.

Across the room, the fire popped, the sharp noise underscoring the tension growing between them. Never before had all his attention been so focused on her and for such a lingering length of time. As a girl of sixteen, all she had wanted was to be seen by him, but she could feel herself unravelling under his incisive blue eyes.

'We can call it a draw, if you'd like.'

She narrowed her eyes across the board. 'No,' she said, smothering a yawn. But another fifteen minutes on, no end was in sight and she was struggling to keep her eyes open.

'Go to bed. We can leave the board as is and finish the game another day.'

'Fine.' She hadn't meant to sound so short, but thought she noticed the corner of his lip tug upwards.

He stood first, coming to her side and offering her his hand. She stared at his upturned palm before setting her hand in his, dizzying as a current of warmth threatened to overtake her. Heat radiated from his skin, power from his touch. His arm brushed along hers as they walked to the door. Emerald's fingers crept up to stroke her throat, a hot flush burning a path up her exposed skin.

They paused in the doorway. She watched his Adam's apple bob with a thick swallow—fascinated by the movement, bewitched by his proximity.

'Miss Doubleday,' Beau murmured softly into the hush of night.

Emerald stared up at him. He was so close she could taste the oaky notes of the brandy on his breath when he said her name. She ran her tongue along the seam of her lips. A ribbon of wanting tied her stomach into knots.

'Pleasant dreams,' he said, releasing her hand.

Had she imagined the gentle caress of his fingers as he let her hand go? Through the sound of her heartbeat throbbing in her ears, she wished him the same.

Hours later, she wondered if he'd been more successful to

that end than she had herself. Once in bed, sleep proved hard to come by, particularly as her mind caught on the twisted branches of an oak tree every time she closed her eyes.

9

*C*old winter wind whipped Emerald's cheeks while she and Sims rode across some acreage of the home farm. She had slept little and poorly, and appreciated something to turn her mind from the man occupying her thoughts.

In addition to all the activity around livestock—cutting hay, feeding the cattle and pigs and poultry, and selecting some for market, for breeding, and for food—there was the typical cold-weather labour of hedging and ditching to be done. Most of the tenant farmers worked on a ten-year cycle, replacing a tenth of their hedges every year, as had the previous Lord Avon.

'Sims?' Emerald called as they came upon the stretch due to be re-laid. 'Is something amiss? Hedging should have started several days ago.'

The steward brought his horse alongside hers, cleared his throat, and looked around as if the answer he needed might be found among the grass or sky or hiding in a bird's nest in a tree.

'Sims?' she repeated, more accusatory than before.

He removed the spectacles he wore and rubbed the bridge of his nose. 'You can appreciate the difficulty of my position, Miss Doubleday. None of us wish to question your authority. Indeed, I hope you understand how much we respect and admire what you have done and continue to do for the estate and those dependent upon it.'

The pique in her voice was ill concealed as she spoke. '*What* has his lordship done?'

The horse upon which the steward was perched did a little sidestep, no doubt picking up on its rider's uncertainty.

'He is considering moving the sheep to some acreage nearer the border with the Roberts farm and didn't wish for hedging to begin until he's made up his mind.'

'It's a smaller plot of land. There is no easy access to water, which is why the previous lord let it be, as I'm sure you know, and no shade, to say nothing of the fact that all the paddocks prepared for grazing are laid out before us. All new hedges would need to be constructed, and what does he intend for this pasture?'

'My understanding is he wishes to increase wheat production and perhaps introduce more cattle.'

Emerald's eyes went wide; her voice pitched up. 'More cattle? More wheat? Has he conveniently ignored our current experiment with the Tullian method? Never mind. There is naught to be done about it at present.'

They rode on, Sims pointing out to Emerald a small storage structure which had to be rebuilt, and together, they stopped at the threshing mill, built by Beau's father specifically for the hated task, so she could observe the work and express her gratitude to those performing it.

She left Sims at his office, her horse at the stable, and without bothering to change, she scoured every primary room on the ground floor until she found Beau with a book in the library.

'What do you think you're doing?'

He looked up from the page, his expression bland. 'Reading. Or I was, but I get the sense you are here to disturb my peace.' With those words, he placed a marker in the book and set it off to the side.

Reading, Emerald mimicked in her mind but swallowed the churlish retort. 'We cannot move the sheep, not this coming spring at any rate, and in the meantime, there are hedges in need of replacement. Nor do we need more heads of cattle, for that matter. Next season we will have an additional three hundred sheep as it stands.'

'Sheep are more profitable, but require more care than cattle.'

'Did you read that in your book?' she sniped, bristling at the way he spoke to her, as if she hadn't even a basic understanding of managing livestock.

'More sheep means hiring more hands than we currently have. That's not an economical concern, but I cannot simply conjure men from nothing to oversee a larger flock. Can you?'

Emerald pressed her lips together. Beau was right on that account. It was the primary reason for the delay in acquiring said sheep. Mr Sims had found several qualified candidates, but one man had broken his leg, another had moved on account of family matters, and the other—well, she simply didn't care for the leering way he'd looked at her. So instead of bringing the sheep on last spring, she'd planned to do it the following. She wished she hadn't.

'You speak to me as if I haven't been doing this for years.'

'I'm speaking as the master of this estate, and if you

continue to rail about like a petulant child, I will speak to you as your guardian as well.'

Fury choked the words in her throat.

'My lord?' Buddle's voice came from over her shoulder and on instinct she turned towards it. 'Monsieur Allard to see you.'

'Show him to the study.'

Buddle disappeared and Beau rose from the sofa, but Emerald stayed firm where she was.

'That is it then?' Everything she had done, continued to do for his estate, and he couldn't even spare the length of a conversation for her? She lifted her chin and stormed from the room. Knowing Beau would turn right to make his way to the study, she went left, and had just turned the corner when she came upon Buddle in company with Monsieur Allard.

The man was tall, good-looking, and a touch sinister in the brow. He stared at her with cold intensity as she approached. It wasn't the gaze of a man imagining what lay beneath her riding habit; it was more unsettling. Emerald refused to look behind her once she'd passed the pair, but she had the creeping sensation he had.

TWO HOURS AT THE PIANOFORTE, several interminable minutes opening and closing a book she wished to read, and the length of a dinner sat staring at Beau's stupid, handsome face had done nothing to quell her resentment of the situation, of his ability to usurp her authority with impunity.

When Emerald retired for the night, she didn't even bother getting into bed. She sat upon the long bench at her windows until the half-full moon was high, the house asleep, her gaze unfocused as she stared out at the undulating landscape in shades of green and black. Either she would nod off and her temple tipping onto the cold glass would wake her and send her to bed, or the sun would peek out from behind the distant tree line and she would begin her day. With a river of irritation coursing through her, she suspected the latter more likely on such an occasion. Beau had behaved with infuriating high-handedness, to say nothing of the strange man visiting him. Emerald's curiosity needed to be sated, but dinner had been her only opportunity to ask questions, and she was reluctant to interrogate Beau in front of the dowager.

Following that line of thought did nothing to improve her mood, not that she had any desire to pull herself from the sulks while in the privacy of her own rooms, but when two figures emerged from somewhere below her, every thought of Beau flew from her mind. She went rigid and pressed her forehead to the window. The glass fogged as her breath came in uneasy little pants, but her whole body went deathly still a moment later when she realised one of the men was her guardian.

Everything stopped—her heart, time, the clouds as they floated above the trees—except for her mind, which whirled through questions and implications faster than she could catch them: What was he doing? Who was he with? Where was he going? Why? Was it the Frenchman? Was he working for the French? Was that the true reason for his return? She hadn't seen the man again, nor had Beau made mention of his mysterious visitor when the family sat down to dine.

Whatever he was up to, given the advanced hour, Emerald was certain it wasn't good. While she would never be so unladylike as to use the word *blackmail*, if she could catch him out, she might be able to balance the recent shift in power. Before she could really think about what she was doing, she slipped into her boots. Mr Babin had made a jest about Beau being a smuggler, but the possibility felt all too real as she watched the pair turn their steps in the general direction of the coast.

There would only be one footman on duty in the front hall, very likely dozing in the chair near the huge door, which made her escape from the side of the house easy. At the stables, Emerald was quiet as a mouse as she saddled Calliope and led her to a block, sending a silent word of thanks to whichever previous lord had thought to erect a separate building as the living quarters for the stable hands and grooms.

Curiosity, the thrill of adventure, the desire to discover Beau's secrets, only carried Emerald so far. Doubt settled over her halfway to Broadstairs, while she considered the danger she put herself in riding alone in the dead of the night. Far above, clouds floated over the moon in whimsical intervals, pitching her into the dark without warning. Around her, air which only felt brisk during the day turned her blood to sludge in her veins and carried a sinister whisper on its current. The trill and chirp of insects ceased. The silence left behind raised the hair on the nape of her neck. Still, she pressed on, telling herself the possible risk he posed to the family, to the estate, to his mother, sister, and herself, couldn't be ignored.

When the buildings of the village came into view, she turned into a copse of trees and dismounted. A sharp snap, like someone trodding upon a dry branch, made her jump. She whipped her head around and squinted into the dark, the ominous sound echoing in her mind, but saw nothing. Emerald tied off her horse with trembling hands. As she left the cover of the thicket, she glanced back at Calliope, a symphony of uncertainty swelling within her breast.

On the high street, only one establishment had light

emanating from it. Emerald couldn't hear anything besides the frantic beat of her heart as she approached the Silver Swan. She took several deep breaths and rubbed the little gold cross that hung about her neck.

Under no circumstances could she enter, not while she was alone and not when any respectable woman would be ensconced within the safety of her home. A peek in the window would have to suffice, and she hoped...well, she wasn't exactly certain what she hoped for since she couldn't be sure Beau was within, or even in Broadstairs at all for that matter. There was no proof of anything besides him leaving Oakmoss, and she'd ridden to the village with nothing more than a hunch guiding her. How foolish it would sound to say so out loud.

With one more deep breath, she forced her feet forward, but before she reached the window, the door swung open. Never in her life had Emerald moved with such speed. She flung herself around the corner of the building, hiding in the little alleyway that ran along the inn and whatever business neighboured it. With gloved hands over her mouth, she held in every cry and gasp. Icy fear wrapped a cold hand around her heart, and she prayed whoever came past wouldn't see her making herself small against the dark stone of the building. The long seconds ticked by. Whoever had left the inn must have gone the opposite direction, and Emerald sagged against the wall, having already decided to make her way home just as soon as she caught her breath.

'You see what I see?'

Emerald choked down a sob as panic overtook her hard and fast. Her body trembled to such an extent her knees knocked together under the drab grey cloak enveloping her. Two men stood at the opening of the alley, the smell of spirits and the stink of unkempt bodies pervading her nostrils even at a distance. The door to the pub slammed open once more, causing her to jump, but they didn't so much as flinch.

'She's a prime article,' said the same one. 'My share from tonight's take for the first go.'

The bitter taste of bile rose in Emerald's throat and filled her mouth. It was a small consolation knowing she would be sick all over them if—when—they came nearer. A third man came into view. The face of Beau's valet was familiar but so out of place in this scene that Emerald's brain couldn't make head nor tails of his presence. From behind him, just beyond her sight, floated a voice that could pierce her heart even in the grave.

'Perhaps I'd like the first go, gentlemen.'

Beau's tone was even and cool as always, but Emerald was filled with dread and disgust at hearing him speak so. Fear warped her perception of this man who she might have despised but had always believed a gentleman. She lived with this man—a man involved in something nefarious, a man who had total control over her for several more months—and she didn't know him even a little. The worst things she'd thought of him proved nothing when compared to what was unfolding before her, as little as she understood it.

Despite the chill in the air, Emerald was sweating. Moisture clung to her spine, the palms of her hands inside her gloves, her scalp under the heavy hood of her cloak. Her pulse throbbed in her temples. The pit of her stomach spasmed. She flexed and stretched her fingers, unable to keep them from going numb, and pushed harder against the wall at her back, trying to keep herself upright.

He was speaking still, but his voice sounded warbled and faraway. The men who'd first found her were no longer paying her any mind, and neither was Saunders. Emerald could flee the nightmarish scene if only her legs would move. She pleaded with her body to turn, to take a step, trying to convince it of the absolute necessity, but her feet remained rooted to the spot.

The men walked off, and a second later Beau came into view. Emerald's chest ached from the frantic beating within. He looked in her direction. She tried to read something, anything, in his bland expression, but her vision was narrowing to a pinpoint at an alarming pace. Her lungs weren't getting enough air. As he stepped towards her, she felt her whole world tilt as everything went black.

10

---

*A*fter Babin had disappeared in the bookshop, Beau had written to Monsieur Allard. Theo Allard was a retired spy and chemist who filled his time with intercepting smuggling boats, letting the Crown take credit for the seizures, and collecting a tidy sum for both the work and his silence in the matter. The pair had met at Cambridge. Theo, still a little wild and not having mastered English to the degree necessary to complete his coursework, had been in danger of being rusticated. The greater consequence, however, had been his father's threat to disinherit him should the school send him home to the country. Beau had offered to tutor him, and when he was recruited by the Crown, Theo was brought on by his recommendation.

Allard was also a man who defied time and space with his uncanny ability to be everywhere all at once. Beau had sent off his note, and Allard had appeared. With him, he'd brought two things. The first, several small pills meant to be used to tie up loose ends or in instances of imminent mortal danger. They were an experiment with hemlock, according to Theo, who'd advised Beau against using the tablets unless he had the time to stay and 'check his work,' so to speak. The second, intelligence on Babin. The man was expecting a shipment of goods before the moon waned and took with it the light to guide the smuggling boats. Theo had also noted Mr Babin's name had cropped up in groups known to empathise with Napoleon and hold similar revolutionary ideals.

Being informed was never enough for Beau. He had to see for himself. A glance at the clock confirmed the late hour. A minute spent listening to nothing but silence assured him the house had long gone to sleep. Beau slipped from his room, the thrill of sneaking around sending a frantic buzz through him. He took one of the unused, or rather, unknown, passageways he'd discovered as a child near the end of the corridor in the family wing. It brought him below stairs where he dipped into another, long-standing muscle memory carrying him swiftly through the pitch black. He spilled into the cold night air with nothing so disgraceful as a whoosh when the door opened in the masonry at the corner of the house. From the outside, the door appeared as nothing more than stacked honeyed bricks.

Saunders was leaning against the stone, hat low, blending into the dark and holding an unlit lantern. 'The horses are tethered to the old oak near the Temple of Health. Figure with the half-moon, we've got enough light to walk and can light the lantern once on the road.'

With a sharp nod, Beau turned his steps, and the two walked in silence, the only sound the steady rhythm of Beau flicking the false bottom of his snuff box. Inside, tabs of belladonna powder sat waiting, although they would hopefully go unused. Plenty of things in nature could be turned into lethal, undetectable substances, including the leaf of the belladonna plant. The Home Office provided arsenic, but

Beau, when forced to extreme measures, preferred something a little more creative and obscure.

Beau's skin prickled, not from the cold January air, but the excitement of doing what he loved once more. He stretched his arm and bent it at the elbow several times, satisfied with the minimal pain in the movement. Crossing the miles to Broadstairs, he thought on their plan and contingencies as well as the weapons on his person, including two pistols, several knives, the snuff box, and a case with poison-tipped needles.

Unbidden, Miss Doubleday's countenance filled his mind. He could see her sitting in the study, talking about a stepmother who didn't want her and a distant cousin who couldn't keep her, her expression resigned. If something happened to him, who would care for her? He shook his head. It was a ridiculous question, one to which he knew the answer. She would, of course, retire with his mother and sister to the dower house or the property his father had willed to his mother, if she even realised it was hers. Miss Doubleday would be cared for as she had been all the years he'd been gone. The answer to the other question rattling around in his mind was less certain and more important. Would she care if something happened to him?

Saunders snuffed out the lantern as they approached an unused barn situated a little off the lane and tied up the horses. Beau had had the chance to walk through it when he'd been waiting on the apothecary and had found nothing to suggest it was being used by the smugglers. Indeed, he would have been surprised if they'd utilised such an obvious spot.

Back outside, his eyes were quick to adjust to the dark. He could see the glimmer of light emanating from the Silver Swan a hundred yards down the road. An open field of waist-high grass unfolded from the barn to the inn and sprawled all the way to where the cliffs dropped off some twenty-five yards behind the inn.

Using two fingers to motion forward, Beau folded over and advanced, giving the inn a wide berth. Near the edge, they dropped to their stomachs, inching ahead till they could peer down at the small beach of Stone Bay. When he breathed in, the brine of the cold ocean air peppered his senses. On the shore, a donkey shifted from side to side while four men loaded crates from a fishing boat into a cart. Squinting, Beau could just make out the fore-and-aft rigging of a bigger vessel a half mile out at sea.

When the boat was empty, the four men separated. Two manned the boat, returning it to the water. The others led the cart by slow steps towards a roughly hewn path from the beach up the low cliff side. Beau and Saunders watched a few moments before glancing at one another. In tacit agreement, they moved further down the bluff and positioned themselves behind a crumbling wall, the remnant of a long-gone watchtower, ten feet or so from where the cart would crest the bluff.

Years of being a spy had taught Beau patience. He was not lost in his thoughts or otherwise distracted when the cart appeared a quarter of an hour later. He had been listening with keen ears and first heard the soft roll of wheels, the tetchy grunt of a donkey, the steady clomp of hooves five minutes before. There was a pause, then the sound of bottles clinking against one another.

'Oi, careful. I don't need to be stinking of brandy when we turn up at the Swan, or especially when I get home to the wife,' barked one of the men.

It was quiet again, and Beau suspected they were sampling the goods brought over on the boat. He heard the sound of shuffling feet followed by a quick quiver of the bottles in their crates, as if one of the men had bumped the cart.

'What did I just tell ye? My coat's as soaked as ye are now.'

''At's the least of yer problems if he goes on with that hare-brained scheme of his,' the other replied with a derisive snort.

The first man scoffed. 'Hare-brained is one way o' puttin' it. I'd call it foolish beyond measure, thinking himself some kind o' modern-day Guy Fawkes. He's forgettin' Fawkes was caught and quartered.'

'What are ye saying?' Suspicion clouded the question.

'Don't be daft. All I'm saying is I think he thinks too much of himself. He's had it easy here for too long. Rather than focus on the estate he's so lucky to have, he thinks of nothing but keepin' his father's legacy alive and squeezin' coins from the English. Greed is a story that begins well but ends poorly. A smarter man would leave on his own terms. He wants to go to the capital, he can go himself.'

Beau and Saunders exchanged worried glances.

'I might consider it, if the price is right.'

'Then you're as big a fool as he. Bigger, even. Runnin' is bad enough. I wouldn't do it if not for Jemmy, but we can barely keep up with the expenses as it is. My father turns in his grave every time I lead a cart up this hill.'

'He'd rise from it if he knew what was comin' in on the boats when there was no moon.' The sinister laugh accompanying this statement crawled over Beau's skin like a hundred tiny spiders.

The cart rumbled onward past where Beau and Saunders were hiding behind the low stones, the conversation fading as if it were being pulled out to sea. When Beau looked up a minute later, he tracked the two men walking towards the backside of the buildings. A glowing lantern in the distance caught his attention. There was a third man behind the book-shop yanking open a pair of cellar doors.

The long, feathered grass provided cover as Beau and Saunders doubled back close to the barn. Once assured of being neither seen nor heard, Saunders said, 'What think you? A drink at the Swan?'

Beau considered their options. The men, any men in the inn, would be suspicious of newcomers and reticent to speak on the subjects in which Beau was most interested. But needs must.

'I suppose we'll have to be our most charming.'

A few minutes' walk brought them to the fringes of the high street. They approached the Silver Swan just as the men who'd escorted the cart appeared between buildings a short ways down.

One of the men came to an abrupt stop at the alley sepa-rating a hardware store and the inn. 'You see what I see?'

The lascivious look on the man's face nauseated Beau. He continued forward, reaching the inn as the door slammed open. Neither man seemed to notice the drunkard as he stum-bled out and collapsed into a heap on the street.

'She's a prime article,' the man continued, and Beau judged him to be the one who had both spilled and drunk the greater share of brandy. 'My share from tonight's take for the first go.'

Beau wasn't sure of the kind of woman he'd find when he looked in the alley—judging by the silence, one who wasn't interested in trading her favours for their coin—but he knew for certain he wouldn't leave her prey to the smugglers in front of him.

'Perhaps *I'd* like the first go, gentlemen,' said Beau in a cool, arrogant accent. As he and Saunders approached the pair, the valet edged around the corner of the building, creating a physical barrier between the men and the woman in the alley. The smugglers were sizing Beau up, greed twinkling in the eyes of the drunk as he no doubt considered how much money Beau carried on his person and the worth of the pocket watch he must be wearing. The other looked fatigued, a trifle irritated, and ready to be done with his business for the night.

'Ah, I can see you're debating whether to fight for your claim. You may attack me, but my friend here won't let you get very far. Trained in Asia in forms of combat I won't do a disservice by attempting to pronounce.'

The man who'd been spilled on said, 'Just making our way to the Swan for a nightcap,' and nudged his friend. But the other hesitated, reaching behind him for the second time during their exchange as if to check whether his knife was still tucked into the waist of his breeches, ready to be plunged between Beau's ribs at a moment's notice.

'Might I suggest a pound each, and we all go our separate ways as if this awkward moment between us never happened?' As he spoke, Beau pulled out his snuff box and took a pinch. A sign for Saunders for how they would react should the shifty man before them choose violence.

The men looked at one another, an entire conversation started and ended with a gaze. The sober man nodded their acquiescence, although his partner scowled.

'Delightful.' Beau pulled a few coins from a purse inside his pocket, gave each man his share, and bid them good evening, although he would not have minded teaching the one a lesson. Behind him, raucous voices rose and fell as the men entered the Swan and the door closed with a cough behind them.

'All right,' he said, tucking away his snuff box. 'Let us be quick with the rest of this business.'

'No good, boss.'

Beau's head snapped to his valet when he heard the phrase used only in times of exigency. Saunders tipped his head towards the alleyway. Beau stepped closer, preparing himself for any number of scenarios, including every smuggler in Broadstairs pointing their pistols in his direction.

There were no weapons or smugglers, much less a mob of them. Flattened against the stone wall, face as pale as the moon above and contorted in absolute terror, was his ward.

*E*verything was dark, but Emerald was warm, snug, and trying to ignore the slow, steady movement rocking her awake. She wished for nothing more than to stay in whatever pleasant dream she was having, and was trying to nestle deeper into the comfort surrounding her, when her memory cleared and her eyes flew open.

Directly above her was the ruthless jaw and sharp chin of Beauden Calverleigh. His strong arms were wrapped around her, carrying her as one might a small sleeping child, as he wove his way through the tree line that followed the main road of Broadstairs.

'Put—' Her intended demand to be released was smothered almost before the first sound reached her own ears. In one swift movement, Beau had dropped her feet to the ground, pulled her back flush against his chest, and clapped a gloved hand over her mouth as the hood of her cloak fell back and gathered around the crown of her head.

'One peep,' he whispered in her ear, his voice firm but not menacing, 'and I will gag you.'

She gasped against his hand, her ribs expanding under the weight of his arm.

'Can you walk?'

Emerald bobbed her head. She was reeling from being held tight to his solid chest and bothered by how easily the lingering feel of his arms wrapped around her overcame the panic she'd felt when he'd approached her in the alley. Beau marched her forward several minutes longer, and she remained quiet, the war inside her between caution and desire depriving her of speech. At her other side, his valet appeared, but the man didn't spare a second glance at her.

'Your horse?' asked Beau.

'In the—' Her voice came out scratchy and mangled. She cleared her throat and said again in a low whisper, 'In the copse at the other end of the high street.'

Beau nodded to Saunders, who jogged ahead to a run-down barn and disappeared inside. When they caught up to the valet, he had already mounted his horse and was leaving through the door she and Beau had just entered. She watched Saunders a moment before the grip of strong hands around her waist startled a strange sound from her.

Without a word of explanation, Beau tossed her atop his horse. It crossed her mind to kick him, to swing for his head, jump down, run away. Except Saunders would likely hear the commotion and chase her, as would Beau, as she doubted her ability to do more than stun him. Besides, her fear had mostly waned. If Beau wished to harm her, she felt certain he would have done so already. And of course there was the matter of where she would even go. Regardless of whatever illegal thing he was involved in, she lived at *his* house.

With uncertain eyes, Emerald watched Beau tuck the wool fabric of her cloak under her, exposing the horn of the saddle.

The feeling of his fingertips working along her leg sent an odd sensation rippling through her, beginning in her thigh and working its way down to the cold toes in her shoes and up to the hot tips of her freezing ears. He slipped a dirty boot into the stirrup and swung himself up behind her in the saddle, his arms slipping along either side of her as he took up the reins.

When they left the barn, Beau steered them towards a cart path inside the tree line, concealing the track a little from view. It was not the way she had come, and quick, disturbing thoughts flooded her mind. They paused, and she heard the clatter of horse hooves approaching. Her whole body tensed.

'It's all right,' said Beau, his breath a wave of warmth cascading down the bare skin of her exposed neck. 'That will be Saunders with your horse. We'll make our way home together.' She could feel the words vibrating in his chest as he spoke. *Home.* A hot tear pricked her eye.

His valet came through the trees, leading her horse Calliope by the reins, and made several odd, silent gestures, none of which made any sense to her. Beau adjusted her between his legs, the hard muscles of his thighs flexing against her hips.

Their pace was cautious, and with every step, Emerald could feel Beau's body work to keep her centred and close against him on the horse. The heat radiating from him, the rhythmic motion, the fall after an unexpected rush of commotion were all taking their toll on her. Her eyelids felt heavy and fluttered against her will to remain awake. She attempted to straighten herself in the saddle without touching the man behind her—all around her, really—when his horse came to a sudden stop, and he snaked one of his arms around her midsection.

The movement startled Emerald, and the distant sound of

rowdy men banished any possibility of falling asleep. Saunders came alongside them and cast a meaningful look at Beau. Emerald tried to turn her head to see how he responded but couldn't do so without twisting. She tipped a little to one side and was met with the firm strength of a lean arm forcing her upright.

Beau peeled off the lane and picked his way through the trees, turning them deeper into the surrounding woodland until the road and cart path alike were blurred through long leafy limbs. The jeering grew closer, and Emerald felt like at any moment the men would burst through the foliage. Saunders dropped from his horse, cocked a pistol that appeared as if conjured by magic, and took up a post behind a thick chestnut tree a little way ahead, the dead branches breaking under his boots as he settled into his spot. His face was obscured, but she imagined his eyes tracking every movement between the wide trunks of the trees while he lay in wait, a predator ready to pounce. She noticed his other hand still held the reins of her horse, but not his own, which was now several feet from him, and she was wondering why when behind her, Beau shifted.

Emerald felt the cold air hit her back and, a moment later, was lifted from the saddle, her waist pinched between his firm, strong hands. He moved her as if she weighed nothing.

Taking her hand, he led her round an old downed trunk and pulled her to her knees next to him. She wondered if he could feel how her hand shook. The quick squeeze of pressure around her fingers was her answer. Her eyes darted up to his face, but his focus was trained ahead. The voices were nearly upon them. With effort, she focused all her attention on the smell of damp earth and wet bark, on the cracked, ridged wood under the hand she was using to stay upright.

There was a round of whooping. The rise of excited chatter enveloped her. Her heart sprang into her throat knowing at any second they would be outnumbered. She thought of the two men from earlier and considered the possibility they were part of the unruly group. Her stomach heaved with the certainty she would not be lucky enough to escape the lecher a second time. Emerald couldn't stop her body from convulsing. Beau said nothing, but he sidled closer to her till they were arm to arm, hip to hip.

As the voices gradually grew more distant, Emerald released the breath she'd been holding, the gentle puff of air shaking on its release. She looked down to where their hands were still joined, wondering if he realised and what it meant, when a shot rang out. The wide bang filled the night air all around them. Beau was on her in a flash, his whole frame covering her own. She could feel his heartbeat through the layers of his clothes and was surprised by how regular, how steady it drummed when her own was so wild. Together they remained in that position until all sound except their breathing faded.

'A misfire, it seems. Too much brandy, not enough sense,' the valet said in hushed tones from the other side of the fallen trunk where Emerald and Beau remained.

With these words, Beau pushed up, taking her with him as he stood.

'Idiots,' he muttered.

Saunders had a firm hold on Calliope and was running a hand between her eyes in a calming motion. She wasn't dancing, but her tail swished and she whinnied with unease. Emerald looked at the other horses. Both remained still, quiet, unruffled. A sharp pang of realisation darted through her. The horses were accustomed to the crack of gunfire. Logic forced her to accept the most obvious conclusion: Her guardian had reason to fire a gun. Often. Suddenly, she recalled Saunders withdrawing his own mysteriously from the air around him and knew by the heavy pit in her middle Beau had a pistol on his person as well. Her mind jumped. Whatever he was doing in Broadstairs, he was prepared to harm someone. Just not her.

Like in the barn, Beau said nothing when he put her on his horse, and the three of them continued on as if the entire startling event hadn't happened.

It wasn't until Oakmoss loomed in the distance, a great dark golden shadow against the night-blue sky, that he ventured to speak. 'You've had quite a shock. Are you all right?'

Emerald nodded against him, determined to think of his lies and deceit, not the solid body and all its latent strength supporting her. But the question, asked with such gentle sincerity, sent a silent tear down her cheek. She would have preferred him to rail at her. She had expected him to. Her tongue darted out to lick the moisture off her lip, and she pushed down a thick swallow, not wishing to give herself away. The effort was for naught. A minute more, and her cheeks were sopping wet. Emerald was overwrought, but not from shock. When her anger and her fear of him faded the closer they drew to Oakmoss, she was left only with nauseating, sinking despair.

A little short of the stables, Beau brought the horse to a stop and dismounted. His fingers curled around her ribcage, his thumbs a hair's breadth from the underside of her breasts. She slid down, doing her best to avert her face but conscious of how her legs, stomach, chest grazed against him. Her feet landed firmly on the ground, but his hands didn't move.

Emerald knew if she tipped up her head, she would find his icy blue eyes boring through her.

He said her name in a quiet, concerned voice.

She bit her lip, shook her head, and refused to look at him.

'Miss Doubleday,' he tried again, this time as his thumb brushed away the tear slipping down her cheek. 'Won't you look at me? Speak to me?'

Her eyes fluttered closed, unable to withstand the aching tenderness of the moment, and hot tears flowed from the tight seams, hiding an expression sure to give her away. She covered his hands with her own, pried them from her person, and fled to the house.

12

*M*iss Doubleday hurried towards the house, and Beau couldn't look away from her retreating form, an unusual mix of anger, annoyance, and concern churning within him. The immediate fury he'd felt after discovering she had followed him had abated after he'd seen her features twisted with fright. He wasn't a brute.

'You can't kill her,' said Saunders.

At his side, Beau's hands clenched, and his mind filled with all the ways he could punish anyone who tried to hurt her. He watched until his ward disappeared through a side door before glaring at his valet.

Saunders, with an impish look on his face, jerked a shoulder. 'You two are little better than cats and dogs. Forgive me for thinking you might see this as an opportunity. All teasing aside,' the valet continued, the levity from a mere moment ago gone, 'this presents a problem.'

A low groan growled out of Beau as he dragged a hand over his face. The valet was right, of course. 'Have you a solution?'

'Not a viable one, unless you wish to leave again, but even that won't replace her memories of tonight. Poor girl looked as though she was being bundled onto a ship bound for the Antipodes.'

The muscle in Beau's jaw tensed at the mention of leaving —retreating, as it were in this case. 'No, tonight's business aside, we can both agree I've been gone too long, let too many others shoulder my responsibilities.'

'Aye, I'm sure it's only your *responsibilities* keeping you here.'

Beau refused to consider the role his ward played in tying him to Oakmoss. He could not act on his attraction nor did she seem to wish him to. He and Saunders fell into silence as they neared the stables. It was no easy task returning three horses without making much sound, but Saunders moved with such graceful stealth that sometimes Beau wondered if the man had been raised by a pack of cats. He hadn't appreciated how much easier it was to spy for the Crown when he wasn't also dodging his mother, sister, ward, and a veritable army of servants. The small staff in his London townhouse were accustomed to his odd habits and odd hours when he was there. More often, he and Saunders were abroad, letting rooms in whatever part of whatever town necessary to complete whatever assignment had been given to Beau.

He stabled Arion and left Saunders to his and Miss Doubleday's horses, sneaking back to his room and stirring the crackling embers of the dying fire while he waited. Beau glanced at the clock when Saunders entered—it was nearly four in the morning—and poured them both a snifter of brandy.

'And here we thought it was just a bit of smuggling,' Saunders opined, taking the glass handed to him.

Beau released a long breath. 'If we take what we heard

about him channelling Mr Fawkes at face value, the questions in need of answers are how will he procure the explosives to blow up Parliament and when is he planning to do so. I'll write Duffy in the morning.'

'If we can get closer during the next delivery—'

'We might hear more of the details. It's worth a try,' agreed Beau, and after a pause, asked, 'What do you think he's bringing in on moonless nights?' The overheard comment continued to disturb him.

Saunders shrugged. 'Can't be worse than massacring the House of Lords.'

They lapsed into silence. Several minutes ticked by before Saunders broached the subject of Miss Doubleday once more. 'As for the other concern, I daresay you may just have to speak with the miss.'

'Saunders.' The tone Beau used was all incredulity. He and his ward barely managed to exist in the same room together, much less have civil conversation. Before she fled, he'd encouraged her to speak to him so that she might unburden herself and find some measure of composure before returning to her rooms, not so he could reveal any of the secrets living within him.

'My lord.' The valet tossed back the rest of his drink and replaced it on the tray atop the sideboard. 'You may either murder her—and it feels incumbent upon me to say I vehemently disapprove of such an option—or talk to her. The choice is yours.'

Beau, leaning against the broad marble mantel, watched the brandy as he swirled it in the glass, avoiding his valet's astute stare when he replied, 'I could do neither.'

'You may remove the man from the aristocracy…'

Saunders appeared unbothered when Beau flicked an

annoyed glance in his valet's direction. 'Yes, yes, fine. I'll speak to her.'

The valet nodded once, pushed away from the sideboard against which he'd been leaning, and left the room in wordless satisfaction.

In the fireplace, the revived flames flicked and hissed as they undulated around the dry oak wood. Beau had long been accustomed to relying on himself, his judgement, his instincts. Miss Doubleday's appearance in Broadstairs had put him in a position as unfamiliar as it was uncomfortable. There was a twinge of emotion deep in his chest accompanied by an unusual longing for his father. Despite all their differences and disagreements, Beau had always been able to depend on the man's counsel.

All at once, Beau dropped the glass onto the thick rug and sprang across the room.

His assumption when they returned had been that she'd retired, exhausted from the night, but what if she'd gone to his mother or roused his sister in a wild state of panic and fear? With a quiet hand, he opened his door. Silence greeted him, and he looked down the hall one way and then the other. Holding his breath, Beau slinked along the wall, pausing first at his sister's door, and when no noise was forthcoming, moving down to Miss Doubleday's. He paused. The edge of the door kissed the plush carpet, making it impossible for him to detect candlelight. Then he heard a sigh, the sound so faint anyone else might think it was only the house complaining of old age. Beau's trained ear knew better.

With his ward tucked away safe in her rooms, Beau was at leisure to stew in all the fury he had initially felt with her for doing something so stupid and dangerous. Except it wasn't only ire thrumming through his veins. As a rule, Beau didn't live in the past; he couldn't afford to in his line of work. But when he had seen her cowering in the alley, felt her shaking against him all the way home, his chest had tightened and an odd pain had pricked the back of his throat. He'd felt helpless, incapable of easing her distress, and he couldn't stop the what-ifs that'd followed him all the way home: What if she'd got lost while trailing him? What if she'd fallen off her horse? What if she'd been hurt? What if he hadn't found her when he did?

What if he'd lost her?

He smoothed his fingers over his furrowed brow and expelled a troubled groan, the soughing sound heavy with longing, exasperation, and the burgeoning agony of worry.

The other question he couldn't answer was how to reprimand her behaviour without accounting for his own. As a rule, he lied for work, but he hated the idea of not being truthful with her. Until he could reconcile himself to doing what he must, Beau would avoid her.

THE DAY AFTER, he turned down the corridor approaching his study just as she entered the room with a footman on her heels.

'He was not at breakfast, and I've already tasked Gwen with searching the family wing, so you may begin elsewhere. When you find him,' she was saying, 'send him here. Enlist the other footmen and Buddle, too, if need be.'

Beau tossed himself into an alcove covered by a large tapestry near where he stood, chiding himself for his spinelessness. The footman walked by, and no doubt several more would in their search for him. He waited, and waited; the rumbling of his stomach was sure to give him away. More than an hour later, she emerged.

'I'm sorry, miss,' Buddle said. ''Tis odd. No sign of him inside, but his horse and curricle are both in the stables still.'

Her growl of discontentment surprised a smile out of him.

When he was certain they'd moved off, he slipped out from his hiding place and into a passageway that would take him to his rooms.

Another time, she caught him up in the hall outside the orangery; the quickness of her appearance in the doorway as he passed came with the heavy suspicion she'd been watching for him. In the two days since he'd seen her, she'd grown even more lovely, her dark features set off by the angry fire shining in her eyes. They were mercifully interrupted by the house-keeper. The gritted smile she gave Mrs Marshall, and the very black look she gave Beau as she walked off with the woman, caused Beau to worry for the dear old lady.

After that, she'd almost found him in the library. He'd heard her kid boots making a soft shushing sound on the marble floor, and had flung himself right over the back of the claret-coloured couch, landing on his healing elbow in a grace-less heap of wool and superfine and praying she wouldn't do more than glance in the room before moving on to the next.

Beau went so far as to invent a cold that kept him from dining with the ladies.

'How unfortunate the English clime does not agree with you,' Saunders had said, straight of face but sharp of tongue, when he turned up to help Beau dress for dinner only to be dismissed.

In truth, Beau was revolted by his own cowardice. Further-more, his recovering elbow had not appreciated the manoeuvre in the library and felt quite tender to the touch.

After taking a tray in his room for breakfast for the fifth day in a row, he made his way to the study, coming up short on the threshold when he discovered Miss Doubleday in the high-backed chair behind the desk, which appeared larger than normal when contrasted with her slender frame.

Beau had prepared himself to see her, but only when he decided to summon her and not a moment sooner. Having previously dismissed every possible start of conversation as unsatisfactory and every lie as insubstantial, with the moment prematurely pressed upon him, he said exactly what he was thinking.

'How fortuitous to find you here. Perhaps I may have a word with you?'

She replied, without so much as a glance his way, 'Perhaps after tea. I'm quite busy.'

'With what?' He stepped further into the room, all but closing the door behind him, torn between maintaining propriety and wishing to keep the conversation private.

'Work.'

He watched her pen scratching away in the ledger in front of her. 'We've spoken of this before, have we not?'

Miss Doubleday still refused to meet his eyes. Her pen shook a trifle, her shoulders had inched up nearer her ears, and redness creeped up her neck and over her sharp cheek-bones. His eyes fell to her chest and the heavy rise and fall of her breasts. He admonished himself and knew he ought to look somewhere—anywhere—else, but his gaze dropped further, and he meditated on the exact rosy shade of her nipples. Her voice recalled him not a moment too soon. Beau willed away the burgeoning swell in his breeches.

'Perhaps it's true other young ladies prefer not to sully themselves with such a word.' She blew on the wet ink for several seconds before dipping her pen into the pot to her right. 'I find having some occupation rather stimulating.'

'Then let me recommend a long walk around the lake or perhaps some time refining your accomplishments. You have *some*, I assume? Netting purses? Speaking a smattering of French? Watercolours, perhaps?' Beau had taken up a post behind one of the two chairs facing her, putting something physical between them. He was being ridiculous. He knew very well he owed a great deal to the probity and strength of character of a girl hardly out of the schoolroom—or so she was when she stepped in after his father died.

A mocking sigh preceded her response. 'Sadly, no.'

'If you have time to sneak out of the house in the advanced hours of the night, you have time to apply yourself to other, more appropriate endeavours.'

Setting down the pen and ignoring the ink spot forming beneath it, Miss Doubleday finally brought her gaze to meet his own. 'Is there something you require, sir? Maybe directions to the library or some other part of the house?' Her words were sharp, but there was caution in her eyes.

Beau set his mouth in a firm line. His fingers twitched, pressing into the leather of the chair they were resting on. 'I require a few moments of your time.'

She tilted her head and smiled in a way one might when speaking to a young child. 'How surprising, given you've been avoiding me for several days. Allow me to return the favour. At present, I'm occupied compiling the order for the rooms needing to be refurbished. New paper for the walls in the green salon, drapes in the billiard room, fabric for the chairs in the yellow morning room—'

'No.'

The only thing that gave away her surprise at his interruption was the quick fluttering of her lashes. But when she repeated the word she drew it out as if she didn't understand the language. '*No*?'

'Hang the refurbishments.'

'Yes, the drapes, certainly, and the paper for the walls, but the chairs…' She cocked her head, her eyes drifting upwards, as if her mind was grinding through what he said.

His patience dwindled, and he felt that tell-tale muscle in his jaw pulse. 'You purposefully misunderstand me.'

'Whatever do you mean, my lord?'

There was an odd tightening in his throat when the last two words rolled from her mouth, sarcastic, disdainful, distrusting. She came out from around the desk, her hands wrapped tight in the fabric of her dress. 'How about a friendly wager?'

His eyebrows went up.

'I'll race you to the folly. If I win, I send my order. If you win, you may have my undivided attention for the ride back.'

Beau's head jerked a little as he worked to understand what was happening. 'You want me to *race* you?'

'On horseback, yes. I certainly couldn't best you on foot.'

He blinked, astonished to discover she had not been speaking in jest.

'Fine. Set the date and time.'

'Now.' She was already moving towards the door but paused to throw over her shoulder, 'Well, a half hour. I need to change.'

He stared at the door, dumbfounded by the rapid turn of events, and struggled against her audacity and his better sense. She was *his* ward, and he could compel her to talk to him without something so ridiculous as a horse race she was bound to lose. Nevertheless, forty minutes later he found himself beside her as she stepped onto the mounting block at the stables.

'Oh, you're here,' she said with what he knew to be feigned surprise. She was baiting him, so rather than respond, he asked her the rules of her little race.

'Quite straightforward. No short cuts. No cheats. We'll go across the down, over the creek, and the first one to reach the folly at the top of the hill wins.' She looked him over in mocking assessment. 'If that's acceptable to you?'

She'd asked such in a way that made him think she'd prefer him to disagree.

'Certainly. Who—'

'William, there,' Miss Doubleday cut him off, gesturing with her crop to the groom walking a short way down the drive. 'He's got a white handkerchief ready when we are.'

Without speaking, they rode to where William was standing, arm in the air, and positioned their horses shoulder to shoulder. When both were satisfied with the placement of the other, she nodded to the groom.

'On yer marks,' William called louder than necessary. 'Get set. Go!' On *go*, he dropped the hand with the handkerchief and the two of them dashed off.

Beau almost felt bad for his immediate, easy lead. *Almost.* His concern had slipped into frustration, and he enjoyed charging the down on Arion, knowing Miss Doubleday was trailing behind. He'd ridden and raced about this countryside more times than he could ever count when he was just a boy. He may not feel at home within the walls of Oakmoss, but outside…

His thought was cut short by the sound of a second set of pounding hooves thrumming in his ears. A little to his left a flash of colour caught his attention, green as the wet grass they raced upon, and for one confounding moment he wondered how she could've possibly caught up to him. In the next, he realised she was going to jump the creek at full speed and shouted out at her, although he was certain she couldn't make out his words.

Miss Doubleday glanced over her shoulder, the devil's own smile on her face, before she folded low to her horse's neck and sailed over the waterway.

Beau kicked his mount after her, but it was only a moment before he knew it was useless. He'd somehow ended up several lengths behind her, and he watched, his nostrils flaring in anger, as she bolted up the hill, slowing only once she passed the folly. By the time he reached it, she was coming round the other side, leaning to pat her horse's shining neck, and, by the movement of her mouth, congratulating it on a job well done.

'If you'd like anything added to the order, perhaps for your own rooms, you need only say so.'

Her smug look, her flippant attitude, sent a swell of irrational fury through him. Or perhaps it was her flushed cheeks, the satisfied shine in her eyes, the regal way she sat upon her horse, and his inability to take her in his arms.

'What were you thinking jumping the creek like that?' Beau hadn't meant to raise his voice, but it sounded loud among the birdsong and swish and swill of leaves in the wind.

'Like the hundreds of times I've done before?' Her eyebrows raised in challenge, daring him to push her.

'Don't gammon me, Miss Doubleday. My father would never let you do such a thing.'

'And he's been gone above four years now. Although I understand how you may not keep track of time the same way as the rest of us.'

A sharp pinching sensation spread through his chest. She'd known exactly where to land her thrust for maximum impact. He ignored the guilt and let indignation guide him. 'You could have fallen. You could have hurt the horse or killed yourself.' Beau's voice shook the air around them like a clap of thunder.

She looked a little stunned by his outburst, but her shock was soon replaced with scorn. 'And then what? You'd have to inform my family?' The last word slipped from her mouth like something distasteful she'd rather spit into a napkin.

It happened lightning fast, the flash of pain he saw in her eyes. He was caught off guard and could see the exact moment her mask slipped back into place.

'Your father never encouraged my jumping—it was more of a hop anyhow—but he showed me how to do so. He considered riding part of my education, particularly as the estate can only be covered in its entirety on horseback. I've *jumped* that creek more times in the last few years than you have in the whole of your life. Now,' she said, turning her horse in the general direction of the house, 'you'll excuse me. I've an order to place.'

Beau watched her go, not bothering to urge his own horse forward. He was out of temper, with her, with his father, and most of all with himself.

13

With a frown, Emerald continued her attack on the pianoforte. Beau thought her free of accomplishments, so perhaps he would overlook her in this end of the house if he deigned to seek her out again. Notes from Beethoven's Symphony No. 5 resonated in her chest and came to life in the long narrow room. She closed her eyes and hammered on the keys with all the impotent fury she felt. A gust of air alerted her to a door opening at her back, but she remained inside the music. Her fingers moved of their own accord, punishing the black and white keys through the swelling coda of the opening movement.

'My, my, child,' the dowager said as she approached the instrument, her delicate applause quiet in the wake of the storm just passed through. 'Your playing improves every time I have the pleasure of hearing you.'

Emerald flushed at the praise, despite knowing her talent extended beyond what was typical of an accomplished young lady. She'd taken to the instrument as a child, sitting on her father's lap as he taught her scales and chords, encouraged her to improvise and follow her fingers wherever they led. When she'd arrived at Oakmoss, playing had made her feel closer to him, and since he'd passed, it was one of the few things requiring so much concentration she couldn't think about him, miss him, mourn him. She often played until her hands cramped and her shoulders curled in so much that Lady Avon worried Emerald would develop an unsightly hunch.

'Although,' the dowager said, taking a seat on the bench next to Emerald, who continued to pluck at the keys, 'your playing is typically…less violent.'

A lopsided half-smile tugged at Emerald's lips.

Lady Avon absently ruffled through the sheets of music before her. 'Better the keys, I suppose, than your desired target.'

'Am I so transparent?'

'Hardly, dear one. You're as good at keeping yourself to yourself as any matron of the *ton*. My son's return was bound to ruffle feathers, yours especially.'

Emerald hadn't realised she'd been tapping on the same key in quick succession until the dowager's hand settled over hers. She was at a loss for how to respond, though many words came to mind—but she wasn't going to call Beau insufferable, idiotish, dangerous, foolish, irresponsible, or entitlement-in-shiny-Hessians to his mother's face.

'I've done you a disservice, letting you take on so much.'

'No.' Then she said it again, discovering there wasn't much else she could add to her denial given the truth of the statement. She would never, ever say so to a woman who provided her not just clothing, food, shelter, every luxury she could want, but also kindness, compassion, acceptance. Nor would she share with the dowager the true source of her disquiet.

There was nothing either of them could do, so why burden another with so great a weight.

Things Emerald hated included peas, long stretches of wet weather, and how at night she watched for Beau's retreating form from her window. Twice more she'd seen him disappear into the dark, Saunders by his side. Once, he had turned, and she was sure he'd been looking up at her window, although she'd let go of the drape snatched in her fingers as soon as she'd seen him pause. She had crawled along the hand-knotted Persian rug back to her bed, not that she'd really believed him capable of seeing through the heavy velvet fabric she'd hidden behind. There was one other thing she hated most of all: the relief she'd felt when she caught a glimpse of him the morning after.

At Emerald's side, her ladyship released a soft sigh, and her lips tipped up in a restrained, wistful smile. 'George would be incredibly proud of you, you know, but I shouldn't have relinquished my responsibilities so easily. Ah, save your protestations,' the dowager said, patting Emerald's hand when she began to object. 'My point is that we now find ourselves in a bit of a tangle. I've been thinking, if you're amenable, perhaps we remove to London for the season. It's long past time, really. It's just that when George passed…' She broke off her sentence and gave one almost imperceptible sniff. 'Be that as it may, I've been remiss in my duties to you. I should have taken you years ago, but my motivations have been selfish in not wanting to lose you, which is bound to happen. Every eligible gentleman from the border to Brighton will be requesting your hand.'

Emerald wondered if the disbelief she felt showed on her face. She was not a Calverleigh in any meaningful way, nor had she much of a dowry—three thousand left to her by her father, plenty for a country miss but woefully short of town standards. She suspected the Beaus of the *ton* would look right through her. Still, the gowns, the dancing, the theatre, and the company would be far more varied than any found in their seaside town. Even if none of that had appealed to her, which it very much did, a chance to remove herself from Beau's presence felt like a lifeline. She didn't trust him, but she was also drawn to him like a hummingbird to nectar. The unsettling combination of those two warring feelings made her desperate for some relief.

'You are too generous with my prospects,' Emerald replied, a playful lilt to her words, 'but all the same, I'd be delighted to have a season.'

The dowager clapped her hands together at her chest. 'Truly? Wonderful. Wonderful!' Her ladyship sprang from the bench with more enthusiasm than Emerald had ever seen before, and she wondered if Lady Avon had never suggested a season because of her own uncertainty at Emerald's reception of the idea.

'Leave it all to me, my dear. March or even early April is when the season really begins, but we'll go down early. You'll need a new wardrobe, of course, and time to get your bearings.'

Emerald nodded along at the plans being made, unable to match the dowager's enthusiasm with her mind otherwise occupied.

In a span of days, she'd been terrified, devastated, angry, annoyed, and now weary.

Beau was putting the entire family at risk with his dangerous behaviour and, she assumed, illegal activities—for why else would he be skulking about in the late hours, with his valet of all people? She desired answers even if she feared them and in addition felt owed some accounting for his return to Oakmoss. Since that awful night, Emerald had begun to wonder if whatever scheme he was involved in was the thing that had pulled him back, rather than responsibility or duty or family.

For days she'd tried to speak with him privately, but for a man with the annoying habit of always being around, he could not be found. The one time she'd caught him in the hall after lying in wait behind the door of the orangery, Mrs Marshall had interrupted with a pressing question from the cook and forced Emerald to retreat.

Once, she'd been certain she'd heard him clear his throat in the library, but when she'd looked inside the room it had been empty. When he deigned to appear in the study after several days had passed, Emerald had wanted answers, but she'd wanted retribution more.

She had delighted in frustrating him and in besting him during their race, but the exhilaration from doing so had been short-lived. Emerald was still without answers, and worse, a pervasive sense of sorrow continued to plague her.

The familiar feeling of anguish which had washed over her once Beau returned her to Oakmoss after that awful night had been a horrid surprise. She'd recognised the feeling on impact: grief. Grief for the man she supposed Beau to be, the one who, despite all his faults, had captivated her for years even from hundreds of miles away. Somehow, in gaining the knowledge he wasn't who she'd believed, she'd lost a piece of who she thought she was.

---

14

*B*eau was locked in a stalemate with his ward. Worse still was the stalemate in which he found himself set against...himself. When he had first returned home and beheld the woman his ward had become in his absence, he had buried his body's initial reaction to her deep down. He had walked into the drawing room, and the moment he'd seen her, his pulse had skittered, his stomach had dropped, and he could see the depth and breadth of a lifetime shared between them. As her guardian, he had a duty to protect her and, in doing so, to ignore every sweet, intoxicating thing about her.

'Buddle, have you seen Miss Doubleday?' he questioned, as he came down the main staircase in the house.

'She's within the green parlour, my lord.'

Beau turned on the ball of his foot to retreat back up the stairs.

Buddle made a little scratching noise, not quite a cough. 'The young lady is with guests, sir.'

Beau stared at the butler a moment longer than necessary,

wanting but refusing to ask whom she was entertaining. 'Thank you, Buddle.'

The door to the drawing room was wide open, and when he entered the first thing he noticed was how the little group was arranged. Louisa and Miss Lyon were seated side by side on one sofa, and directly across from them on the other, Mr Lyon and Miss Doubleday. Beau quelled a rising flicker of jealousy.

'Brother.' Louisa smiled brightly. 'What a charming surprise. I'd not thought you indoors today. Do join us,' she said, gesturing to one of the open chairs sitting at a right angle near the edge of the sofa.

'Yes, do.' Miss Doubleday reasserted the invitation, as she was the hostess of the small party, but Beau could tell by the flat line of her mouth she was displeased to do so.

For one rare, mischievous moment, a sensual smile curved his mouth. He let every ungentlemanly thought play across his face for a mere fraction of a moment while his hungry gaze raked over her. His eyes came to rest on her face. Colour touched her cheeks. She crossed one ankle over the other, unwound them again, and brushed her hands over her dress.

Beau took a seat just as she rose to offer him coffee, a rasp of agitation in her low, silken voice. He accepted, forcing himself to focus on Lyon and not on the natural sway of her hips as she walked to the cart on which the coffee things were laid out. Lyon, who would make a fine match for some other woman, but not his ward.

Before he had a chance to tell her how he took his drink, she was handing him a cup. His gaze drifted from her to the coffee—black, as he preferred, but he also took it with half a sugar cube. Miss Doubleday crossed to her seat. He took a sip and tasted the exact right amount of sugar, as well as something else, cinnamon maybe. Beau looked up from the cup to find her scrutinising him, but only for a moment before she flicked her stare back to the little group, which had returned to their conversation while she'd served him.

'How are you finding Kent, my lord? Much as you left it?' Miss Lyon asked.

Beau hadn't seen the young lady since her first season out and thought the years had been as kind to her as they had her brother. 'In many respects, yes, but some things have altered beyond recognition.' As if by their own will, his eyes slipped towards his ward before returning to Miss Lyon. 'Is your aunt Margaret well?'

'She suffered a severe attack of influenza for a fortnight after Michaelmas but has recovered and is as stout as ever.'

'I'm pleased to hear it. I am also quite overdue in paying her a call. Her cook makes the best cakes. Whenever I visit, your aunt has a way of making me feel little more than a schoolboy.' He felt Miss Doubleday watching him, noticed her head tilt in consideration, and was desperate to know what she was thinking. It was as if he was suddenly possessed by an irrational desire to please her and to show her there was more to him than whatever dark things she suspected. Mr Lyon laughed, drawing Beau's attention from his ward.

'It's not just you,' the younger man said. 'It seems as if she is always either chiding me or patting my head, but either way, I feel more like a boy of ten than a man of five-and-twenty. Another few years and my bones will creak when a storm is coming.'

'Says he as if he's one foot in the grave!' exclaimed Miss Doubleday. 'I am not so many years behind you, and your sister even fewer. Have we nothing left to look forward to?'

Beau sipped his coffee, his jaw clenching as he swallowed.

He did not care for her teasing response or the ease of their interactions. None of it was surprising. The Lyons had been visiting their aunt for ten years or more, ever since it was decided the brother would inherit her estate. Earndale Park was not large by comparison to Oakmoss. But it earned, he guessed, almost four thousand pounds a year. Certainly the income was enough for Mr Lyon to support a small family in comfort and allow for some elegancies, particularly if the rumours of him and his sister inheriting a little wealth from their grandmother proved true.

'Are you fishing for a compliment, Miss Doubleday, because you know I'll be gallant in my response?' Mr Lyon turned his whole body towards her as he spoke, all but excluding the rest of the party from their conversation. Beau took another sip of coffee to hide a scowl and began to make a list of all Lyon's faults, beginning with his insufferable amiability. 'Your best years are ahead of you, as you no doubt know, and your best dances, if you consent to be my partner at our final assembly before my sister and I leave to London for the season next week.'

'That sounded as much like a compliment to yourself as it was to me,' replied Emerald. 'But I'm afraid Lady Avon has a prior commitment.'

Mr Lyon nodded to Beau. 'Would it be so bad for your guardian to accompany you? We are in the country, after all.'

'Not at all, but I was remiss when I failed to mention her ladyship has requested her son's escort that evening.' Miss Doubleday looked to Beau when she spoke, the glint in her eyes daring him to contradict the lie.

Beau was a kettle over the fire coming to a boil, both impressed with how easily she lied and angry with her for doing so and preventing him from taking the opening Lyon offered. He opened his mouth to mount a protest when Buddle came into the room to announce the arrival of Mr Babin.

'I'd thought to pay a call on his lordship,' the man said, looking at Beau first before taking in the small party as a whole. 'Do not let me interrupt. I'm happy to return another time.'

'Nonsense,' Miss Doubleday said, rising. 'You are welcome to join. It's only coffee and conversation, getting our fill before the Lyons leave for town. If your business is private, you may break away at your leisure, but do let me pour you a cup.'

Beau studied the man as he took a seat directly opposite himself, surprised that Mr Babin would pay a call, given they had no more than a slight acquaintance.

Mr Babin accepted the cup of coffee from Miss Doubleday with a grin, but turned to Beau with a sharp, purposeful look and asked without preamble, 'Did you find what you were looking for in Broadstairs?'

'Broadstairs?' repeated Louisa, her voice and face reflecting her surprise as she looked at Beau.

Miss Doubleday said nothing and looked into her own cup, taken by a sudden interest in its contents.

'It was as quaint as I recall, the bookshop especially. It seemed you were rather familiar with the place yourself.'

'The proprietor was a close friend of my father's. I've spent countless hours there over the years.'

Beau sipped his coffee, ignoring the curious and confused faces around him. 'Was your father as prodigious a reader as you?'

It was possible Mr Babin boxed or was a sharp shot with a pistol or had any other number of traits cultivated for running illegal goods, but unlike Beau, he had not trained the emotion out of his expressions. The gentleman's chest flared, his eyes narrowed, his jaw jutted out then back to its rightful place. Beau held the man in a cool stare, almost daring him to say more.

'Quite.' Babin's lips pinched in a smug smile. 'How did you enjoy the fine brandy at the Silver Swan? Not the kind of haunt I pictured you at, known among smugglers and whatnot.'

Babin said so in an offhand, almost affable way, but Beau knew a threat when he heard one. Out of the corner of his eye, he saw the cup and saucer in Miss Doubleday's hand wobble.

'I suppose that's why they have such a fine selection.' Beau had no interest in correcting Babin's erroneous assumption he'd made it in for a drink. The greater distance he could put between his ward and that night, the better.

A small fire crackled in the grate, and Louisa set her cup down on its saucer, the tink of bone china ringing loud like a shot in the tense silence.

'Let us move on from the conversation about brandy and books—not that I don't read my fair share, but I can't say it's the topic I'm most interested in when in the company of three fine ladies. Yes, Esther, I'm including you,' Mr Lyon added with a teasing smile for his sister.

Beau turned to him. 'Do share with us your topic of choice.'

Mr Lyon positioned himself almost fully facing Miss Doubleday. 'Whether my favourite neighbour will grace us with her presence in London? I go to appease my father and mother, but your company would make it all much more bearable.'

'If you continue to talk so, it won't be long before my head is too big to fit in the carriage and soon after the ballroom,' she replied with a smile, and placed her hand on Mr Lyon's forearm in a friendly gesture that would have elicited a growl in a lesser composed man than Beau.

'Are you not your own man, Lyon? Certainly you may remain in the country should you wish it.' Annoyance and anger, irrational as it was, were burning in Beau's chest as he worked to keep his countenance.

Miss Doubleday swivelled to face him. 'The *ability* to do something does not mean it should be done.' Her tone was sharp, her rebuke clear.

Louisa stood abruptly. 'I'm going to refresh my coffee and take a turn about the room. It's a pleasure to stretch one's legs after sitting so long in one attitude. I'll be glad when the gloomy weather clears, and we once more find ourselves strolling under clear blue sky. May I get anyone anything? Here, Beau, let me,' she said, taking the cup from his hand as she passed.

In his sister's meandering speech was her own subtle disapproval of his behaviour. It stung not because she was more than a decade his junior, but because he knew himself to be acting foolishly, ungentlemanly even, at least towards Mr Lyon. The man was guilty of nothing more than being friendly with Beau's ward; it wasn't Mr Lyon's fault Beau could not act on his own feelings for Miss Doubleday.

His sister thrust his cup back into his hands, and he took a sip without looking, realising as he held the hot liquid in his mouth that she'd used equal parts coffee and cream and an entire lump of sugar. The sweetness pinched at his jaw.

'Mr Lyon, allow me,' Louisa said, reaching for his cup. 'Cream and no sugar?'

He nodded, giving over the little saucer. 'Quite right. I too cannot abide such dreary days as these. Although winter has been unseasonably fine, we can all agree. How are your lessons progressing, Miss Calverleigh? Sorting out your right foot from your left?'

Louisa's back was to the rest of the room. Yet Beau could see her profile and watched the light pink tinge spread over her cheeks. The little smile playing about her mouth while she poured Mr Lyon's coffee—just as he preferred—made Beau think it wasn't from embarrassment. She carried the saucer with both hands, saying to Lyon as she did, 'You will have to wait a year till my own come-out and see.'

Beau looked at his sister, a little shocked by the cheeky nature of her reply.

'The prospect of such fine company in the metropolis certainly increases my own interest in attending for the season,' commented Babin. 'I cannot fault Lyon for wishing to write his name on your dance card. Should I be so lucky to find myself in your company when there is the possibility of dancing, I do hope you'll leave a space for my own name. Perhaps we might not leave our next meeting to chance, however, and instead plan on a ride when the sun returns,' Babin said, directing his attention to Miss Doubleday.

When she consented, Mr Babin beamed at her, but then glanced in Beau's direction and offered a small smile, without amusement but full of contempt and satisfaction.

15

'Would you care to join me in the study, Babin? I'd not thought to ask if your call was more than social in nature,' said Beau as the company in the green parlour stood to leave.

'I've trespassed on your hospitality long enough, my lord.'

Beau held an arm out, signalling for the man to follow the rest of the party out, and said with false pleasantness, 'I wish you a good day then.'

'You take care,' Babin countered with emphasis, through a smile that was little more than bared teeth.

Beau set the threat aside and thought nothing more of it until he was ambushed on the road to Broadstairs that very night.

Saunders had gone ahead after helping Beau dress for dinner to sit at the pub, watching, listening, observing. Three more times they had visited Broadstairs, but only once were the men moving goods. The distinct lack of glass tinking against glass made them suspect it was a shipment of gunpowder. One way or another, they needed to confirm their suspicion, by luck, by coercion, or by opening the cellar doors themselves.

As Beau neared the barn where they had previously stabled their horses, an aura of expectation settled over him. His blood thrummed, his skin tingled, and a minute later four men on horseback were upon him.

He felled one with a throwing knife to the soft tissue where shoulder meets chest from a distance of several metres. He waited for the other three to come nearer, then dropped from the saddle and sliced through the Achilles of another. From the trees came the scurry of birds woken by a thunderous scream.

One man had turned his horse in the direction of the village. His friend called out, 'Oi! Where de ye think yer goin'?' but received only the fading pound of hooves in retreat for an answer.

'You and me then, guvnor. The boss wants ye roughed an' I'm happy to oblige. Keep comin' where yer not wanted and it'll be much worse for ye.'

Beau would've chuckled at the misplaced confidence if he hadn't been annoyed. A flailing boot caught him in the face as he yanked the man from his horse and quieted his yapping with one punishing jab.

With a little shake of his head, Beau walked to the man with the knife in his shoulder and pulled it out. The man howled.

'May I suggest dousing the wound in some of your illegally procured brandy sooner rather than later? This knife has seen more men than your preferred brothel.'

Beau wiped the blood off on the inside of his black coat, tucked the knife back into the custom lining of his boot, and left them to meet his valet.

'LET US HAVE A LOOK,' Saunders said the morning after, speaking to Beau as if he were a small child unwilling to remove his hand from his scraped knee.

With a grimace, Beau pulled the roughly hewn pack of ice from his left eye. Saunders sucked in a breath.

'Indeed.'

Beau roused himself from the chair in his bedroom where he'd been sitting. The ice in his handkerchief had begun to melt and he deposited both in the bowl at his elbow before walking to the mirror to survey the damage himself. It wasn't so bad as he'd expected—the skin under his eye was mostly pale yellow with hints of purple and blue. Not the worst he'd had, not by a long shot.

'I pinched some of her ladyship's Pear's Almond Bloom,' said Saunders, removing a small tin from his coat pocket.

Beau's only reaction was a mildly disapproving stare.

'If you'd get your own like I suggested…' The valet let his sentence trail off as he dipped a finger into the powder and began patting the bruised skin. 'What will you tell the ladies?'

Beau inspected his eye. The powder helped, but nothing would cover the evidence of last night completely. 'Nothing. A clumsy mistake. Too stupid to explain.'

When he descended to the breakfast parlour and responded as such to his mother's inquiry, she let her gaze linger on him several seconds, pursed her mouth, and then returned to reading the society pages of *The Times*. Louisa, who entered a short time later, went so far as to suggest he ought not to ride while foxed. Given he'd never been in his cups around his mother or sister, he wondered where she'd get such an idea. But, as he had no better explanation to offer, he let her assumption stand and made for his study before finishing the bacon on his plate.

He turned the corner just as a flash of muslin disappeared into the music room and called out to Miss Doubleday, reaching the door just as she reappeared. Her expression was one of strained tolerance, but her clamped lips parted in surprise when she noticed his black eye.

'We are past due for a private conversation, Miss Doubleday.'

'Another time. This day is given over to *refining* my accomplishments.'

Beau winced and blamed it on his injury.

'What happened to your eye?'

'Nothing. Silly, really. If you have a moment.' He gestured behind her to the music room.

She remained standing firm in the doorway. 'I don't.'

For a long moment, he looked at her, as if his will alone could convince her to unfold a little. 'It would not please me to compel you, but as your guardian, I will if I must.'

Her black brows slanted into a frown, but Miss Doubleday didn't acquiesce and allow him into the room behind her. She brushed past him, the fabric of her skirt rustling against his breeches. 'Miss Doubleday,' he called, trailing behind her through the corridor. She turned down a set of steps at the back of the house, and he followed her until they came to a stop in the kitchen. The work within halted, everyone turning to stare at the pair. A few faint gasps and a quiet murmur of astonishment rippled round the large, open room.

'Stay,' she ordered him, disappearing into a storeroom and returning a moment later with a small jar of something in her hands. 'Come.' They retraced their steps, and once in the privacy of the music room, she closed the door. 'Sit.'

'Do you always speak to gentlemen as you would a dog?' he asked, doing as she bid and seating himself in one of the chairs along the wall.

Miss Doubleday came to stand in front of him, so close he could wrap his arms around her, bury his face against her taut abdomen, and drink his fill of her clean, citrus scent. She unscrewed the lid, and he silently accepted it as she held it out for him to take. He watched her ring finger swipe through the contents of the jar still in her hand. 'As far as I know, curs fight, gentlemen don't.'

'Who said anything about a fight?'

'I suppose I was wrong to compare you to a dog—they're incapable of lying. Close your eyes.' With her ring finger, she began to dab the bruised skin around his eye.

Beau tried not to focus on how her touch felt, the warmth of it under the cooling sensation spreading over his tender skin. 'What is that?'

'Arnica jelly. It will help with the pain and bruising. You can reapply as often as you'd like, but I suggest forgoing the powder next time—it acts as a bit of a barrier between your skin and the ointment.'

For the first time in more than twenty years, Beau blushed. 'Where did you learn to use it?'

'Mrs Shackley. Her husband—'

'Farms wheat and turnips.' He opened one eye to gauge her reaction, but if she was surprised or displeased to discover he knew who his tenants were as well as she, she gave none of it away.

'I fell off Calliope jumping a hedge near their cottage. My fault, not the horse's—I overestimated my ability. Luckily, the only real damage done was to my pride. Mrs Shackley saw from her window and rushed to check on me. Then she soothed my frayed nerves with a little tea and sent me home with some arnica for the soreness and bruises she knew I'd have after a tumble. I've sworn by it ever since.'

'And why the basket the Shackley family receives for Christmas every year has in it a fine canister of Twining's tea?' Beau hadn't realised his eyes had drifted closed again till he felt her finger gliding along the fine edge of his lashes. When her hand came away, he immediately missed the intimacy of her touch, the concern articulated with just a finger. He forced his eyes to open.

Her mouth was set in a stubborn line. 'Why are you back?'

The question hung in the air like moisture after a heavy rain.

'Because Oakmoss is my home.'

'It has been for all the years past. Why now?'

'You wish me gone again?' Beau didn't know why the answer mattered to him, but he asked the question anyway.

'I wished you here when we had a year without summer and many of the crops failed. I wished you here when the Hamiltons' barn went up in flames, and when scarlet fever took three of the Jones children and two from the Bowers. I stayed up so many nights wishing for your return that I ran out of stars to wish upon.'

'You need not say more.'

'Quite right. I've had my turn. What are you doing here? Or maybe the more important question is, what are you doing in Broadstairs?'

Beau lowered his gaze, observing how much better his eye already felt. When he looked back at Miss Doubleday, her face was clouded with unease.

'I cannot say.'

'Cannot or choose not to? You sneak about like a shadow—'

'Once.'

'Two more times, I've counted to date.'

Beau held the bland expression on his face. Once then she had missed him. 'You've been watching me? I'm flattered.'

'Of course you are.' She snatched the jar from his hand and returned the lid. 'You slink about, with your valet, no less. You turn up with a black eye, which I know is related to the sneaking. You know I know it's related to the sneaking.'

'And so you would like us to know it together?' Her expression pinched, and this time he let the corner of his mouth tip up. 'My concerns are my own, Miss Doubleday.'

'My concerns are also yours, are they not? Tell me then, what would happen to me if my guardian were to perish or be imprisoned? I am entirely dependent on the generosity of this family. My life would be uprooted once again should the estate's present owner—that's you, although it's occurred to me perhaps you've yet to fully realise it—finds himself inconvenienced.'

Her speech deflated him; worse, he couldn't offer her any guarantee of security or assurance. It was the same problem his father had had and what had precipitated their ferocious row before Beau left for the last time.

'I cannot—'

'Those words again,' she said, sounding equal parts exasperated and angry, and whirling away from him before taking hard steps back. 'Are you working for the French? Who was that Monsieur Allard, and why haven't you mentioned his visit to anyone?'

'He's a friend I met abroad, and no.'

'You're a smuggler then? Why else would you be by the coast in the dead of night?'

'The man ready to accost you was a smuggler. I am not involved in anything illegal. You may stop convincing yourself otherwise, although I realise your urge to uncover my flaws is strong. I'm glad we have made our way to this overdue subject. Never, ever again do something so foolish.'

She gasped. '*I'm* the foolish one?'

'Does that come as some great surprise to you? Had I not turned up when I did, you would have been ruined at best, killed—accidentally or otherwise—at worst.' He knew both those things had been thrumming through her mind that night, but he spoke them aloud anyway. She had seen him leave the house twice more, and he needed to be sure she was too scared of the consequences to follow him again. Her face was alive with emotion, and he suspected she wished to protest but knew he was in the right. 'It may not suit you, used to having your own way as you are, but you've no right to interfere in my concerns and no claim on how I spend my time or with whom. If you follow me again and are lucky enough to be caught by me and not some lecher, I will lock you in your room till you come of age.'

Miss Doubleday bristled, and as close as she was, he could see her grind her teeth behind her tense lips.

'And stay away from Babin.'

'Why?'

'As your guardian I'm afforded the privilege of not explaining myself to you.'

'You're right. It's much more fun this way. Shall I wager a guess?' she asked, raising her fine, arched brows, and lifting her eyes skyward in feigned contemplation. 'Accomplice or rival.'

The muscle in Beau's jaw ticked.

'Ah, I see I'm right about one of them. You need not confirm which; I'm satisfied with my own answer. But tell me, if I fail to heed your instruction, what will you do? Club me and drag me back to your lair?'

'If needs must.' Beau pushed up from the chair, forcing her to take a step back. In a softer voice, he said, 'Thank you for this,' with a vague wave to his eye.

She held out the little jar for him to take, his bare fingertips grazing the soft skin of her upturned palm as he did so. He studied the lines crisscrossing her hand for a moment. His breath suddenly stuck in his chest. How easy it would be to lift her hand, dip his head, and place a light, searching kiss there for her to hold. His lips parted with the thought. An aching need to touch her, to be touched by her, made the hand holding the jar shake ever so slightly. He withdrew, the sharp pain of restraint making his muscles ache.

With a nod, he turned to leave the room. Only years of training away every impulse kept him from looking back.

16

With a furrowed brow, Emerald looked at her open palm as if a seedling might sprout from its centre, trying to understand what had captivated Beau. She turned to look after him, her mouth opening in question, but he had already disappeared down the long hall, leaving her to her confusion and irritation.

Pacing the room, she told herself that the root of her concern was self-serving. It wasn't wrong to tell him her life would be uprooted should he be so stupid as to get himself killed, but Emerald was struggling against the niggling feeling underneath—the feeling that if he should cease to exist, somehow she would too. Inhaling as deep a breath as she could manage, she held it a moment, then exhaled slowly and gave her head a little shake.

Before retreating to her rooms, she peered into the corridor, looking in both directions, not that she really thought Beau lingered anywhere near.

When he made no appearance at dinner or in the drawing room after, Emerald had the unwelcome suspicion she wouldn't find him anywhere on the grounds of the estate had she the desire to go looking. It was futile to put that thought from her mind as she stared out her bedroom window into the dark night, intrigue and concern making sleep impossible. Her fingers fidgeted with the fabric pooled in her lap. Outside, the faint, faraway hoot of an owl reached Emerald's ears, her senses heightened while she waited for some sign of his return.

She rolled her neck to release the tension then tipped her forehead into the cool pane of glass. A wave of grief and longing for the previous Lord Avon swept over her—for someone she could turn to, someone whose counsel and guidance she could depend on. After her father died, Lord Avon had been the one to pull her from her sadness, one ride at a time. Those were the moments she'd felt listened to, felt like someone cared about what mattered to her, her wants and dreams. He had promised her a season, promised to find a man worthy of her. She'd wished for nothing more than a chance to find a husband she could love and who would love her in return, a home of her own, children whose joy and laughter would ring through the halls. All she hoped for now was some measure of control over her future.

The following morning, Beau was not down at breakfast, nor was he in the study when she stepped in to balance the accounts, and she debated how long she would wait until she asked after him. Distraction came in the welcome form of a summons to the dowager's sitting room, but still Emerald found herself searching the great expanse of green for a moving speck of black.

'Em? Emerald, dear?'

Emerald jerked her head from the window of Lady Avon's room. 'Yes, ma'am?'

'I asked if you prefer the strand of pearls and diamonds over the diamonds on their own. Perhaps we ought to take both—diamonds are a must for your first ball in London,' the dowager said, holding up a delicate necklace of bevelled diamonds set in gold that increased in size as they drew nearer the large centre stone.

There were cases upon cases of jewels set out on the dressing table. Emerald couldn't recall her ladyship wearing much jewellery at all, and her eyes had nearly doubled in size when she and Louisa first entered the room. The young girl who still lingered somewhere in Emerald was in awe of it all.

'Are emeralds too on the nose?' Louisa asked, lifting a box containing a diamond and emerald choker with matching earrings and a stack of bracelets.

'Not at all, only not quite fitting for a girl in her first season.'

Emerald smiled and shook her head. 'I am hardly that.'

'In London, that's exactly what you will be, and we cannot afford a misstep.'

It was a polite way of saying no one could be exactly sure how the *ton* would receive Emerald.

'Do not think me in the frets, dear, only conscious of what it means to be a young lady embarking on her first season. You will soon discover it's not at all uncommon to have as many foes as friends, only you must treat them all equally. Or you must when you are a green girl. Although years have passed since my last stay in town, I am far from friendless, you know.'

Emerald stifled the laugh bubbling up in her and covered it with a little cough. Between both sides of the family, the Calverleighs were related to a half dozen peers and however many more families of ancient lineage. Before Lord Avon's passing, he and her ladyship had removed to town for the season every year, and Lady Avon's elderly aunt had been brought to Oakmoss to stay with Emerald and Louisa while they continued their studies.

Her ladyship would send letters describing all the fashion and balls and fêtes. The theatre and opera and routs. Little more than a girl at the time, Emerald would lay awake at night, imagining herself shimmering under some excessively large chandelier, a handsome suitor leading her to the floor. She would remember the times as a child when she would drape herself in sheets, pretending they were wildly elegant gowns, and twirl about the drawing room while her father played the piano.

A dreamy sigh broke into Emerald's reminiscences.

'I can't wait for next year,' said Louisa, a faraway look in her eyes.

Emerald smiled. 'Is another year long enough for you to stop tripping over your own feet?'

'I'll have you know I've made excellent progress in the last weeks,' the younger girl said, with her nose in the air and feigned accents of superciliousness before giggling. 'By next year, I'll be as fine a dancer as you.'

'Better, if I dared to make a wager.'

'You can't possibly think so!'

The dowager, still mulling over the options in front of her, interjected as a mother was wont to do. 'You both dance beautifully.'

Emerald and Louisa shared an amused glance.

'Your dance card here is always full,' the younger girl continued.

On a laugh, Emerald responded, 'You can't possibly know such a thing.'

'I do. Because I always demand you tell me everything

after. So unless you've been lying to me for years, from the number of dances you participate in, I can surmise your dance card is always full. And from such a detail, I can glean that you must be a very elegant dancer. Of course, I've seen you here at home myself, but 'tis not the same as a ball or assembly—and because I've two working eyes in my head, I'm certain of your loveliness. We can all agree sharing a dance is often the first step towards sharing a life, and if you liked a gentleman here, you wouldn't be going to London.'

'Lou!' Emerald couldn't hold back her laugh.

'What I'm saying is you'll have more, and better, prospects in London, and I very much hope you find a gentleman to your taste. You have such a great capacity to love and nowhere for it to go.'

Emerald was touched, and a little embarrassed too. 'I've you and your mama.'

'But your heart can accommodate so much more.'

In her mind, an image of her younger half-sisters formed. Emerald wondered what they looked like now and if they even remembered her. She didn't miss Whichwood or the friends she'd had as a child or the winding paths she used to walk—that life had long felt as though it had been lived by someone else. But she couldn't think of her sisters without a touch of sadness.

'Goodness, you're making me feel quite maudlin.'

'I've just the thing for that,' Louisa replied, walking to the dressing table and returning with a tiara. She secured it to Emerald's head, stepped back, and studied her work with a lip caught between her teeth. 'Is there such a thing as too many diamonds? Let us find out.' Lou layered as much of her mother's jewellery as she could on Emerald—stacks of bangles, brooches sagging the satin of her dress, enough necklaces to weigh down Emerald's tense shoulders—and continued until they were laughing so hard the sparkling headpiece precariously topped on her head fell with a thud to the thick carpet.

Hours later at dinner, when the first course was served and there was still no sign of Beau, Emerald felt herself fraying at the edges, concern and anger peeling away her hard-earned and fire-forged layers. Under the table, her legs bounced, and she struggled to keep her composure as the dowager waxed poetic about her own first season.

'Brother!'

When Louisa cried out, Emerald resisted the impulse to jerk her head towards the door. Instead, she set her spoon next to her bowl, swallowed the lump in her throat, and willed her face into an inscrutable expression before looking in his direction.

'My apologies. Business kept me longer than anticipated.' He went to kiss his mother's cheek before taking his seat, and Emerald watched the consternation on that woman's face melt with the gesture.

'We were just discussing our plans for London,' said Louisa, with innocent enthusiasm reserved for the young.

Beau looked to his sister, but his eyes quickly flicked over to Emerald. 'What plans are these?'

'Mama is taking us down for the season. I am not out yet, of course, but Emerald is and has never had a season in town, which seems a great shame. The assemblies and dinners we have here can't compare. Not that I'd know, but it seems an obvious statement.'

'I see.'

'You're displeased.' His sister frowned, and Emerald wondered how his opinion could still matter so much to her.

'Perhaps he's worried that our presence will somehow

impinge upon his own pleasure. By all accounts, there's not a single ballroom in the capital in which you have failed to find contentment at some point or other, if the papers are to be believed. Although perhaps you've forgotten the steps in the last five years.' Emerald addressed him with such airy accents someone unfamiliar with her might easily overlook the barb. Or maybe it was more an indictment.

It had been her wish to provoke him, a little form of punishment for the worry he unknowingly caused her, but his response was a languid blink, a long pause, and finally, 'Are you so surprised to discover I am fond of dancing? Do you feel such pleasure is reserved for the fairer sex?'

'Beau is a wonderful dancer. Do you remember,' Louisa said, a wistful smile softening her countenance, 'when I was very little and you would let me stand on your feet and called it dancing? Oh, how you would twirl me around the blue drawing room.'

'Because you said it made you feel as if you were dancing among the clouds and stars and the sun in the sky. And only until Father came round. Then it was on his feet you wished to dance.'

Emerald could very well imagine a young Louisa saying such things. The blue drawing room was one of the most elegant on the ground floor, papered in pale shades that appeared to shimmer when the light streamed in through the long windows. The drapes were the colour of the sky on a moonlit night, and every piece of furniture was cream, cerulean, or aquamarine. When she glanced over, both brother and sister seemed adrift in the past, and Emerald suddenly felt like an intruder in a moment, a memory, a place that could never belong to her.

'You're for the marriage mart then, Miss Doubleday?'

The dowager sighed. 'Beauden, really, she's not a piece of cattle going to auction.'

'No doubt he'd prefer I was.' Emerald made the comment into her spoonful of soup. The subject of the marriage mart, however, had animated Lady Avon, who began to speculate, more to herself than anyone else present, as to which eligible gentlemen would be in town. Her chatter prevented her from hearing Emerald, but Louisa snorted into her wineglass. When Emerald peeped at Beau out of the corner of her eye, he was stern-faced and had paused in chewing the food held in his mouth. She swallowed her own soup with a little smile lingering at the corner of her mouth, but her victory was not to last.

Since he was the only gentleman present, they never separated after dinner. He used the opportunity to draw her apart from his mother and sister, keeping Emerald back in the hall as the other two women made their way to the drawing room.

'I was surprised to learn you consented to a season.'

The rich timbre of his calm voice at her side filled her with a strange inner awareness she wished to ignore, and so she said matter-of-factly, 'Because no man wants a penniless wife with no connections?'

'Because I thought you content to keep busy here, with me,' he replied, undaunted by her provocative words.

'If I remain, when you marry one day, I will find myself relegated to the dower house with your mother, where I'll fade into spinsterhood and obscurity after having given the best years of my life to managing an estate to which I've no claim. As pleasurable as such a life sounds, I'd rather take my chances in town.'

'You are quite serious then about making a match while in London?' he asked in his usual cool tone, but Emerald thought for one quick moment there was a glint of displeasure in his eyes.

'Will you forbid it?'

'The trip or your marriage?'

'Either. Both.'

'The trip? No.'

Emerald curled her fingers into her palms until the nails threatened to cut the skin. 'Would you prefer I remained and waited for Mr Lyon or Mr Babin to make me an offer?' She had the satisfaction of seeing his countenance grow taut and grim.

'Are you in anticipation of such?'

'Does it matter?'

'My father desired you to find a worthy match. You may not see it as such, but I will do my best to act in accordance with his wishes, even if we are not always in agreement on the methods.'

She scoffed, and it sounded like a boot crunching gravel. 'Your father…'

'Has his spirit offended you?'

Emerald's lips parted, and she looked around as if the words she wished to speak had fallen out one at a time and she needed to gather them all up in order to form a sentence.

''Tis nothing,' she finally said, her whole body heaving with effort as it struggled to hold everything in. She turned to walk away, but his hand on her arm prevented her. With little effort he halted her steps and turned her body. She was facing him once more, but so close the silence could hardly fit itself between them. Emerald licked her suddenly dry lips and watched him watch her. His eyes dropped to her mouth.

'Tell me.' It wasn't a question. It was a demand.

She shook her head as the breath in her chest hitched.

'Miss Doubleday.'

Emerald tried to control her voice as she spoke, but it cracked nonetheless. 'Whatever faults you felt your father had, real or imagined, he was kind, compassionate. Few men in his position would have taken on a girl like me of no relation. It was a testament to his goodness, his integrity, the loyalty he felt to the friendship shared between him and my father. To know that one is seen, valued, where there is the least expectation of such is a great gift. *You*'—he flinched at her emphasis—'show up with expectation but without word or explanation, and tell me after all the years I've given to you, you might deny me the one thing I want. The one thing I have some little control over.' Her body tremored as she released the words.

'What is it you want?'

Again, she shook her head, feeling foolish for letting the conversation get as far as it already had.

'Please?'

Never, not in this lifetime or the next, had she thought the man in front of her would ever use that word. She brought her eyes to meet his, hoping the unshed tears remained so. For once, his expression was open, his gaze not cold but sincere. He reached out a hand, as if he might take her own in his. He let it drop back by his side, and she felt the emptiness in her own. Still, she could not voice her most private wishes, not aloud and not to him with so many years of acrimony between them. Even as she realised what a thin line separated love and loathing, his earlier words ringing in her ear: *We are capable of feeling both at once and in equal measure.*

---

17

*B*eau had been desperate for her to reveal a little of herself to him, to confide in him her wants, dreams, desires. Instead, she sewed her lips up tight and left him with nothing to do but lead her to the drawing room, where she sat as far away from him as possible and kept herself occupied by playing backgammon with his sister, making the occasional comment to his mother when the dowager's soliloquy on a London season necessitated it.

Miss Doubleday had not appeared at breakfast the following morning. 'Gone riding,' his mother had succinctly put it when he'd gone so far as to inquire, and as he ambled down one of his favourite paths through the park, he wondered if he would catch sight of her.

'Beau! Beau!'

He turned just as Louisa pulled up alongside him in her little gig. 'How well you look driving a handsome pair of horses, Lou.' In truth, his young sister appeared quite grown up driving her own pair, and very much like their mother.

She bowed her head at the compliment. 'Let me take you up. Martha doesn't like when I go fast enough to overtake the little turtles near the pond,' she said with an amused look at the maid next to her.

When Beau looked to Martha, the poor maid was already standing, ready to jump if she must. He suppressed a smile and offered a hand to help her down.

'No groom?' he asked once he'd seated himself next to his sister.

'Emerald doesn't think it necessary when I stay inside the park.'

He kept his thoughts on the immeasurable extent of his ward's authority to himself, and asked, 'And what does our mother think?'

'Oh, you know.' Beau imagined his sister would have added an airy wave of her hand, had one been free. 'She's rather lucky we're both so good, is she not? Short of eloping with the baker's son, I don't know she'd ever stop me from doing anything that might secure my happiness.'

'Would eloping with young Stuart make you happy?'

Her light laugh flitted away as if it had wings. 'I've missed your teasing, brother.'

Beau detected a note of melancholy in her words. 'How kind and ridiculous you are to say so.' After a pause, he pressed, 'And Father, do you miss him terribly, sweetling?'

'In the beginning, of course. It was like an awful pit of despair opened inside of me and was trying to consume me from the inside out. The pain now is not so terrible or bitter. Instead it's more a dull ache or a wistful feeling when I think of everything he's already missed and everything yet to come.' She cast a quick, assessing glance in his direction before adding, 'This might sound strange, but sometimes Emerald reminds me of him.'

'Oh?'

'Little things. She murmurs to herself sometimes when she's working, like he did, and even makes some of the same faces. It was she who nudged me into visiting tenants on my own—tricked me, really, making me think it was my idea because I was so grown up. Just the way he used to get me to do things I didn't want to or didn't think I could.'

His sister, it seemed, could wax poetic on Miss Doubleday endlessly, and his curiosity outweighed his desire to switch to a new subject, so he refrained from interrupting her.

'I see in her his steady determination, his kind but firm resolve, his desire to help others. She had enjoyed teaching some of the children in the village basic arithmetic and reading, and I think she would have spent more of her time doing so, if not—' Louisa broke off, and Beau knew she'd figured out that finishing her sentence would also mean drawing attention to his absence. A sliver of silence wedged between them, and he let it expand. How the conversation continued would be decided by his sister.

Beau stared out at the different shades of green woven together in the Kent countryside. In spring, there would be fragments of yellow when the rapeseed blossomed. He loved the land, the care that crops and livestock necessitated, the harvest and sustenance Oakmoss provided for tenants and farmers. Each time he rode out, his heart swelled with gratitude. He hadn't missed fighting with his father or being redundant, but he had longed to sit under his favourite oak tree, to run his fingers through the grass and feel the blades flutter with life. Beau had begged his father to understand.

Roots and bark, great stalks of wheat, the first daffodils of spring, carried with them the changes in his heart without ever questioning his constancy, his dedication and devotion to them.

Louisa spoke again, her voice calm, quiet, serious. 'You were gone too long, Beau. You don't need me to tell you that. People think children are silly or deaf and therefore cannot comprehend what happens around them. It was always obvious to me, the discord between you and Papa. Not to say you and he didn't get on, only that I know it was easy for me to be Papa's child and less so for you.' Her eyes remained focused ahead on the little path down which they travelled, but he could see what it cost his younger sister to expose herself and him. 'And Emerald,' said Louisa with a dramatic sigh.

Beau thought his sister would say more. When she didn't, he pressed, 'And Emerald what?'

Louisa was quiet a long, thoughtful moment while she composed her thoughts. In the distance, Beau registered the calming sound of running water. Part of the estate ran all the way to the coast, the furthest reaches of the property cut up with little inlets and shallow coves.

'She would be mortified to receive our pity, but it's near impossible for my heart not to squeeze with compassion for her if I spend even a moment thinking about how she wound up here, or even how her life has played out since. You know, Father began taking her out to ride the estate because it was one of the only things to interest her after her own papa died— that, and playing the pianoforte. It would be impossible for another to fill the space left in one's heart by a parent, but sharing ours helped.'

Shame made Beau feel hot all over. 'She's done very well here.'

'Because she's had to. I'm not cross with you, you know, and if you tell me you've been away doing something important, I'll believe you, of course. But even though it may seem like everything is well, that's not an indication it's also been easy.'

Louisa allowed them to lapse into their private thoughts as she pulled her gig into the stable yard and accepted Beau's hand to help her down.

'You go on,' said he. 'I think I'll go for a ride.'

'But the weather is turning.'

Beau shrugged, gave her a scoot forward, and turned away.

FROM THE DOCTOR Beau visited in Broadstairs, he had learned the man who'd spoken of Jemmy the night he'd watched the smugglers was a Mr Poughill, son of a clergyman and father to half a dozen children, including one who survived scarlet fever as a baby but suffered lasting effects. And that Mr Poughill helped the current elderly clergyman in the church garden and cemetery every Wednesday.

When Beau approached, the man was on his knees ripping weeds from a long-forgotten grave despite the fat drops beginning to splatter the gravestones. Mr Poughill glanced up to see who was standing next to him, his eyes narrowing. Beau stood with the pretence of paying his respects, but said quietly after a moment, 'I believe I have the honour of addressing Mr Poughill? Don't stand. Continue as you were.' He looked down over his shoulder, meeting the man's suspicious gaze.

'I recognise you. You were outside the Silver Swan some time ago.'

'Good memory.'

'I wasn't foxed, and neither were you.'

A little muscle at the corner of Beau's lips twitched in appreciation. This man was no fool. 'This isn't the only work you do.'

'No, sir. I'm the butcher as well.'

'Of course you are, but that's not the work to which I'm referring.'

There was a notable pause. 'I can't say I understand you.'

'Come now, you've already introduced the Swan into the conversation,' and, a little impatient to get on with things, Beau added, 'Your son Jemmy is a fine young lad.'

The man threw down his spade and made to stand. 'You leave my boy—'

Beau turned his head a very little. 'I've no intention of bringing harm to your son, but for your safety, his, and my own for that matter, I'd really rather you avoid drawing any unwanted attention.' The church was situated a short distance from the village, and the cemetery behind the main structure. No one was about, but Beau had no desire to explain away his presence or their conversation. Mr Poughill dropped back down. 'Am I right in thinking you smuggle to pay his medical expenses?'

The man gave a terse nod. 'I don't feel good about it. I was raised to know better—to be better'—he cast his eyes skyward as if seeking forgiveness—'but with Jemmy—'

'Just so. What if I could help you, your son?'

Suspicion clouded the man's face.

'Yes, it sounds too good to be true, does it not? You're right to look at me so. I can help, and will, gladly, but require something of you in return, just as you suspect.' Beau had Mr Poughill's attention. 'First, tell me what Babin pays you.'

'Two pounds per haul.'

Beau reached into his coat and retrieved a billfold from which he withdrew ten pounds of one-pound notes, handing it to Poughill, who protested. 'Take it, and tell me what you know of his London plans.'

The man put the money in his coat pocket, looking at his hand like he couldn't believe it had held such a sum at once. 'Not much. He rants about what he sees as injustice for Napoleon. Talks about retribution for France. To be truthful, I didn't take it much too seriously until several barrels of gunpowder arrived. The copper hooping has French manufacturing marks.'

'Have you a date and time?'

Poughill shook his head. 'After Easter, I think he said. The barrels are coming over six at a time. Based on what I've heard, I'd say he's got three more shipments to wait on.'

'But you haven't alerted the authorities?' Beau's tone was curious rather than censuring.

'Mr Babin, like his father before him, is not a man many would cross. At least not those who know him here in Broadstairs. There is no choice between men I've never met and keeping my own family safe. That's just the way it is.'

Beau considered the man before him and his own brand of morality. 'You're not afraid of speaking with me?'

'I didn't say that, but you said you could help my Jemmy.'

'Indeed I did.' Beau proffered another ten pounds under the astonished eyes of Poughill. 'Keep me apprised of Babin's movements, deliveries, the like. If you're worried for your safety, you may leave your correspondence with the doctor. He and the apothecary will send Jemmy's bills to me from now on.'

When Beau returned home and told his valet what he'd discovered from Mr Poughill, Saunders let out a long whistle. 'I guess we're for London.'

'Indeed.'

18

*B*eau checked his pocket watch as he made his way to the pub in Ramsgate where he was meeting Allard. The day had begun with a hard cold rain, and although the wet had moved on, the bustling seaside town remained quiet.

He was just passing the bakeshop when the door opened, and a young woman stepped into his path. He reached out to steady her.

'Miss Doubleday,' he said with surprise in his voice. 'This is not your usual day to complete your errands.'

Her brow quirked, and she took a determined step back, forcing him to release her. 'I have a usual day?'

'Tuesdays, but twice you've gone on Friday.'

She looked both baffled and mistrustful and made a short humming noise. 'I see. How observant—curiously so.'

Beau was only paying half attention to his ward's words. Several storefronts down, Babin stepped out of the black-smith's, looked over his shoulder, and turned in their general direction. Beau didn't think they'd been seen, but the more distance he could put between his ward and a man he knew to be dangerous, the better. He would do whatever necessary to keep Miss Doubleday from Babin's attention and out of harm's way.

'Come,' he said in a voice that brokered no opposition.

'I beg your pardon?'

'Do not yelp, scream, or otherwise draw attention to us. Do you understand?' Before she could agree, Beau wrapped an arm around her and all but dragged her down the dim little passageway between the bakery and the haberdasher, the two buildings close enough to make it impossible for sunlight to wedge itself between them.

'Whatever do you think—'

He ruthlessly cut her off, pinning her against the grey stone wall at her back and covering most of her person with his own body. Against his chest, he could feel her breasts rising and falling at an erratic pace. Beau put his left cheek to her right, working hard to ignore the graze of her soft skin against his stubble as he turned his head in to whisper, 'My apologies, Miss Doubleday. Bear with me a moment longer.'

Beau's breathing was even, calm. He'd spent years facing enemies, the unknown, and death more times than he could remember. He'd learned to give the impression of control even as panic swelled within him. After several minutes passed, he peeled himself from his ward.

'Where is your horse?'

'Tethered outside the barrister's.' Her brows drew together in concern and confusion. 'What are you about?'

'I'll escort you to your horse, and you will ride straight home. Do you understand?'

'I hear what you're saying, but I've yet to stop in at the

milliner. I promised Louisa a new bonnet for mastering the steps of the quadrille.'

Laughter shook his voice when he asked, 'Is she really so bad?'

The look his ward gave him was sheepish and all the answer he needed, but she nodded and sighed through a smile. 'It's a good thing for all involved she's got another year before making her come-out.'

They stood staring at one another, a rare moment of accord drawing them closer. Her lips had parted, and the movement of her tongue running over them captured his notice.

'Miss Doubleday,' he whispered, his index finger trailing the line of her gloved hand from wrist to fingertip with a featherlight touch. He could hear the shaky breath she drew in.

'Yes?'

Her face was upturned, her dark eyes like two pools of ink. Kissing his ward, and in public no less, was wrong, ungentlemanly, a miscarriage of power, and something Beau was certain he was about to do.

'Oi, I know ye.'

Miss Doubleday jumped back, but Beau, both grateful for and upset with the interruption, turned to face the grating voice with his typical composure and immediately recognised who it belonged to. Judging by the tiny, stifled choke at his side, so did his ward.

'Ye stole that chit out from under me, but where's yer friend now?' he said with a sneer, his glassy eyes running the length of Miss Doubleday, who had stepped closer to Beau and shuddered against him.

'It's not stealing when I paid for it. You were handsomely compensated, were you not?'

The man grunted. 'Silver can't suck my—'

'That's quite enough,' Beau said. His ward's posture had gone rigid enough to snap.

'I'll say when I've had enough. You can leave us, or I can make ye leave us, but leaving us you'll be doing.'

As the man took a wobbly step forward, Beau cursed under his breath. Without his partner's steadying, sensible presence, the drunkard chose violence.

He looked at Miss Doubleday. 'Stay.'

It was the work of a moment for him. Beau stepped away from her and lunged just as the man drew a knife from the band of his dirty trousers. Grasping the man's wrist, Beau twisted until the hand holding the blade released it. The fool had hardly enough air to breathe much less to yelp as Beau stood behind him. Threading his right forearm in front of the man's throat, one strong bicep flexing into his windpipe, Beau's left hand pushed the other man's head forward.

In seconds, the smuggler went limp, and Beau gently slumped him against the wall. Beau reached into the shabby coat pocket for the flask he knew must be there, unscrewed the cap, and poured a little over the man's waistcoat before placing it in his open, relaxed hand.

Trying to ignore Miss Doubleday's stare burning at his back like heat from the summer sun, Beau pulled the snuff box from his left breast pocket and flicked open the false bottom. He licked his finger, dipped it in the powder in the box, and rubbed the powder on the man's gums before using a little brandy to rinse his finger.

Rising, he said with a lilt to his voice, 'Really, Miss Double-day, we've got to stop meeting like this.'

'You've just killed a man, and you make a joke?'

'You think I've just killed a man, and your response is to chide me for what you feel is a poorly timed joke?'

Her eyes narrowed, but she held her tongue.

'He's not dead,' supplied Beau without a trace of emotion. 'But when he comes round, he won't remember anything from today, and perhaps nothing from yesterday either.'

Miss Doubleday fingered the button on her cape situated at the base of her throat. 'It's unbecoming and unchristian of me to say so, but I struggle to find compassion for a man who would force himself on a woman. All the same, it's a relief to know you've not sprung a man from his mortal coil, as I'm beginning to suspect you have in points past and may have done had I not been here to witness the altercation.'

Beau could not deny this, so opted for silence. He held out his hand for her to precede him down the length of the alley which lay between them and the flag-way. She took two steps and turned back on him.

'You could have done that in Broadstairs.'

He tipped his head in silent acknowledgement of her statement.

'Where did you learn how?'

'Do you think the answer I give you will be truthful?' Beau preferred to redirect the conversation, although he found leveraging her distrust in him almost as distasteful.

She cocked her head and chewed her lip before shaking her head no.

He took her elbow once more, guiding them forward while she observed him with cautious, depthless dark eyes. She opened her mouth as if she might speak, before closing it and keeping whatever thoughts she'd considered sharing with him private.

Beau led her straight to her horse. When she made to step on the mount, he wrapped his fingers about her middle and settled her atop the beast with ease. His hands lingered. The feel of her was becoming an addiction he could ill afford.

'I'll see you at dinner.' His words were prosaic but felt intimate in their reassurance. She nodded, and Beau took a single step back. Their eyes met for a long moment before hers slipped from his face to the road ahead. He turned on his heel and made for the pub.

$\mathcal{T}$he easy way Beau had subdued that horrid man was all Emerald could think about on the ride back to Oakmoss. It had been done before she'd had a moment to sort out what was happening, and by a man who did such things as naturally as one might inhale and exhale. Shock, confusion, and disgust at such a violent display were all feelings which should have been roused in the breast of a gently bred female, but Emerald could conjure nothing beyond amazement. With his attention to his dress, impeccably manicured nails, and soft curls arranged with a deft hand, Beau had executed the manoeuvre with exquisite precision and ruthless brutality that surprised her.

She returned directly to the estate at a sedate pace, adjusting her ideas with each slow step. It was Emerald's grand and faulty hope that by the time the sweep came into view, her mind would have sorted itself into some semblance of tranquillity and even perhaps an answer or two.

After giving a perfunctory smile and a kind word to the stable boy, the butler, and the footman, Emerald found herself at the door to her rooms without really knowing how she'd come to be there.

Her hand settled on the gold knob, the cool metal like ice against her hot palm. She hesitated, her gaze drawn down the corridor towards Beau's door. There wasn't a sound on the floor. Even her own breathing had halted, and with a quick look first left then right, Emerald released her hand.

Mindful that she was well on her way to Bedlam, she kept her steps light, but there was nothing to be done about the excessive way her heart thumped in her chest. Raising her hand, she rapped on the door to Beau's room. She had not expected any response, having left him standing in the road in Ramsgate. Still, she pushed the door open, only a little at first, and whispered into the large room a soft 'Hello?' that went unanswered.

Emerald closed the door behind her and wasted no time in making a dash for his writing desk. She did not know precisely what she was looking for, only hoping it would make itself known when her eye landed on it. All she wished for were answers to the questions multiplying in her mind. There was a letter from a cousin and a sheet of paper with the title of a book she'd been speaking of written upon it. There was a volume of poetry that Emerald pushed aside, but a moment later she found her eyes once more resting on the title. Picking it up by the spine, she shook out the pages, the breath in her throat hitching as another letter fell to the desk. A letter signed by Monsieur Allard, but not written in French or English. The words were perhaps Spanish or Portuguese, but as she understood neither, all of it was nonsensical.

The letter was clutched in her hand when she heard Beau's muffled voice in the hall, and panic seized her. Emerald spun around the room with wild eyes, seeking a place to hide herself. There were doors she could pass through, but she had no idea where they would lead. Just as someone pushed into the room, she scurried under the great mahogany bed. Even as a child she had never done such a thing, or she would have known what a terrible decision she was making. The space was confining, and if Beau sat upon his bed, she might well be crushed under his weight.

She heard his voice giving orders for a bath to be drawn, which Emerald found curious, until considering perhaps he wished to wash the day from himself before dinner. A footman assented, and then she heard the door close. A pair of polished Hessians passed in front of her, most of the boot hidden by the valence on the bed.

In the middle of her prayer that he did not accidentally sit upon her, Emerald paused to consider how he was home much earlier than she had supposed. His business must have concluded in a quarter of an hour, perhaps half if he had galloped home, whereas she had only walked. She was still considering this when Saunders entered.

'Your boots, sir?'

'The boots I can manage on my own, but I'll accept your help with the coat.'

There was a little movement in the room and the sound of fabric rustling.

'This is not so unlike the time in Denmark,' said the valet into the silence.

'Perhaps this time I can avoid taking a bullet. Or a blade.'

Beau's tone was sardonic, but Emerald's stomach clenched at the thought, and she couldn't help wondering where he'd been injured.

'Builds character.' Saunders's voice moved further away as

he spoke, and Emerald imagined him going through one of the other doors to a dressing room.

'Yes, I believe it ranks alongside helping others and keeping one's word,' Beau said dryly. She heard the creak of the chair as he sat. One boot dropped to the floor, then the other.

The valet murmured as he shuffled along the far side of the room. 'In good company with honouring one's responsibilities and duties.'

Under the bed, Emerald's eyes went as wide as two dessert plates, and her breath caught in her chest while she waited for Beau's reply. None was forthcoming, and the next voice she heard belonged once more to the valet.

'Odd, is it not? How no one discusses the complexity and contradiction of such things—duty to family, duty to country, responsibility to dependents as well as oneself.'

'Saunders.' Beau spoke the name with cool authority and an unmistakable warning Emerald didn't understand.

The reply, or rather rejoinder, was an exaggerated fawning, 'Sir. If there's nothing else?'

There was a pause. Finally, Beau said no and dismissed the valet. Emerald heard the grunt of the door opening and closing, leaving her alone with Beau in his room. He stood. The quiet shushing of fabric felt loud in her ears. His waistcoat dropped to the floor, followed a second later by his shirt. Her breath hitched, and although she'd been hiding her mouth behind her hand in an effort to quiet the sound, Emerald was certain he could hear it. The moment was dreadful in its intimacy, and her body burned from the inside out as if someone had struck the tinder box right in her belly.

Emerald turned her head and laid her cheek to the floor. With a shaking finger, she lifted a small bit of the valence a meagre inch—just enough to catch a glimpse. His sculpted back stole her breath away, not just the musculature of it, but the scars. Not heaps of them, but enough to know he had faced greater dangers than a belligerent drunk.

He was turning, but her body refused to release the valence and tuck herself away once more. Emerald was captivated—her eyes pinned to the sturdy black branches of the tattoo stretching up his arm and the dozens of smaller limbs reaching across his shoulder and over his heart to touch his collarbone. The leaves were growing sparse. They were shades lighter in colour too. An ode to the oak in winter. It reminded her of those framing the drive and scattered throughout the estate.

Sneaking into Beau's room had proved a grave mistake. She would suffocate under his bed, unable to breathe when faced with the beauty of his body. The hard edges defining the muscles in his stomach and sinew carving out his ribs. The swell of his biceps and the thick veins running through them. Those arms had held her, protected her. Her mouth went dry with the memory of his heat, his hardness, against her on the forest floor. A light sprinkling of hair ran in a dark line from his chest down his stomach and disappeared into his breeches. She wondered how soft it would feel under her fingers if they were to graze along the ridges of his abdomen.

He was not big and broad and brawny, but sleek, lean, predatory. Emerald could feel his strength and vigour in her fluttering pulse, calling to her like a siren's song.

There was an unfamiliar ache at the juncture of her legs. Emerald was too scared to squirm, but she rocked her hips a little side to side and pressed her pelvis against the ground, trying to find some kind of relief. The small movement made her limbs tingle. She did it again, stifling a breath when a little twinge of pleasure shot through her.

A door in the room opened. The sound startled her, and she bumped her head as she withdrew under the bed, grateful Beau's attention was on the footman, notifying him his bath was ready. Beau disappeared, but to her horror and dismay, the door did not close behind him. A moment later she heard the slosh of water and a deep moan so articulate of sensual satisfaction she became hot all over. Her core throbbed, her palms were sweating, and down her back she could feel dampness soaking through the thin linen of her shift.

Emerald dragged in a shaky breath through her nose and exhaled it through her mouth in a futile attempt to regulate her erratic panting and calm the frenzy making every nerve in her body tender to the touch. She was unravelling and desperate to escape, but without knowing where the tub was positioned or how he sat within it, she would not dare to walk past the open door. There was nothing to be done, so she rested her forehead atop her hands, willed him to leave his room directly after he finished his bath, and then, without realising it, fell asleep.

ithin a minute of entering his room, Beau knew someone had been there. Within two, he knew it was Miss Doubleday—and that she remained. With such delicious information in mind, he purposefully ordered a bath. She could not attempt an escape while he bathed if he left the door between the rooms open. Then, with his back to her to hide his amused expression, Beau removed his shirt while reconsidering his previous belief on torture as barbaric and unnecessary.

He was certain she could see the tapestry of scars on his back, evidence the life he lived away from Oakmoss was not so frivolous as she believed. When he turned, he revealed the whole of his tattoo and wished he could watch her watching him. Beau would give up his title and lands to know what she thought of the damage to his body and the art stretching across his chest.

A footman entered to announce his bath. There was a muffled thud in the background, and Beau bit down on the tip of his tongue to stop both a laugh and his smile. The footman's

eyes darted in the general direction of the noise but he made
no other reaction.

'That's all, Andrew.' Beau always preferred bathing unat-
tended, particularly with Miss Doubleday tucked under
his bed.

Beau walked into his bathing room, indulging in a wide,
self-satisfied smile while he stripped the rest of his clothing. As
the hot water slipped around his body, rigid with constraint,
he released a throaty, primal noise, notes of longing, desire,
and indulgence cutting through the steamy air.

One hand rubbed his chest, while the other closed around
the hard evidence of his arousal. He allowed himself several
long strokes, skimming the tender head with the pad of his
thumb on every rise while he imagined burying himself inside
her. A deep moan rose up from his belly. He sank under the
water and expelled a breath. Hundreds of little bubbles rose
around him, each one a piece of his fracturing restraint.

In one swift motion, Beau pushed himself up to standing.
Warm rivulets rushed down the landscape of his body,
catching in its contours. He looked down at his erection with
narrowed eyes. Hands to hips, he huffed and waited. Minutes
later, he was able to step out and retrieve his banyan without
his arousal parting the fabric of the robe.

Beau was undecided on what he wished to do next, but
when he stepped back into his bedchamber, he heard a quiet
murmur followed by slow, rhythmic breathing floating from
underneath his bed as he drew closer. Carefully, he lowered
himself to his knees and peeked under the valence. His mouth
curved with tenderness.

Miss Doubleday's eyes were closed, the perfect petals of
her lips parted. Several pins in her hair had come loose. He
couldn't resist. With this heart in his throat, Beau wrapped one

silky black curl around his finger, rolling the strands between his thumb and forefinger. Her faint hum brought him to his senses.

After pulling the bell for Saunders, Beau waited and greeted the man with a finger to his lips. In near silence, the valet helped Beau dress and left as quietly as he came. With a last lingering look at his bed, Beau left his room.

As MUCH AS he enjoyed knowing his ward had trapped herself under his bed, he was even more diverted by the furtive glances she cast his way at dinner hours later, particularly after his mother commented on how revitalised Miss Doubleday looked. She demurred at the compliment, but couldn't prevent her gaze from slipping his way, if only for the briefest of moments. Beau sipped from his wine to avoid smiling outright.

He ought to have been furious with his ward for any number of reasons, not least of which included her total want of propriety and her invasion of his privacy, but far from feeling rancour of any shade, he was delighted with her antics and found her both admirable and amusing.

The small party retired together to the drawing room after dinner. The dowager, seating herself in a chair near the fire, pulled some embroidery from a basket and entreated Louisa to recount whatever lessons she'd had that day. For her part, Miss Doubleday was looking through a small pile of books stacked up on an end table when Beau approached and challenged her to a game of backgammon.

His voice was even, his face devoid of emotion, and after regarding him with hesitation for a brief moment, she acquiesced. The board was always set up at the opposite end of the room near the long windows, which afforded them some privacy.

'May I say, my ward, I am quite in agreement with my mother. How refreshed you look this evening.'

Her eyes narrowed subtly in clear challenge, and he treated her to a rare warm smile that held a touch of approval.

The game began, and he allowed them each to take several turns in silence. When her shoulders relaxed and her mind had turned to the game, he said, 'You have something that belongs to me.'

There was tension in her neck and a touch of pink tinging her cheeks, but she met his gaze evenly and replied in a firm voice. 'Oh? I cannot even begin to fathom what that might be.'

'Miss Doubleday.'

'My lord guardian.'

He broke eye contact, rolling the dice and moving his pieces almost by rote. 'If you are unwilling to return the letter, it's incumbent upon me to warn you that you will not approve of the means by which I will reclaim it.' When he looked up from the board, her stare was both hard and baffled before she recovered her spirits.

'And if I keep it close to my person?'

Beau pushed aside thoughts of tearing her dress from her lithe body and instead employed a tactic that had long served him well. He sat as he was, made no riposte, offered no apology or contradiction to her intimation, not a single expression that might indicate any unwillingness to do what needed to be done.

With a little huff of annoyance, Miss Doubleday reached into the bodice of her dress.

Beau pushed down a dry swallow.

She pressed the missive into his hand, the paper warm from being nestled against her breast.

A flurry of sensation swelled his chest. He slipped it into his coat pocket, catching a hint of her sweet, clean aroma as he did so.

'How did you know I was there?'

'Are you aware you drool while sleeping?'

The huff of air sucked in by his ward was so loud, so shocking, as to draw the attention of his mother and sister.

''Tis nothing but a handsome, if unexpected, manoeuvre,' he tossed over his shoulder to quell their questions without bothering to turn round.

Burning, reproachful eyes met his when he looked up from the board to Miss Doubleday. 'I do not,' she hissed between clenched teeth with a glance beyond him to ensure they were once more alone in their conversation.

'You are able to observe yourself while you sleep? How fascinating. Someone somewhere will want to study you, to be sure.' For a full minute, she answered him with nothing more than hardened features, her lips pressed so firmly they were ringed in white, and a withering stare capable of shrinking a lesser man than the one with whom she was faced. 'It was only a little, nothing to put you in a pucker, and if you feel it necessary to be cross with anyone, be cross with yourself. No spy worth his salt would ever sleep on the job.'

'I was *not* spying,' she countered in a frosty voice.

He tilted his head to the side for a studied moment. 'Oh? Tell me, what title have you assigned to your furtive undertakings then?'

Miss Doubleday took a deep breath and rolled her dice. With airy defiance, she said, 'I was merely investigating.'

Beau's deep, gentle laugh rippled in the space between

them, surprising them both. The curious sound had the effect of expunging the heat from her eyes, leaving behind an expression not unlike that of a confused puppy.

'My apologies, Miss Doubleday. You had not expected me after so soon departing my company. Had I been mindful of your wish to ransack my chambers, I could have avoided putting you to the blush.'

'Ransack! Well, I—' She broke off, seeming to catch the light in his eyes, the crinkles at their corners a sign of his restrained mirth. 'You *tease* me?'

'Shocking, to be sure, but what else would you have me do? Cut up at you? Retrieve the magistrate? A trifle excessive, if I may humbly offer my opinion on the matter.'

'You haven't answered the question. How did you know?'

'That my letter was in your possession, or that you tucked yourself under my bed?'

Her eyes flicked towards his mother and sister. 'Both.'

'You must think me a poor correspondent to assume I would not notice one of the few letters in my care missing. Are you fluent in Portuguese, Miss Doubleday?'

'I am not. The language is not one in which most ladies receive instruction—or men, as I understand it. What other secrets are you hiding?'

'Plenty, but allow me to reassure you, you would not have discovered any single one in the letter from Monsieur Allard. We often correspond in foreign languages simply for the practice and pleasure of it. And such letters serve as excellent red herrings, do they not?'

Her pretty mouth opened and closed several times without a single sound escaping. She had dropped her eyes once more to the game in front of them, each drawing out their turns longer than necessary.

'Emerald.' Louisa's sweet voice sliced through the thick silence. 'When you're finished winning, perhaps you can help me understand what Byron is trying to say with his verses. Do you think you'll meet him in London? 'Tis hard to believe we leave on the morrow already.'

Miss Doubleday pushed back her chair, but as Beau prepared to protest, he realised she had in fact won, although he couldn't recount bearing off the stones settled snugly in their pocket at the edge of his home board.

He rose from his seat. 'If I don't see you before you leave, I wish you a pleasant journey to London.'

'Thank you.' Her body swayed where she was standing before she turned on her heel, and he wondered if she was as reluctant to leave him as he was to watch her go.

'Miss Doubleday?'

She looked back over her shoulder at him, her ink-black eyes pulling him into an abyss. If he couldn't find a hold, he would lose himself forever.

'Save me your first.'

'In London?' Her brow wrinkled. 'Is there one you had in mind?'

'All of them.' Beau brushed past his ward where she was rooted in place to search out the mind he had apparently lost.

21

'What think you of these gloves?'

With a questioning murmur, Emerald looked towards her friend Esther. 'I beg your pardon. I was wool-gathering.' Emerald hadn't been doing any such thing, but she wasn't going to confess how much her mind had been occupied by her guardian since she left him for London several days prior, turning over whether he'd meant what he'd said about claiming all her firsts. What her heart wished for and what her mind convinced her to believe were two different things.

'These gloves, aye or nay?'

He had handed all three ladies into the carriage, but neither she nor he had been wearing gloves. The feel of his warm skin against her own had felt like a tiny fire built between their hands. Emerald blinked to clear her mind of Beau and looked at the pair of yellow kid gloves her friend was holding. 'Not so complementary to your colouring as the light green.'

'Shopping with you is far superior to shopping with other young ladies. Most are either too polite to tell me the truth or wish for me to buy something unflattering to make themselves appear to greater advantage.' Miss Lyon set down the yellow gloves and picked up the other pair. 'Besides, if I purchase these, I don't see how I can avoid also taking home this charming hat,' she said of the satin and straw bonnet with a flat crown, delicate pink and white flowers, and light green ribbon perched on a nearby hat stand.

'Oh!' exclaimed Emerald. 'You've reminded me I need new silk gloves for the theatre tonight.'

'What will you wear? I shall never forgive Mama for engaging us in some dreadfully boring evening playing cards with her dowdy friends. It would not be so bad except Mrs Kettleman plays for stakes so low even a clergyman could sit at the tables. No one would mistake me for a gamester, but I find if I must sit through such an evening, I'd at least like the opportunity to walk away with enough coins for some fripperies. Never mind that. I asked a question and am desperate for the answer.'

With a chuckle, Emerald described her gown of pale blue satin with a matching tulle overlay embroidered with large blue and cream flowers and speckled with iridescent pearls. 'There's a band under the bust as well that appears as if it's shimmering when caught by the candlelight.' She looked around and picked up a ribbon from another table. 'Similar to this.'

Miss Lyon cocked her head. 'It's quite pretty. As if a frozen lake has been woven into fabric.'

Emerald felt a whisper of heat creep up her neck as she studied the ribbon in her hands. Without realising, she had selected an entire ensemble in the same shades as Beau's eyes.

'What I wouldn't give to be there this evening. Lord Avon has one of the best boxes. You will have a great vantage point, although I suspect it's you who will be the object of most interest.'

From the day she'd been plucked from Whichwood, Emerald had known how unusual it was for a girl who clung to the bottom rungs of the gentry to be sent away to live with a grand family. When she'd first arrived at Oakmoss, there'd been sidelong looks and curious whispers behind hands. But the Calverleigh family was one of power and wealth, both of which had smoothed the road to Kent.

London was something else altogether, where lords and ladies old and young shopped for a spouse who could improve their connections or fill their coffers—and where all her knowledge of weather patterns, hothouses, greenhouses, kitchen gardens, animal husbandry, crop rotations, and the like would be both useless and a cause for scorn. 'I confess, to be an object of such intense interest and scrutiny is a situation with which I am a little familiar, but here in town I feel much more exposed and find myself fighting off the remnants of unease.'

'Emerald.' Miss Lyon stepped forward and put a hand on her friend's shoulder. 'There is no one I know who can wield composure like a weapon as well as you. If there is a benefit to your personal history, it must be the way it has taught you to face uncertainty with courage. All you have to do is go on as you started. That is to say, be brave and brandish kindness as if it were a rapier.'

As the carriage carrying Emerald and Lady Avon slowly moved through the long queue towards Covent Garden, Emerald first fidgeted with the diamond and pearl bracelet that sat on her wrist over her long white gloves. After she spun it and spun it again, she moved on to the necklace at her throat. One large pearl was at its centre, nestled in a cluster of diamonds, and a pearl drop dangled just above the swell of her breasts. The dowager had given her the exquisite piece as a come-out gift when they had arrived in London.

'Get your fidgets out now, dear,' the dowager said, looking out the window with a playful smile tugging her lips.

Emerald coloured, the flush on her cheeks matching her dress of pale pink satin. Her maid had laid out the blue dress, but after her unfortunate epiphany at the modiste's, she'd requested the pink instead. The puff sleeves were decorated with the smallest rosettes Emerald had ever seen, and spangles and pearls rose from the hem like a firework over the skirt of the dress. Louisa had been waiting at the foot of the stairs to see them off, and she had declared Emerald the loveliest creature she'd ever seen. It was a silly exaggeration, and Emerald had said as much, but the sentiment was genuine, and she'd kissed the younger girl's cheek before saying her goodbyes.

Stepping from the carriage in front of the theatre, she brought her head up to find at least half of the patrons moving towards the doors had craned their necks to look behind them as word spread of her and the dowager's arrival.

Lady Avon took Emerald's hand and threaded it through her arm, giving it a little pat as she did so. Emerald kept her chin high and chose to be fascinated rather than embarrassed. It was, in fact, a wonderfully wild sensation to know so many people were interested in her.

Speaking through the smile on her face that never faltered, Lady Avon addressed her. 'The *ton* is nothing if not meddlesome. Officiousness was inevitable, whether we took you to town years ago or now. Pay it no mind. You are a novelty at the moment, but fascination wanes as quickly as it comes on. Ah, Lady Lane and her niece, the new Duchess of Hazelhurst, come this way. Quite the stir that young lady caused last year. I couldn't open a letter without some mention of Miss Emory, as she was before marriage. You will like her exceedingly.'

The mention of the duchess perked Emerald's ears. She recalled the dowager reading bits from the letters she received while they took their breakfast or sat by the fire after dinner. Emerald most often let the information wash over her. To hear of persons living grand lives in town was entertaining, but not something to which she could feel any connection. As the women approached, she wished she'd paid better attention or stored some of the intelligence away in her mind.

In a sea of stares and whispers, Emerald was pleased to be greeted with a genuine smile and captivating green eyes that sparked with amusement rather than speculation.

'It's a pleasure to make your acquaintance,' the duchess said as Emerald dropped a curtsey. 'I'll admit I'm enjoying the stir you've caused. It's much more pleasant to be a spectator rather than a participant.'

Such a statement left Emerald at a total loss, as did the curious way the duchess was looking at her. A thousand questions swam in Emerald's mind. The woman couldn't have been more than four- or five-and-twenty, but there was something about the Duchess of Hazelhurst, a quiet confidence, a sureness in herself which Emerald wished to possess.

'Let us pretend we are the best of friends and walk to our seats together. The Avon box is situated near our own, and if I don't appear there soon, no doubt my husband and his very broody countenance will come looking for me,' the duchess added, slipping her hand around Emerald's arm. 'As it turns out, this has become a poor habit of mine, one I've no interest in correcting.'

'What has, Your Grace?'

With a mischievous smile, the duchess clarified, 'Stoking the fire, Miss Doubleday.'

22

*E*merald had enjoyed the theatre—the tragedy more than the farce—but was aware throughout of the stares drifting her way and the whispers that followed. The dowager, in the carriage on the way home, reminded Emerald again of her novelty and how quickly such a thing would wane. 'The more you are seen, the less you will be spoken of,' Lady Avon said.

So, the day following the theatre, Emerald could be found looking at the Elgin Marbles at the British Museum. And the day after that, she attended tea and cards at the home of Marchioness Lawmore, an old friend of the dowager and a woman who introduced Emerald to more hostesses whose invitations would matter most during her first season.

It had been a shock to Emerald, despite knowing the dowager and her husband had come down to town regularly before his death, to see how many friends she had, how welcomed she was, how much deference was paid to her. At every opportunity, she pulled Emerald forward, saying things like, 'I don't know what I'll do with myself when some fortunate gentleman whisks her away from Oakmoss,' or, 'She's such a part of the family, I'm always shocked to hear someone refer to her as Miss Doubleday.' The words were sincere; Emerald never thought otherwise, but she also knew what the dowager was doing by signalling the family's full support. Her dowry might not compare to that of an heiress, but a man who married Emerald could depend upon her connection to the Calverleigh family.

'Oh, Em, how lovely you look,' remarked the dowager as Emerald came into the drawing room, the demi train of her white silk satin dress trailing behind her. 'If Beau isn't already receiving letters of interest on your behalf, he will after tonight to be sure. How wrong it was of me to keep you cooped up in the country for so long.'

This expressive speech sent a streak of heat across Emerald's cheeks. The dowager was taking Emerald to her first ever private London ball, given by Lady Cawdry. Emerald spared an unkind thought for the man who'd requested her first set but was once more absent from her life, even as her rational mind told her he never meant to dance every first with her and was easily able to concoct all sorts of reasons he might say such a thing just to tease her.

'Everyone is anxious for the season to begin in earnest, myself included, and tonight will be a crush, I'm sure,' remarked the dowager as she bundled Emerald out of the townhouse on Grosvenor Square.

She shoved her nerves deep down on the short ride and reminded herself that in Kent she'd had full control of an entire estate—surely a ballroom was nothing compared to that. By the time she and the dowager were stepping to the forefront of the glittering crowds, Emerald's chin was lifted, her eyes sparkled as if she was keeper of a great secret known to only her, and the poise and grace she'd honed over her years at Oakmoss carried her through like one born to the highest rungs of the *ton*.

'Quite the crush, is it not, Miss Doubleday?'

'Mr Babin.' Emerald smiled. 'I was not sure we would see you in London, and I cannot say I anticipated your company at a ball.'

'I arrived only hours ago and found myself swept up in a friend's evening plans. The surprise is not an unpleasant one, I hope?'

'In a city where I know almost no one beyond my own small party, any face from Kent is a welcome one.'

'How do you find London thus far?'

'There is so much to do and to see I hardly know where to begin. With a little more time, perhaps I'll have my bearings.' Emerald glanced at the dowager, who was in conversation with several women she recognised from her afternoon of tea and cards.

'Is it just you and the dowager down for the season?'

Emerald laughed. 'You mean is my guardian here, and can we expect a repeat of the scene from the drawing room?' Mr Babin smiled at her jest, but a sudden flutter of uncertainty rippled in her stomach as she recalled Beau's warning.

'A man with not one but two diamonds to keep watch over cannot be faulted for his dedication to the task, although I suspect his motives for one vary from the other.'

There was much to make of his little speech, and Emerald wasn't sure which part garnered the greater share of her attention.

He put a hand to his heart. 'My apologies, I've overstepped.'

'No.' She shook her head, even though she felt perhaps he

had pushed the bounds of what was proper, given their tenuous connection. 'Only I do not follow and am not quite certain I should seek clarification.'

'We are nearly neighbours, are we not? I'm a simple man, but it would take one much simpler than I not to notice the way he looks at you is not at all the same way he looks at his other charge. I had thought perhaps such was at the root of the tension in the drawing room that day.'

Emerald willed away the colour stealing up her neck. 'Not at all. Quite the opposite. We're rather spiky where the other is concerned.' To her own ears, the nonchalance in her voice sounded forced, but she hoped it wasn't so for Mr Babin. He held her in a long, contemplative gaze, as if weighing the truth of her words. 'How do you know the viscountess?' she asked, hoping to change the subject. She had a hard enough time pushing Beau from her mind despite the large stretch of country separating them and had no wish to allow the man a significant portion of her concern when he was nowhere near.

'I don't, not personally, anyway. Her son is an acquaintance of mine with whom I've had some business dealings. It's him I have to thank for my invitation to tonight's event.'

'Are you enjoying yourself?'

'Yes, and if you consent to dance with me, my pleasure in the evening will be complete.'

She agreed. If she refused, she would be forced to sit out the rest of the dances. When they stood across from one another, waiting their turn, Emerald said, 'You consider us nearly neighbours, and yet we know so little of one another, or at least I about you.'

'I am an open book. You only have to tell me what it is you wish to know.'

'Oh, I suppose whatever you're willing to share.'

'You know I've two sisters. One lives outside of Brighton, and the other in Yorkshire. My mother spends most of her time at one or other of their houses; she finds it too depressing to remain in the home she shared with my father. He passed some time ago, and I miss him often.'

Emerald softened a little. 'I quite understand the feeling. My father used to say, "*après la pluie, le beau temps*," and I've repeated it often.'

'You speak French like you were born there. I've longed to hear it spoken so beautifully. My paternal grandmama is French, though of course it's not so fashionable to say so now.'

'*Is*? She benefits from good health then?'

'Indeed,' confirmed Mr Babin. 'But she's quite old now and lives near Dunkirk with a cousin and two dogs nearly as blind as she is,' he added with a fond chuckle.

Their turn was next, and the movements of the dance limited their conversation. He returned her to the dowager at the end of the set, expressed his delight in spending a half an hour in Emerald's company, and bid her a good evening before moving on to secure his next partner. The rest of the night passed in a blur of silk and superfine, and by the time the carriage was called to return her and the dowager to Avon House, Emerald's feet were sore and her head swimming with new names and faces.

Still, despite partners who had been agreeable or handsome or even the few who dared to be both, when Emerald snuffed out her candle, the only man occupying her thoughts, much to her dismay, was the one a hundred miles away at Oakmoss. A sudden heaviness pinned Emerald to her bed, and it was with effort she lifted a heavy hand to rub the pain in her breast so acute its origin could be nothing other than a broken heart.

23

'*R*eally, Beauden, you ought not to make a habit of such entrances,' his mother said, glancing up from her book as he walked into the morning room of the Calverleigh townhouse on Grosvenor Square.

'I sent a note signalling my intention to join you in town shortly after you departed, and you replied with a long list of engagements to which you'd committed, underlining the ones you thought I'd most enjoy. It's hardly a surprise.'

The dowager made a quiet murmuring sound more to herself than to him. 'A mention without date or time, but you are known to do as you please.'

He stiffened a little at her comment. 'I am also known to keep my word. Where are Lou and Miss Doubleday?'

'Your sister is with the dancing master. Poor dear will get all the steps sewn up in the right order eventually. Emerald is at Hookham's with Mr Abbott. She made his acquaintance at Lady Cawdry's ball the other night. He seemed quite taken with her.'

A ball he'd been loath to miss, but he'd learned Babin was

leaving Kent the same day and used the opportunity to steal into the man's study through a window on the ground floor and riffle through his correspondence, a gambit which had supplied the names of two co-conspirators but no firm date.

'Henry Abbott?'

'Unless you know another.' His mother studied him with unabashed curiosity. 'What is that look for, Beauden?'

'She ought not to spend so much time in his company, or any at all.' Beau remarked, shuffling through the newspapers on the rosewood end table near the sofa once more.

'Goodness me. The Abbotts are a perfectly unexceptional family, the children as much as the parents.'

Unexceptional was right. There was nothing notable about Henry Abbott, other than he was the absolute wrong type of man for Miss Doubleday. 'She can do much better.'

His mother's gaze drifted up once more, her full attention now settled on him, an interested gleam in her eyes he didn't care for. 'Do you think so?'

'Don't you?' he asked, a little offended on Miss Double-day's behalf.

'I think Henry Abbott is well mannered, from a good family, and not unpleasant to look at.'

'What I heard you say is he's boring and has had the good fortune not to be horse-faced.'

His mother closed her book and let it settle between her palms. 'Interesting you should interpret my words so. You know, as well as anyone, a man with a comfortable income and some connections is a good match for Emerald. With her fine countenance, she may secure a baron, or if she is very lucky, a viscount with the means to marry where he chooses, but she will not land a nonpareil and knows better than to try.'

A wave of anger washed through Beau. 'Should not she

also have the option to marry where she chooses? Why is it Father never enlarged her dowry?'

'I could not say. He discussed the idea with me on more than one occasion but, as you know, never acted. You may do so, of course.'

He could, and should. No one would deny she deserved it. But just as he opened his mouth to say so, he snapped it closed. More than he hated feeling his ward was limited in her choices, he hated the idea of her being courted for her dowry and not her intelligence or kindness.

'You know, it has only just occurred to me I could as well. How embarrassing to admit I'd never considered such a thing to be in my power, but I've money from my own mama.'

'Funds you intended for Louisa, no?'

His mother lifted a shoulder. 'Yes, but Lou already has plenty and won't mind sharing. Besides, I've long since considered Emerald another child of mine.'

'But she's not,' he quipped, almost before his mother finished speaking.

'How ungenerous of you to say so, although I can suppose why you're anxious to make that distinction,' the dowager retorted with a smirk.

'I don't take your meaning.'

'I'm certain you do, but if you wish to play the fool, Beauden, this one time I'll let you. A nod to your honour and diligence in observing the sweeping impropriety of pressing a suit upon your own ward.'

The astonishment Beau felt was not reflected on his face nor in his demeanour, but his mother's frankness was unwelcome, if only because she dared to hint at feelings Beau had been trying so hard—and failing—to ignore.

'I commend you on your forthright speech. Now, you only

have to say how angry you are with me for my protracted absence, and we may be done with it.'

Shock paled his mother's face. There were few as English as she in her ability to overlook conflict and discomfort. She gave a little sniff. 'I am not—'

Beau didn't let her finish. 'You are. Very much so, and rightly too.' He could tell she was surprised to hear him say so by the slight widening of her eyes. 'Father knew why I was so often gone. He didn't approve, which is perhaps why he never mentioned such a thing to you. For him, duty to Oakmoss took precedent above all else. But I needed to carve my own path. I am very glad I did, though I know I stayed away too long. At the moment, I cannot say more, but I hope you will believe my life away was so much more than balls and hunting parties and will accept my apologies for leaving you and Louisa alone in your grief.'

The dowager sat quiet and still. Her countenance had softened, but the look in her eyes was not one of forgiveness. She rose and walked to where he stood, drawing one of his hands to hold between her much smaller ones.

'I thank you for what you have said. I have been angry with you, but only a very little for myself. What claim can a mother have on her grown-up son? I felt your absence—keenly, as any parent would, and so did your sister. We often wished for your return, but we were not the ones most impacted. Do you understand?'

Sourness settled in the pit of his stomach. He had known, almost from the day of his arrival, who'd suffered the most under his prolonged sojourn, and not once had he explained, apologised, or shown his ward any sign of appreciation. Miss Doubleday had not done it for him, he was all too aware, but she had done it without being asked, without complaint, and without any expectation of gain.

In response to his mother's question, Beau gave a concise nod. He then kissed her cheek, withdrew his hand, and departed to his rooms, where he would be left at peace to castigate himself.

He was not a man worthy of Miss Doubleday, and wasn't sure he could be, but he was certain of one thing: If anyone deserved to know what had kept him away, it was her.

24

---

*E*merald fidgeted with her elbow-length white gloves.
'Are you enjoying your first season, Miss
Doubleday?'

She started at the sound of Beau's voice, feeling breathless
and a little lightheaded as he drew nearer. When the dowager
had casually mentioned his presence in the house the day
prior, Emerald had found herself only half paying attention to
what happened around her as she waited to set eyes on him,
needing to see his person for herself to believe the truth of his
mother's words. Had he come for her? Her conscience warned
her to guard herself against such insidious thoughts, but the
spinning of her pulse had its own story to tell.

'Certainly,' she replied, pretending all her attention was
absorbed in trying to secure the button in the delicate keyhole
on the inner wrist of her glove.

'Allow me.'

Emerald thanked him, hoping she didn't sound as flustered
as she felt. She watched as he pulled his own gloves off and
held them out to her. Instinctively she reached for them. Beau

took her other hand, and rather than extending her arm towards him, he brought himself closer. Her heart jolted, and in an abstract way, as if the hand weren't her own, she considered how very fine it looked in his. The bare tip of his thumb drew several caressing circles on the tender flesh of her wrist, sending a shock of awareness through her body.

'I intended to follow you and my mother directly to town and was sorry to miss your first ball.'

Her heart quickened. 'Oh? It's no matter. I assure you our pleasure in the evening did not suffer.'

'No?' His gaze ensnared her.

She shifted under the disbelieving gleam of droll amusement in his eyes and turned towards a painting on the wall to hide her confusion.

He secured the wayward button in its loop and held her hand, inspecting the rest of the buttons. Emerald thought she felt his fingers graze the side of her own as he released her. Or maybe she only wished it was so. She swayed on her feet, dizzy from his proximity, and her chest rose rapidly with her quickening breaths. When Lady Avon came down the stairs, Emerald swallowed with relief.

Each in possession of one of Beau's arms, the three of them walked into Almack's at quarter to eleven. Their arrival set off a deafening furore as the assembled company released gasps of astonishment and cries of delight to see the earl returned. The crowd bobbed and swayed, consumed with excitement.

Emerald had heard on occasion discussions between Lord and Lady Avon regarding a good match for their son—the right match—and felt, at least philosophically, she understood what had been meant by that. What she learned as the crowd parted for them to take their place, with every pair of eyes turned in their direction, was that she knew nothing.

Oakmoss, and the villages and towns surrounding it, had been her whole world for almost nine years. The estate might have been Beau's, but she saw his return from the perspective of one who belonged, observing an outsider attempting to make a place for himself where one no longer existed. London, however, appeared to be his to rule if he so wished. Mothers rushed to daughters. Young ladies who'd smiled at her before eyed her with critical stares and bent their heads together behind gloved hands. Gentlemen squared their shoulders and lifted their chins as Beau walked past.

Lady Avon released Beau's arm to clasp the hands of an older woman approaching whose long plumes of ostrich feathers tickled the faces of everyone she passed.

Emerald spoke in a soft voice for his ears only. 'When I suggested over dinner ages ago there was not a single ballroom in the capital in which you had failed to find contentment, I'd meant to provoke you. Had I any notion of how revered you are, I would've employed a better barb.'

'Revered?' he repeated with a low, rumbling chuckle.

The sound settled in her belly and warmed her like a hot brick.

'You've been gone for years and still everyone here clamours for you.'

Beau turned to look at her, a playful smile lurking in his eyes. 'You don't.' The musicians struck up the first notes of a quadrille. 'I believe the pleasure of leading you out is mine.'

Emerald felt a little flustered at the idea of dancing her opening set at such a revered place with a man such as he. 'How gallant you sound.'

'Did you suspect my request for your firsts a jest?'

'Wasn't it?' she asked, pleased with the indifference in her voice.

'You know it was not.'

Her stomach swooped. 'But you missed the Cawdry ball,' she pressed, revisiting the topic despite being afraid his response would prove she was not so important to him as his request made her feel.

'I did. I broke my word. The choice was met with agony. One day, when I can, I will tell you more, if you'd like, and you may weigh the worthiness of my excuse for yourself. In the meantime, would you rather I leave you with the wolves?' he asked, glancing over his shoulder to the matrons flocking towards his mother.

'It's you they hunt, not me.'

'You don't see what I see, if that's what you think.'

There was an unfamiliar light in his eyes when he spoke. Emerald, her mind whirling from their conversation, sought refuge by turning her attention to the bustle of people around them. He led her to the floor, with real or feigned blindness to the stares following them. Which it was, she couldn't tell.

The dance began. His hand twined around hers, and excitement thrummed in her bones. He lifted their joined hands overhead and took a step towards her, coming so close the thin line of propriety disappeared between them. Beau's leg brushed her dress. His boldness sent a tremor of wanting straight to her very core. An expressive glow lit his brilliant eyes from within, and despite a rush of pink to her cheeks, she couldn't tear her gaze away.

When the dance forced her to turn from him, the smell of tobacco and oakmoss and spiced vanilla plucked her senses like a vibrant chord.

'You dance with natural elegance, my charming ward.'

She eyed him with what she felt was open suspicion. 'What

is it you're hoping to gain with such flattery, Lord Avon?' The address felt awkward coming out of her mouth. She rarely called him by his title. She rarely called him anything at all. Years of distance between them prevented her from feeling comfortable calling him by his given name, but *Lord Avon* felt reserved for the one she'd known and loved and missed dearly. By his shuttered expression, she wondered if he felt the same.

Beau replied, his tone teasing, 'Some conversation is expected when dancing.'

'Conversation, not compliments. Such a thing is not in your nature.'

'No one would accuse *you* of flattery.'

She expected a blast of cool air when she looked up at him, but his eyes shone bright like a full moon and held a gentle challenge. They were separated again, and Emerald was grateful the dance made it impossible for her to issue a response because she had none—rather, none she could share with him. She was too uncertain to admit, least of all in a crowded ballroom, how he figured in her mind as the most handsome man she'd ever seen or how drawn she was to his sharp mind and veiled strength.

For the remainder of the dance, they were quiet, and Emerald expected him to lead her back to the dowager at the end of their set. Instead he folded her hand over his arm and said, 'Allow me to procure you a glass of lemonade.'

Emerald wasn't thirsty and she didn't much care for lemonade, but something was shifting between them, a change in the cosmos, his star and hers coming into alignment. The awareness of the change clung to her like the bodice of the blue dress she wore, the one with the ribbon matching his eyes.

'Why did you do it? Run the estate?' Beau tipped his head towards hers to keep the words between them.

The unusual hint of confusion in his voice caused her eyes to fly to his own. 'Someone had to.' It was a statement said without anger or accusation.

'Sims has worked there nearly thirty years and is capable of managing, maintaining as it were, to say nothing of the house staff. You know as well as I do they could plod along if needs must. Much like you know that's not what I was asking.' His manner was mild, subdued almost. Emerald's instinct to open for him rubbed against her desire to protect herself, even as a whisper in the back of her mind told her it was much too late.

There were only a few others in the room where refreshments were being served, and Beau offered her a glass of ratafia while taking a cup of orgeat for himself. She gave him a sidelong glance.

'I've never seen you drink lemonade. Ratafia, on the other hand...' His sentence trailed off, and he steered them to an attached withdrawing room, where they sat knee to knee on a chaise longue, the door open.

Emerald took several sips of the drink, her mind whirling, her heart striking hard against the bone cage containing it, knowing she was on the verge of revealing one of her greatest fears to a man she only half knew.

'When one has been abandoned once,' she began, her eyes downcast and focused on the ruby red liquid in her cup, 'one fears it happening again. But if one makes herself invaluable to the place and the people...' She couldn't bring herself to meet his gaze, but his gloved finger tilted her chin up, not giving her a choice. The mix of pain and understanding writ clear across his face almost broke her, and she shook her head to clear her eyes of the tears forming. 'Why did you stay away?'

'I've no such worthy answer. Work took me away, but guilt kept me from returning.'

She didn't understand and said so.

'Before I left the last time, we'd had a ferocious row, my father and me. He felt my work posed too great a risk to my life and the Calverleigh name. I felt he didn't—wouldn't—understand why I desired to feel useful in my own way, to establish an identity not directly linked to his own. Although I wrote, I never acquiesced to his wish for reconciliation. Towards the end, he mentioned something of great import and expressed a wish to speak to me. He asked me, very directly, to return home at the soonest possible moment. I ignored that request, too, and then it was too late. The next letter I received was yours.'

Of all the emotions Emerald anticipated feeling, the sharp sting of empathy wasn't one of them. At least she had been able to say goodbye to her own papa. Without thinking, she reached out and gripped his hand with her own. His fingers pressed into her palm, and he stared at their white gloves layered over one another until she shifted on the chaise. He set his cup on a side table near at hand before taking the one she held and doing the same. The movements happened slowly, like the two of them were underwater, pushing through imperceptible resistance. Beau took her free hand in his, giving a little squeeze as he did so.

'Miss Doubleday. Emerald.'

She was drifting. Music and chatter from the other room faded away. If there were still people in the tea room, Emerald couldn't see them. The feel of his hands holding hers, the reverent way he spoke her name, carried her away to a time and place where nothing existed but them.

'I am so sorry—for leaving you to shoulder my responsibility, for making you feel there was no other choice, for not thanking you or appreciating you as you richly deserve. I cannot make amends, but I can make a promise.'

Emerald listened first with bewilderment and then with her mind reeling. Her stomach fluttered like a murder of crows took flight, and a knot of hope lodged in her throat.

'I promise to be present, to do better.'

Emerald deflated. She hadn't really expected a declaration, had she? But his phrasing— She cut the thought short, relegating it to the back of her mind with all the others till she could pick it apart in the privacy of her own room. Her face was upturned, studying his, and whether it was his hands pulling her forward or her leaning in of her own accord, she didn't know, but she came so near she could see his entire history in his eyes. He dipped his head, bringing his lips so close to hers they ached. Her eyes fluttered closed, every thought vanished, but the kiss she waited for never came. She felt his heat drift away from her and opened her eyes, mortification blossoming in two red spots on her cheeks.

It did not surprise her when he released her hands, but her mouth dropped open when he removed his gloves and began to undo the button at her wrist he had secured earlier. When that sensitive spot of flesh was once more exposed, he traced along her veins with the soft pad of his thumb before bending down and touching his lips to it in a delicate kiss that sent shivers over every inch of her body. In silence, he buttoned her glove once more, returned his to his hands, and stood, saying, 'It's long past time I returned you to my mother.'

Emerald couldn't sort out what had just happened, if the kiss to her wrist had been his way of easing her embarrassment, and whether such a thing was worse than suffering the humiliation of not being kissed at all.

He led her back to the dowager as some other gentleman came to request her next. Beau relinquished her hand, his inscrutable expression issuing the final, devastating blow in a series of events that left Emerald bewildered.

Her new partner's easy conversation was no match for her wayward thoughts or her defiant gaze, which wandered more than it had any right to do to where Beau stood until he disappeared from her sight altogether.

Emerald expected to see him once more in the carriage on the ride home and prepared herself for awkwardness between them, but when she and the dowager stepped outside, she was informed he had departed some time earlier.

Nothing that had happened during the course of the evening could escape scrutiny, and all Emerald had to decide was whether she preferred starting at the beginning or the end. When she settled into bed, she determined to examine every interaction from the moment he found her fiddling with her glove, but as she set forth to do that, her mind raced to their moment in the withdrawing room, then back to their dance, then forward to him leaving Almack's entirely. Instead of taking any kind of logical approach and sewing up the scenes and the feelings each engendered into anything remotely resembling sense, Emerald drifted off just as the morning sun pushed out the dark with only two things clear in her mind: She had hoped he would kiss her; he had walked away instead of doing so.

25

*B*eau slipped out of Almack's overcrowded rooms before desire brought him back to Miss Doubleday's side. He knew tasting her would be his undoing. With her willing, upturned lips, he had come too close to claiming her as his own. She was still his ward and would be for another fortnight. Disappointment, confusion, and embarrassment had flooded her expression when he pulled away, and his gut twisted, the pain in his middle his penance.

On the way to London, he'd promised himself he would keep a respectful distance, but the more he saw of her, the more he *wanted* to see her. He craved being in her presence. When Saunders came up to help Beau out of his coat once he returned home, he hadn't warned Beau off so much as said the path he was on only ended with death. It was his valet's notion of romance.

To his surprise, all three ladies were at the table the following morning, and Miss Doubleday was spreading an indecent amount of jam over a roll while speaking to his sister.

'Louisa, have you an interest in getting ices or candies? I

find myself wishing for some fresh air and a sweet treat this morning.'

'Of course you do,' Beau said, reviewing the selections at the sideboard. When there was no reply, he looked over to see three sets of eyes—questioning, curious, and guarded—pinned on him. Miss Doubleday had gone still in her chair, the tendon in her neck strained. 'What? You mean to tell me you've never noticed your desire for sweets coincides with your late nights? The morning after the assembly in Ramsgate, you had two mugs of chocolate, Louisa made some mention of tarts the morning after you went to the Cawdry ball, and I can always tell when you've stayed up too late working because Cook sends up honey cake with the rest of the usual breakfast fare.'

A faint flush dusted Miss Doubleday's cheeks, and she turned back to Louisa, who shrugged in return, but said, 'I have a lesson with the dancing master. Would you like to join me in the ballroom instead?'

'I would offer my escort, dear,' chimed the dowager, 'but I'm hosting some ladies for tea.'

Beau sipped from his cup of coffee. 'I'll take you to Gunter's, if you would like.'

His mother's eyes widened as she looked across at Miss Doubleday. Louisa held her fork suspended mid-air on the way to her mouth. All he was interested in was his ward's response.

'All right.'

They were mostly quiet on the walk to the shop, but when it came time to order, she said, 'Let me guess, the Mirabelle mousse?'

He felt his face betray a flicker of surprise.

'You've talked about those plums several times at breakfast and during dessert, and oh, let me think,' she said, pretending to count silently to herself, 'at least a dozen times since you've returned.'

'I most certainly have not.'

'There was a plum cake, plum tart, plum jelly…' She let her words trail off into a smile, and he couldn't look away. 'One would think you ate Mirabelle plums exclusively while away from home.'

Ices in hand, he guided them to a small open table near the front of the bustling tea shop.

'You must at least give me credit for my good taste in sweetmeats. Have you ever eaten something as delicious as a ripe, sweet plum?' As he said it, he imagined her biting into the fruit, a little juice running down the corner of her mouth, his finger reaching out to wipe it away. His reverie was cut short when he noticed her happy expression falter and her mind retreat somewhere far away.

'Yes,' she eventually answered. 'White cake with fresh wild strawberries and a hint of rhubarb.'

'Has Cook made that often? I can't say I've ever had the pleasure.'

'No. At Whichwood, our cook would make it each year for my birthday.' She dropped her lashes to hide her hurt but he heard it in her voice all the same.

'If you had told my mother or father or Mrs Marshall directly, Cook would have been happy to make it for you.'

'I'm sure she would, but birthday cake doesn't taste half so good when one has to ask for it oneself.' The little smile accompanying her words was sad, not quite reaching her eyes or even enough to bring out the small dimple in her right cheek he had recently discovered, which fascinated him.

'Do you miss Whichwood?' He was playing a dangerous

game—asking a question to which he wanted to hear only one specific answer.

'Are you hoping to send me back?'

'I wouldn't dream of it.'

Miss Doubleday eyed him not with incredulity as he may have once suspected, but something more akin to deliberation as she appeared to weigh her response. She took a dainty bite of her lavender ice and said, almost defiantly, 'You won't like my answer, but it's no. I don't miss it. I did, at least what it represented, for a long time. But not anymore.'

'I like your answer because it is honest.'

'And you? Did you ever miss Oakmoss when you were away?'

Beau allowed himself a quick, scornful snort, hoping his own honest response wouldn't start a war to rival Napoleon's after the progress made the night before. 'No.' He was unsurprised when her expression changed. 'You don't like that answer. The quick pinch of your lips forever gives you away.' He waited for her to strike out with some acerbic comment, but she remained silent. 'I missed my family, the familiar paths through the wood, taking the little boat out to the middle of the lake and watching the clouds go by. But I never felt connected to my ancestral home the way one ought, perhaps because I always wished to be more than just an heir.'

There was a pause as they considered one another in equal frankness. He had set two paths out before her and knew, as she sat across from him, her intelligent, shadowy eyes assessing, that she was choosing which to take.

'Did you always wish to be a man who steals about in the darkest hours of the night? Who could fell another as one might hail a hackney or solicit a lady for a dance?'

This close, with crisp sunshine filtering in through the thick glass of the window, he could just discern the rich brown of her irises from the black of her pupils. She was his choice. If he wished to be hers, there was only one way to answer.

'Yes.' With the word, he unfurled for her, inviting her to see his truest nature. He would hide nothing from her, do anything for her. Between them, time took a breath. The moment was measured not in silent seconds but in flashes of memory flickering with new meaning.

Her eyes widened and her mouth rounded into a little 'o' as she stared at him with considerable astonishment. He suppressed his humour at her reaction by taking the last bite of his ice.

'As a boy, I often imagined myself as some secret agent uncovering dastardly plots and conducting secret liaisons to ferret out dangerous criminals. The reality is far more complicated and has kept me from home for too long—or rather, I let it keep me from home too long. In my mind, I imagined returning to Oakmoss as I left it, as I remembered it when my father was still alive. My rooms remain unchanged, but everything else... My mother's hair has greyed—'

'As has yours on the sides.'

He skimmed his fingers along the short hair just above his ear, a reluctant smile ruffling his mouth. 'Louisa has grown a foot, and you, you...' Beau couldn't finish the sentence. Not here. Not when she looked at him in such a way. Not while she was his ward.

Somewhere in the shop, a glass slipped, shattering when its fragile curves hit the floor and sending a shock of sound rushing between them.

Beau cleared his throat, Miss Doubleday smoothed the skirt of her dress, and in unison, they rose from the table and walked out the door.

26

_____

$\mathcal{T}$he walk from Berkeley Square to Grosvenor Square began as a quiet one. Beau's heart raced, and there was a subtle quake in his limbs, reminiscent of his early days on assignment, but he found the uncertainty of knowing what thoughts were whooshing through Miss Doubleday's brain more disconcerting than anything he'd faced in his line of work.

She was doing her best to keep her face forward, placid, untouched by his revelations and who could say what else, but several times her eyes slipped his way, by turns curious and scrutinising. Once he thought she looked inexplicably dissatisfied.

As they left Berkeley Square behind, she ventured to say, her voice tinged with unusual shyness, 'I thought perhaps you were avoiding me, when you didn't return with us from Almack's.'

'Never,' he said, and, keeping his tone light, added, 'except when I hid outside the study for more than an hour and the

201

one time I threw myself behind the couch in the library when I heard you coming. After that night.'

She whirled on him with a sharp gasp. 'I *knew* it!'

'While we're speaking of hiding, did you really wake up under my bed and think your presence there had gone undetected?'

Miss Doubleday began her answer with an imperious lift of her chin. 'Mayhap I did. It seemed just as plausible, more so, some might argue, than the alternative: you finding me and *leaving* me there.' There was amusement sparking in her eyes when she brought them to meet his own.

Beau was enchanted and let his laughter kindle in the air between them. 'The alternative, my dear ward, was my sitting in a chair and biding my time till you crawled out. I think, given the choices, the one allowing you to preserve *some* dignity was the correct one, no?'

Her dark eyes slipped his direction, a dangerous gleam sending a shiver of warning down his spine. 'You undressed *knowing* I was there.'

He adored her firm, purposeful way of speaking, and her willingness to challenge him, spar with him.

'Perhaps I mistook your intentions in entering my room,' he drawled.

'You never.' She met him with a stern-faced expression, but he knew she was fighting off a smile by the twitch at the corner of her lips.

As they turned onto Grosvenor Street from Davies Street, a cry of 'Thief!' disturbed the quiet, warm accord brewing between them. An urchin rushed around the corner, his small body knocking into Miss Doubleday's legs as he ran like the devil himself was at his back. She would have fallen backward had Beau not been there to catch her, and she toppled into his arms with a stunned little cry as the pair watched a well-dressed merchant give chase, although the young boy was already gone from sight.

Beau righted her, inquired if she was all right, and cast a quick look over their surroundings.

'Fine. A little shaken. And I feel terribly for that poor boy, although there are not so many of them as I expected to see in London.'

It was a naïve statement, and one Beau wasn't sure he was willing to correct yet, but her assessment held some truth. It was unusual to see a street urchin in this part of town. The crimes they got away with in the seedier parts of London could see them hanged if committed and caught in Mayfair. The boy, the given hour, and Beau's general wariness made him suspicious, but if the charge had been deliberate, it made no sense why the urchin would run into her and not him. He said none of this to Miss Doubleday, but picked up her hand and placed it snug in the crook of his arm, keeping her close to his side for what remained of their walk.

He felt a silly rush of pleasure when she didn't immediately disentangle herself from him when the door to Avon House opened. Even as she turned to face him, she let her hand rest till the very last moment.

'Thank you, for today.'

They stared at one another, and Beau hoped it wasn't only he who heard the subtle song of change flickering between them. Any reply he might have made was prevented by the arrival of a courier with a letter. He took it, and by the time he looked back to Miss Doubleday, it was only to see her retreating up the stairs.

The sender was written out as *J.B. Brown, Esq*, a cover for the Home Office. Waiting till he was in his room to break the seal, he cast a quick look around and considered finding new hiding spots for missives he could not immediately destroy.

The letter was as expected as it was short. Two sentences. The first requested his immediate presence at the Home Office; the second instructed him to burn after reading. Despite the clear orders to avoid work while he recovered at home, Beau had dashed off a letter to his boss as soon as he had heard Babin compared to Guy Fawkes and many more missives since.

He retrieved his greatcoat from the chair upon which he'd just placed it, walked back downstairs, and began the mile or so walk to the Palace of Whitehall, where the government's offices were housed. Upon arrival, he turned down a smaller street, home to several law offices and other sundry business fronts, and entered the door framed under the letters *J.B. Brown & Co.* He proceeded through one long corridor, two short ones, and three separate doors, the last bringing him into the back of the Foreign Office within the Treasury building.

His boss, the esteemed Lord Duffy, and the gentleman's fresh equerry were waiting, a grave air hanging about the pair.

'By all means, take your time,' Lord Duffy huffed.

'I walked.'

'You and your walking,' grunted Duffy. 'You could have a carriage for every day of the week and yet you *choose* to walk. Never mind. No time to explicate your odd habits. Where is Babin now?'

'At this very moment?' Beau lifted a shoulder. 'His lodgings, his club, on his way to Westminster to blow up the House of Lords?'

Lord Duffy scowled, but the equerry's face went grim and dreadfully pale.

'Rest easy, boy, Duffy here knew it to be a jest. Babin doesn't yet have the explosives needed, and Parliament won't reconvene from their Easter break for nearly three weeks. Before we move too far beyond the subject, I was enjoying a walk through Mayfair this morning with my ward when an urchin barrelled into us. She would have crumpled to the ground had I not caught her. Curious, no?'

Duffy's brows spiked towards his hairline. 'Well, if you're intimating the man had something to do with the scuffle, I daresay you may be right, given what happened to his father.'

Surprise registered on Beau's face. He stamped it out, but his voice still pitched up when he said, a little stupidly, 'Mr Babin?'

The older man was too stoic to tug at his cravat, but his hand touched it briefly before returning to the desk where he was sitting. 'Are not your estates in the same county?'

Beau acknowledged they were. The peculiar tendrils of uncertainty snaked through him, and his limbs tingled with dreadful anticipation.

'I suppose we've kept you from home quite a bit.' Lord Duffy paused, looking as uncomfortable as Beau had ever seen him. Beau glanced to the equerry, who wore a terrified if confused expression but bore nobly the sheen of sweat gathering at his brow.

'Let me clarify. I understand his father was also a smuggler, but I fail to comprehend what that man has to do with anything presently,' said Beau, a touch of exasperation in his reply.

'Babin the elder was indeed a smuggler—a mighty good one and prolific in the quantities of tea, tobacco, and brandy he was able to move. It took more than a year for us to build a case against him—you were in Brussels at the time—and even with a solid case built, given the challenge of trials and unreliable witnesses, all might have fallen apart had he not used one of the inlets on your family's estate.'

Someone less familiar with Beau might think he hadn't heard what had just been said to him, the way he sat so still it was impossible to tell if he was even breathing. There was a sound in his ears—he'd heard it before, like the high winds of a storm whipping past.

The last letter he received from his father came to mind, the contents of it turning the plum ice in his stomach to stone. Before this moment, Beau had often considered whether his father had only been saying there'd been something of great import he'd needed to discuss just to bring Beau home. But it had been this; he was more than certain. And he needed to know the rest.

'My father and I did not have the benefit of open communication before he passed.'

Lord Duffy nodded in understanding. 'There had been some poaching concerns at the same time.' Beau remembered his father mentioning as much in his letters. 'Your father was out riding with the gamekeeper when they spotted Mr Babin. According to your father, little more resulted than a staring contest. He suggested Babin got turned around looking for coastline closer to his own estate, cautioned them to watch out for poachers, and bid them a good evening.'

'There was never any mention of a trial, and I saw Babin's death announcement—' The only reason his attention had drifted to the notice to begin with was the familiar name from Kent. Even now, Beau couldn't recall a single detail from it, as uninteresting as it had been.

The equerry was fiddling with a pen, trying to mend the tip, and sent it clattering to the ground, earning him an unimpressed glare from Lord Duffy.

'If you weren't my only sister's son,' Duffy mumbled before turning his attention once more to Beau, who, for his part, was glad to know how the young man remained employed. 'Pour me a drink,' Duffy barked to the equerry, who startled at being spoken to and once more dropped the pen. 'No, make it two.'

Duffy waited until Beau was holding the glass before he continued.

'The problem with men like Babin is all their power is derived from fear. But your father was a man impossible to ignore or intimidate. A man whose power derived not just from his title or wealth, but from his integrity, his willingness to act, the relationships he built with others. When the older Babin learned your father was willing to be a witness and speak against him, he hanged himself before a trial could be scheduled, and the family put in the papers that he'd passed peacefully at home after a short illness.'

Beau, who had done nothing with the glass in his hand besides hold it, threw back its contents in one gulp, enjoying the burn and momentary distraction from the deluge of information he'd just received.

'That's—' The sentence broke off in Beau's mouth.

'A lot? I thought it might be,' Lord Duffy said, nodding to his nephew to bring the decanter over again.

But Beau shook his head and held up a staying hand. 'No, thank you. I prefer to keep my head about me.'

He doubted this was the way the meeting was meant to unfold, and there was still more to discuss as it related to Mr Babin's plans, but there was no room in Beau's mind for anything else. He excused himself, and Duffy let him go, steepling his fingers under his chin as he bid farewell.

Beau thought to take the long way home, not that there were enough miles in all of London to walk his thoughts into some kind of order.

27

_____

'Oh.' Emerald's breath caught. 'I beg your pardon.' She had come into the portrait gallery on the second floor, intending to take up a seat across from the previous Lord Avon's picture as she often had at Oakmoss when puzzling through something occupying an inordinate amount of space in her brain. Except the thing taking up residence in her mind was sitting on the bench in front of her. Beau made no response, but slid over, making room for her next to him.

She hesitated. Her thoughts were muddled, and had been for much longer than the night at Almack's, if she was at all prepared to be honest with herself. After parting on the steps once returned from Gunter's, Emerald had seen nothing of him for two full days. His empty seat in the breakfast parlour had felt conspicuous, and the dowager had gone so far as to remark on his absence at a poetry lecture, saying he'd planned to attend.

Beau was a man in possession of arresting good looks, whose countenance she would describe as intimidating, inscrutable, or, on a good day, apathetic. But the man on the bench wore a pensive expression, and when he finally let her see his face, his clear blue eyes appeared clouded with sadness and pain, perhaps even regret. Picking her steps carefully, as if a tree branch might swell up from the floor and trip her, she joined him.

Emerald took it upon herself to open the conversation, confessing in little more than a whisper, 'I sometimes speak with his portrait in the long gallery at Oakmoss.'

'Does he reply?'

'Not always.'

'I am one-and-thirty and only just learning how little I knew him, will ever know him.' There was a hint of bitterness underpinning his words and something else she couldn't pick out, but which made her want to comfort him all the same.

'Who can claim a comprehensive understanding of their parents? I certainly cannot. We polish and tarnish their memory by turns. Today you feel he is a stranger to you. Tomorrow you'll realise you pinch the bridge of your nose when your thoughts are faraway, the very same way he did.' His eyes shifted to her. 'You do, you know. And when you sit in the chair behind the desk in the study, and the light shines in just so—' She cut herself off with a little shake of her head.

'How did it happen?' Beau dropped his gaze to his inter-laced hands, hiding himself from her again.

It mattered not. She'd spent long enough with him to know that asking the question hurt him, and no matter the answer, hearing it would hurt too.

Emerald rubbed her chest, painful memories she had shoved down from that time quick to resurface at the slightest provocation and wrap around her heart like the thorned stem of a rose.

'We were at dinner, the four of us, like any other evening.' She paused, her throat constricting as she remembered thinking Lord Avon looked a little strained as the covers were removed and the first course laid out. She had glanced from him to Louisa to Lady Avon, wondering if the others noticed his wan countenance as well, but the conversation had remained casual and comfortable. 'I looked down to my plate. There was artichoke soup and turbot and lamb. Your mother was saying something to Louisa about how fine her drawing of the home wood was. My thoughts had turned to Which-wood and how very far away my life there felt. The clang of a fork hitting a plate drew my attention.'

The sound, startling and abrasive to her ears, had caused her to whip her head up. Lord Avon had wilted at the head of the table. For the space of a breath, everyone had sat stunned. Then, chaos erupted. Her ladyship had thrown back her chair, words of frightened concern ringing out, each louder and more frantic than the one before.

Lord Avon had looked across at Emerald. It could only have lasted a second, but time had stretched long between them. The moment would haunt her forever. His stare hadn't been frightened or confused as perhaps she'd expected. It'd been regretful, mournful even, and he'd opened his mouth as if he would say something. Before any sound had a chance to wend its way out, his whole form had slumped from the chair.

'Your mama tried to rouse him, and Buddle was already sending one of the footmen for the physician while directing two more to carry your father up to his rooms. Everything that could be done had been done in a trice. Even the physician appeared as if summoned from the air.'

None of it had mattered.

'Poor Louisa was too shocked to even remove herself from

the table and was carried up by one of the footmen. Her ladyship sat with him through the night, only sleeping on the chaise in his room when I insisted and took her seat in the chair. But by dawn—' Emerald choked on the words she was trying to say. 'By dawn—' On her cheek, she felt the warmth of a soft handkerchief. She couldn't remember when she'd begun to cry or even when she'd turned away from Beau, whose typical staid expression was twisted with compassion, sorrow for their shared loss.

'He was gone.' Beau finished the sentence for her, and she nodded in confirmation. 'Did the physician say why? Did he have any idea? Papa was so healthy.'

Emerald noticed the pitch of his voice change. Not in the way that sometimes happened when people couldn't comprehend a loss. It was tight, searching. So were his eyes as he watched her and waited for the answer.

'The physician said your father had, for the better part of a year, been mentioning some tightness in his chest.'

A trace of relief softened his hard features. She would have missed it, had she blinked or sneezed or done a thousand other things that took less than a second to complete. It was curious, and when she was less embedded in her own grief, she hoped she would remember to ask him about it.

'We should have known. I should have. I should have made him do something.' The previous Lord Avon had not treated her as an equal. No one would have expected him to do so, but he had listened to her and considered her ideas, questions, and requests with fairness and an open mind.

Emerald had discovered that the pain of losing one parent was not multiplied when losing another. Rather it took on new colour, grew new tangents, was expressed in new ways.

'There was nothing for you to do.'

She shook her head and sniffled. In the drawing room before dinner that awful night, while she and Louisa had been looking through a book of illustrations, she had heard Lady Avon ask his lordship if he was all right. The worried note in her voice had caught Emerald's attention. Even as Lord Avon reassured his wife he was quite well, Emerald had noticed him clearing his throat several times and rubbing his chest. Lady Avon had looked as if she would've protested, but the door had opened and dinner was announced.

'I'd seen him press a hand to his heart. I can't say how many times, but enough that I shouldn't have ignored it.' Emerald was powerless to prevent one sob from tumbling into another until her whole body shook.

A pair of strong arms wrapped around her, and she turned her head into Beau's waistcoat, trying to muffle the awful, ugly sound coming out of her.

'Let it out, my darling girl. Let it all out.' His words were soothing, reassuring, and Emerald released her hands from her face to curl them into his coat, as if she could bury herself inside his warmth and strength. 'It's not your fault.'

'It is.' Her voice was hoarse, her words muffled.

'It isn't.' With care, Beau pried her away from him, taking her puffy, tear-stained face between his hands so she could not hide from him. 'Look at me,' he insisted. 'No matter how good the person, we all walk this earth for a limited time. You are not at fault for my father's death. Or for your own's.'

'Why?' She hiccupped on the word. The wound now open was impossible to close, and her body shook like wiry boughs in a bruising storm. 'My mother, my father, your father. What is it about me? Why won't people stay?'

His thumbs smoothed her brow, the anguish in her cheeks. 'You have my mother and Lou.'

'Lou until she's married. Your mother until Lou has her first confinement. All these years are just…waiting, waiting to be left again.'

'Me.'

Between his palms, Emerald shook her head, her face twisting in an ugly grimace as she spoke. 'You until you find a wife.'

'Me.'

'You until you go away again.'

'Me.'

'You until—'

'Me, dear one. Always.'

Emerald closed her eyes against the burn of fresh tears and was grateful for the little mercy Beau showed by pulling her close once more. He rubbed her back and murmured calming sounds into the hair at the crown of her head. But even as her weeping abated, she hesitated to pull herself away from him. One more minute, she promised herself, again and again until everything faded but him holding her, his arms a shelter from the storm within. Each rise of his chest a reminder of the living, a lifeline to forgiveness, hope, the sublime.

She had cried herself to sleep and only realised it when her lashes beat against her cheeks. Emerald knew in an instant where she was. Being held close to his chest wasn't a sensation her body would ever let her forget. She mumbled out a quiet protest.

Beau shushed her. 'You are mine…' The rest of his words faded, and a minute later, he was letting go and she was sinking into something soft and snug.

She grasped the lapels of his coat. He folded his hands over hers, and with gentle movements released her hold. There was a pulse of something warm, soft, on her forehead, and then he was gone.

When she opened her eyes again, it was to the low glow of a candle. She was in her bed, unsure if she was waking from a dream or in one, the sprigged muslin dress she'd been wearing replaced by her nightclothes.

'You're awake, miss,' Gwen said, coming to the bedside and holding out a cool compress for Emerald, who turned a questioning look at her maid. 'You had yourself quite a cry, if the puffiness about your eyes is any indication. When this one begins to warm, I'll trade it with another. Half an hour or so should set you right. Then we'll call for a tray and get you settled for the night.'

Emerald peeked at the clock before she adjusted the compress over her eyes, becoming aware of their heaviness as Gwen spoke. The events that had brought her to bed at seven in the evening took a firmer shape in her mind.

'Such a right one, his lordship. He waited for me to respond to the bell and seemed quite concerned for your well-being.'

Emerald was thankful for the cloth over her eyes, obscuring any reaction that may have given her away.

'I hope you're feeling more the thing, miss. I know a good cry always sets me right. A good cry and a hearty meal. I'll let Cook know you'll be ready to eat within the half hour.'

Blood pounded in Emerald's temples. She wished the memory of their exchange remained buried—not so she might relieve herself of the chagrin that accompanied the knowledge she'd ruined Beau's cravat and allowed him to witness her in such a miserable state, but because she wished to ignore the brilliant turmoil of her mind as she turned over one thought with frightful clarity again and again: She had shown him the shadowy part of herself, and he had answered not with his own darkness but with light. A voice she would hear always, anywhere. An answer, a vision, a beginning.

28

*B*eau had already gone twelve rounds with Gentleman Jackson at his boxing club in Bond Street when Mr Lyon showed up, his eyes wide and eyebrows high as he studied Beau's tattoo.

When he spoke, however, he said, 'How do you do, Avon? Your return to town is all anyone can speak of. I'm not at all surprised to find you here preparing to defend yourself against the matchmaking mamas.' He laughed at his own jest, his jovial disposition in stark contrast to the grunts and groans knocking around the club.

Beau rolled his eyes as he dodged a left hook. 'Care to join me?'

Lyon looked a little awed by the invitation and agreed. Stepping up to the mat, he removed his coat, waistcoat, and boots. The bell sounded, signalling the end of the current round, and he took his place, looking more confident than Beau had expected. They squared off, Beau in happy anticipation of putting Lyon through his paces.

'Your form is good,' Beau said to the younger man after a

minute or two, 'but you hesitate. Outside of these rooms, little pauses such as those could cost you dearly.'

He moderated himself a little, certain Lyon couldn't take the full force of his strength, but then he did not wish to subject the man to it either. Beau had Jackson, Saunders, and Allard for such purposes.

More dangerous than Beau's strength was his skill. His footwork was unmatched even by Jackson himself; he was a master of feinting and baiting, and he possessed a deadly combination of accuracy, speed, and power.

Lyon watched him with cautious eyes as they moved around one another.

'Did you think I invited you to box just to thrash you?' asked Beau, genuinely curious to learn the answer.

'It crossed my mind.' The wary way Lyon answered made Beau chuckle. 'You have known me in face and name the better part of my life, but in essentials, we do not understand much of the other.'

'And?' Beau asked, landing a punch to Lyon's ribs.

Lyon grunted. 'And the few conversations we've shared in recent history have been'—he faltered, absorbing another punch—'serrated.'

'You appear on familiar, even intimate, terms with my ward and my sister.'

'Esther and I have been friends with Miss Doubleday almost since her arrival at your estate. Only in the last year or so has Miss Calverleigh been joining us for tea or the occasional picnic,' replied Lyon, his jaw jutting at the perceived offence. 'I am no fox in the henhouse, my lord. I would say your care does you credit, but how convenient for your concern to align so neatly with your homecoming.'

Beau had no interest in being maligned by a pup who

thought himself the pinnacle of gentlemanly principles and who would describe iniquity as anything preventing him from securing his place on the dance cards of his partners of choice. Beau did not pull his next punch, but he did lend a hand to Lyon when the young man fell to the floor.

Lyon brushed himself off, throwing a leery sidelong glance at Beau. They squared up, tapped knuckles, and began another round.

'You are right. In essentials, we are practically strangers. I'm past due in becoming better acquainted with my younger neighbours, such as yourself and Babin.' Beau's statement was only half true. He knew plenty about all the estate owners, big and small, in his part of the country, but not all of the knowledge had been obtained by neighbourly methods.

'Babin is a good fellow.'

'You are well acquainted?'

Lyon shrugged, and Beau let him land a hit. 'He's an Oxford man. I went to Cambridge, like yourself. He's a year or two ahead of me anyhow and seems to keep busy with his home and fields. A neighbour introduced us at an assembly last year. Mentioned I'd be inheriting my aunt's estate and would one day be woven into the fabric of the area in a more permanent way.'

'A piece of advice, if I may?'

With a subtle tip of the head, Lyon acceded.

'Use caution where Babin is concerned.' Beau knew Lyon wasn't involved in Babin's business dealings, but being present in town, being a friend, and being naïve was enough to put the young man at risk.

'Because he's of French descent? I'd not thought you so closed-minded as that.'

'Is he? I had no idea,' Beau lied.

'Babin was shortened from Babineaux by his father when he came over in the nineties. If I recall, he still has a grandmother there, maybe an uncle or some such, on the coast.'

'Interesting,' was the best Beau could do. 'But no, not because he's French.'

'Who's French? Besides me,' Allard interjected, his accent softened after spending more than half his life living in England. 'My apologies for the interruption, but I'm in need of a private conference with Avon.'

'Then I suppose I ought to end the round,' replied Beau, knocking Lyon down once more and helping him back up with the same effortlessness.

The younger man pouted. 'Next time, you need not go easy on me.'

Beau picked up a towel to wipe the sweat from his bare chest. 'See what your ribs have to say about it tomorrow and the day after.' He turned to Allard. 'A moment to refresh myself, and we can go.'

The two men made their way down St James's Street, along Pall Mall, and turned down the bland lane on which J.B. Brown & Co. was situated and where Saunders was waiting. Cutting through the little maze of halls and doors, they spilled into Lord Duffy's office with such energy the equerry spilled tea on his waistcoat.

Beau apologised with a sardonic curl of his lips before turning his attention to Duffy. 'What have you learned of Babin's accomplices? I assume that's why Allard came to fetch me.'

Duffy nodded and picked up several sheafs of paper on his desk. 'Jude Hensell is known to us. He worked as a spy for the French and has been inflaming revolutionary groups in the North. Henry Fournier, we've determined, is supplying barrels of gunpowder from France, likely aided by Babin's grand-mother, who lives on the coast. But Charlie Newling remains a bit of an enigma. We've been unable to find even a record of his person.'

'Babin's lack of originality is disappointing,' Saunders ventured, as the men digested this information.

Beau agreed, but said, 'He's still got time to surprise us.' It bothered him that in the letters he'd seen in Babin's study, those which had been intercepted and opened by the Home Office before being resealed and sent on, and the ones he'd received from Poughill, not a single date had been mentioned, for an act of mutiny or otherwise. 'We're missing something.'

'One of our best codebreakers has been through every piece of mail Babin's received since you first wrote. Most of it borders on the mundane, with a few mentions of card parties, family dinners, the theatre,' replied Duffy, sounding a little affronted. 'He isn't stupid enough to blast the building before it's filled with lords, and I confirmed the location of the stock-piled gunpowder myself. How many shipments are left? One?'

'One,' confirmed Beau. 'Babin has been receiving them at regular intervals. If the pattern holds, six days from now will be the final one.' Which still left a week or more before Parlia-ment reconvened. Another detail that rubbed against his instincts.

Duffy dragged his long bony fingers along his jaw. 'Then in six days we'll be waiting for him at the storeroom. I'll be in touch,' he said, dismissing them.

Outside, the three men exchanged uneasy glances.

'I suppose that's what happens when you get used to being in charge, being right,' remarked Saunders.

'Go on to Avon House,' said Beau. 'Have Wallace settle you in the study. I'll be there directly. I've got a quick errand.'

His errand to the jeweller to inspect the stones for a ring he was having made was quick, and Beau trotted up the steps of Avon House less than an hour later. On the first-floor landing, he turned towards his study only to be greeted by his ward.

'Your valet awaits you in the study.' The emphasis she put on *valet* was not lost on him. 'Along with another gentleman, or so I suppose him to be, but perhaps he's only a fleshy apparition.'

'Have you seen many spirits? I'd not thought you a connoisseur.'

Emerald walked alongside him as they approached the study door. He could feel she wished to say more, and she opened her mouth before pinching it closed several times. With a hand on the handle, he said by way of consolation, 'Perhaps a game later, if you are inclined.'

'We're for Lady Abercrombe's. Her husband had a portrait commissioned for her fortieth birthday.'

'She turned forty the year I turned three-and-twenty. How fine for her that the members of the *ton* have such short memories.'

The corners of his ward's mouth hooked upwards, and he felt inordinate pleasure in winning even a ghost of a smile from her.

'Will you be there?'

It was the first time she had ever asked him directly about his plans, and her interest warmed him like the first rays of spring sun after a long, sorrowful winter.

'I had other interests in mind for this evening. But I recall once having promised never to interfere with your pleasure, so if it would please you, you may depend upon my presence.' His answer was forthright, and the chance she might demur or deny him caused a little twinge of uncertainty to fist around his stomach.

The pale pink tinge to her cheeks and the sweet, slow smile brightening her already lovely face was his reward, and it remained with him long after he shut the door to the study behind him.

---

29

*T*he doors between the drawing room and study flung open, sending Emerald stumbling backward. She flailed, imagining her ignominious demise as she reached for one of the heavy brocade drapes to her right. A heartbeat was exactly how long it took for Beau to catch her swinging arms and steady her against his chest.

'Next time, perhaps you will reconsider eavesdropping.'

Emerald huffed and pushed herself away. 'I was—' She stopped when she caught the glint of amusement in his eyes. They had moved into unfamiliar territory, a place where the stiffness between them had bent, where hope and fear came into existence in equal measure. 'I was not having a very good go of it. Next time, maybe you'll be more considerate and speak louder.' She gave herself a moment to take in his open face, this peace between them, and then said, 'If I asked, would you tell me?' Like the sky outrunning the sun, his expression darkened. The gentle tone he employed when answering came as a surprise.

'Information is power. Power is dangerous. You are mine to protect.'

'As your ward, you mean?' Her voice rasped low, faraway to her own ears, and although she was speaking to him, she was having trouble focusing on anything besides the tempting crescents of his mouth.

Beau palmed her cheek, and she turned her head into the intimate touch. His thumb traced the outline of her mouth before he dragged it across the fullness of her bottom lip. Closing her eyes, she pressed her mouth to the warm, pulsing flesh of his finger, nipping the tip as he slipped it between her lips.

When her eyelids fluttered open, his bold, burning gaze consumed her, and the surge of blood in her ears made a sound like *mine, mine, mine.* She needed more, needed to know at last what it would be like to feel his kiss. Emerald stepped closer, letting the heat of his body rake her over. Beau ran his hands down the length of her arms, her bare skin burning in the wake of his touch, and threaded his fingers through her own.

Her mouth went dry. She could feel the pound of her pulse in her quivering stomach. Against the delicate fabric of her chemise, her nipples hardened, and her core throbbed with a rush of wet heat.

'Emerald,' he whispered, tipping his forehead to rest upon her own.

She couldn't hide her reaction to him, her uneven breathing, desire spreading a vibrant flush over her chest, the hint of moisture gathering on her palms. The hollows of her body filled with yearning. In every uneven breath a wish to be claimed.

'What was I before you? A night grown too cool, too quiet.

A flawed prayer forgotten by morning. A man against himself. Summon me into existence. In your hands I am formless, unfastened. Bury me in your deep sweet, in your grief, in your splendour.'

Her skin prickled in anticipation as he nuzzled the hollow of her neck, her jaw, the sensitive shell of her ear. She had no faith in her voice, but her heart said *I'm yours* and beat against his in a soundless vow.

'I'd ask you to forgive the interruption, but let us all agree it's for the best,' Saunders said in mild, dispassionate accents from the doorway.

Emerald jumped backward but was prevented from going too far by the tight grip of Beau's hand still linked with hers. He released it once she stilled, and she ran both hands down the front of her dress and over her hair before tucking them behind her back.

'A moment, my lord.' Saunders tipped his head in the direction of the study.

With a look towards Emerald, which she interpreted as *We're not finished*, Beau preceded his valet back into the study. Saunders turned to follow, and Emerald made for the relative safety of her own rooms. Although no amount of time spent in quiet reflection would permit her to forget his hushed words, their despair and tenderness. Her spirits soared with the realisation he cared for her and sank just as quickly when the scene she relived in her mind again and again never ended with a kiss. She was beginning to wonder if she'd ever taste his yearning. The doubt sent a single tear down her cheek. She swiped it away, determined to regain her composure before leaving the house for the evening.

She and the dowager were engaged to dine with some of Lady Avon's friends, and despite taking tea with Louisa in the sun lounge, writing a letter to her stepmother in the library, and meandering past the study door once or twice more before departing, Emerald did not see Beau again while at home.

With her arm threaded through the dowager's, they entered Lady Abercrombe's already crowded picture gallery. Emerald, paying no mind to what was being said to her, scanned the faces for one familiar and dear, her breath bottled in her chest, her slippered foot tapping a staccato rhythm under her dress. Her heart dropped when she couldn't pick out his lean build, his sharp, square shoulders, his brilliant, clear eyes.

'I had thought the earl planned to be in attendance this evening.'

'Did he say so? Last I heard, he had engaged himself for a card party with friends, but when you get to be my age, you've long learned to accustom yourself to the whims of young people,' the dowager answered in her steady, easy way, but the climb of her eyebrows and the curious way she regarded her made Emerald feel exposed. She resisted the urge to fidget.

'Yes, well, I daresay we could be shoulder to shoulder and still not find each other in this crush.'

'What a charming picture you two ladies make.' A male voice interrupted their exchange, and Emerald, releasing the dowager's arm, turned to see Mr Babin at her other side.

'Mr Babin, how do you do?'

'Very well, Miss Doubleday. This private gallery rivals some of the finer public ones I've had the pleasure of visiting. Do you sketch or paint in watercolour?'

'I cannot claim any such talents. My time has been given to animal husbandry and horticulture, although those may not weigh so favourably with the *ton*.' She smiled at the absurdity of it all. 'I hope I am nevertheless at least able to appreciate the skill required to achieve a well-composed piece of art.'

'Do you appreciate the dramatics of a big reveal as well?'

Emerald laughed. 'Don't we all? I'm convinced the turnout is due to the thrill of anticipation more than the joy of viewing a portrait of a woman who stands in front of us.'

'An astute observation, Miss Doubleday.'

Emerald's mood soared when she heard Beau's voice, but she held tight to the smile wishing to form on her face. She had no desire to let others in. 'A compliment? I am in disbelief.' His blue eyes sparked. He understood.

'Babin,' he said with his most glacial stare.

'What a happy reunion we have here,' chimed Mr Lyon, joining the group with his sister on his arm.

'I could think of at least a dozen other things I'd rather be doing,' Esther stated, with a subtle roll of her eyes in Emerald's direction. 'But after the fuss last year, I'm awash in curiosity to see Mr Wilson's work. His paintings can no longer be found in most public galleries, and it seems his commissions have all but dried up too. I just overheard he wouldn't even have had this one if not for being Lady Abercrombe's nephew.'

'Fuss?' asked Emerald.

It was Mr Lyon who answered. 'Scant on the details, but it seems he made quite the enemy at the Royal Academy last season.'

'Come, Charles. Mama beckons,' said Esther on a sigh. She took a step, but paused to say to Emerald, 'I need a new scent. Care to visit Floris with me tomorrow?'

Emerald inclined her head in agreement.

'I'll call for you at two,' stated Miss Lyon, dragging her brother away by his arm.

Mr Babin also excused himself, and the dowager had slipped off some time ago, leaving Emerald standing alone with her guardian.

'Are you enjoying your evening?'

She replied with light censure, 'Quite well, no thanks to you.' In truth, she wanted only to return to the drawing room, to finish what they'd begun, and in the absence of such a possibility had lingered on his words, the way her body formed to his, and what it could all mean until her mind was as scrambled as the eggs she'd eaten for breakfast.

'Would you care to lay specific charges at my feet? Perhaps I may redeem myself—and your evening—yet.'

His tone was serious, but Emerald suspected he was teasing her. 'You're quizzing me.'

He smiled. 'I'm only following your lead.'

'It's a shame you're not always so amiable.'

'Is that why you drive me to distraction? For your own enjoyment?' Beau's eyes were as clear as the diamonds around her neck but blazed down on her like the sun itself was reflected within them. Somehow during their exchange the distance between them had lessened. Emerald forced her lungs to fill with air, wondering if he could hear it whooshing through her.

She wanted for a witty reply, something to maintain the foreign lightness of the conversation, but his question, though teasing, had caught her off guard, and she struggled to do more than blink at him.

'You'll forgive me while I delight in my achievement. I've never seen you speechless and feel I ought to appreciate the relative quiet.'

His face held a challenge, and Emerald, released from her stupor, opened her mouth to utter some retort only to clamp it closed instead, making a show of holding her lips tight together and issuing a challenge of her own.

'You wish to gratify me? No, not you, dear ward. You wish to punish me by forcing me into conversation with other guests. I know how you delight in vexing me, and as I'm committed to your pleasure, I'm left with very little choice.' His eyes dropped from hers and roamed over her body—the gaze lustful, lingering, and touching even the most sensitive parts of her hidden from view. Her centre seized with desire. 'Your humble servant, ma'am.' Beau eased back into the throng of people filling Lady Abercrombe's rooms.

Emerald watched his back as he retreated. The image of what lay under his fitted coat sent a shiver through her.

A crowd gathered at Lady Abercrombe's beckoning, and Emerald took her place next to the dowager with only half a mind for what was happening around her. After the curtain dropped, revealing a downright ghastly painting of the woman, Beau's eyes caught hers and held them in a fulminating stare. Like the last leaf falling from a bare branch, the vestiges of caution protecting her heart slipped from her hold.

'You and your guardian appear to be on better terms with one another.'

Emerald was startled to find herself in the company of Mr Babin once more. After he had walked away earlier, she'd not spared another thought for him.

'It's much easier to share a home with someone when one is not always at odds with them,' she said, keeping her face and focus forward.

'True.' He nodded. 'There was a time I suspected his interest in you was unbefitting his position as your guardian, and it would only be a matter of time before I'd be offering you congratulations. But, alas, I suppose intuition remains stronger in the fairer sex.'

She couldn't prevent the flush creeping up her neck and hoped it went unnoticed. The familiarity with which he spoke to her was unwelcome and unappreciated, and she opened her mouth to excuse herself when rescue came from a surprising quarter.

'Miss Doubleday, a pleasure,' exclaimed the Duchess of Hazelhurst, reaching out a hand for Emerald's.

When Emerald looked to where Mr Babin had been standing at her side, reluctantly prepared to make the introduction, the space was empty.

'Forgive me if I overstepped. You did not appear to be enjoying yourself in your previous conversation.'

Emerald was a little taken aback. One of the earliest things she'd mastered at Oakmoss was her composure, or the ability to imitate it. 'Was it so obvious?'

'No.' The duchess offered a kind smile. 'Not at all.'

'What think you of Lady Abercrombe's new painting?'

The duchess's enigmatic green eyes flashed. 'Would you prefer an honest answer or a society one?'

Emerald's brows drew together in a wrinkle of confusion, but she asked for the honest answer through a crooked half-smile. Her Grace angled herself towards Emerald to afford them whatever privacy could be had in such a crowd. 'She only hired Wilson because he's her nephew, as I'm sure you've heard by now, and'—she paused, drawing her eyes up to Emerald's—'because I refused it.'

Emerald's eyes widened. It would've been futile for her to make any attempt at hiding her surprise. 'You're a painter?' The question was stupid but the best Emerald could manage while she tried to recall anything the dowager had mentioned about the young woman next to her.

The duchess's mouth twitched with amusement. 'Shocking, I know.'

'Yes, but wonderful too. To even dare dream of such a thing. The most I've ever dreamt of is a home and family of my own. How trite that sounds by comparison.'

Her Grace found Emerald's hand and gave it a squeeze. 'There's nothing trite about wishing for something—or someone—to call your own.'

A hot sting assailed Emerald's eyes, and she fluttered her lashes, embarrassed by her visceral reaction to the duchess's words and the sincerity with which they'd been delivered.

'Come, let us take a turn. I'll introduce you to my husband, and if it would distract from whatever weighs on your mind, I will tell you all about the scandal I caused last year.'

Emerald chuckled, enchanted by the woman, and let herself be guided through the throngs of people who seemed to float apart to make way for the young duchess.

'I hope you do not feel it forward of me to express my wish that we may become friends.'

'You're a duchess. Is impertinence not one of the pleasures accompanying rank and fortune?'

The duchess beamed. 'How I do enjoy being right. Although, I've only been a duchess less than a twelvemonth. All the rest I spent steeped in propriety, or near to it.' She paused her speech as they passed a pair of fair-haired ladies whispering behind their fans. 'So many of the rules we follow we do so out of fear.'

If the woman's striking veneer were to be peeled back, no doubt one would find her made up of grit and backbone and purpose, and in her, Emerald recognised a kindred spirit.

'Once you know who you are, Miss Doubleday, and what wish is foremost in your heart, be bold.'

The words were quick to root in Emerald's fertile mind.

She had been looking for Beau as they made their way round the room, her eyes scanning every face for the only one that made her feel as though an entire garden bloomed in her belly. When she spotted him, his mouth curved into a private smile just for her. Even as she moved beyond where she could see him, she knew he was watching her. The very same way she knew she never had and never would love another man so long as there was breath in her lungs.

---

30

*B*eau trailed some twenty paces behind his ward as she and Miss Lyon departed Floris, made the right onto Duke Street, and then took a quick left to walk down Piccadilly. He couldn't prove the urchin running into her after Gunter's hadn't been an accident, but he also suspected it'd been a crime of opportunity—perhaps Babin had seen them in the tea shop and taken the chance to act. Knowing what he did about his father's role in ending the elder Babin's smuggling operations, and how the son very likely assigned some guilt to the previous Lord Avon for his father taking his own life, Beau was able to craft a motive for the action.

Babin had good instincts, which was a shame, given how he used them. The night prior at Lady Abercrombe's, he had watched Beau and Emerald. Although Beau had been conscious to keep his distance for most of the night, he knew in the end it didn't matter. Babin had already determined hurting her would hurt Beau. And Emerald, when she'd agreed to go shopping with Miss Lyon, had told Mr Babin exactly where she would be and when.

Despite a morning cooled by bracing air left over as winter rolled into spring, Mayfair bustled. The road was busy. Carriages carried esteemed persons from here to there, vendors pushed carts heaped with wares ready to sell, and the flag-way spilled over with dandies on the stroll, footmen carrying precarious stacks of boxes, and young women like his ward walking arm-in-arm with friends.

He and Saunders wove in and out of the crowd, Beau keeping his eyes trained on Emerald's back. She and her friend paused in front of a stationery shop. Miss Lyon dashed in, leaving Emerald waiting near a cart piled high with fruit, her maid close by with two bags from Floris in her hands. She had just turned to say something to Gwen when a hackney, rushing from behind an oppressively large carriage, lost control and came careening at her. Beau was too far away to do more than call her name, which could not be heard above the din of the busy street. There was a frightened whinny, a terrible crashing noise, and a ghastly shriek that sent fear sweeping through him.

As one, Beau and Saunders rushed forward, pushing their way through the knot of people already gathering. His breathing was shallow and ragged, and when he got to the centre of the group gathered, the cold hand of fear had wrapped tight around his heart. Curled on the ground, unmoving and with her head lolling away from him, was his ward. At her side, her maid. The lady had a small hand on Emerald's shoulder and was shaking her with more strength than one would suppose possible in a woman of diminutive size whose primary activity was selecting gowns and dressing hair.

Miss Lyon reappeared, package in hand, and released a horrified scream at the sight laid in front of her.

'Emerald!' Beau called her name twice as he knelt down, his voice trembling and panicked. He ran his hands along her neck, back, and arms, checking for broken bones. When he didn't find any, he rolled her over so he could see her face, taking her in his arms as he did so. In the background, Saunders was dispersing the crowd and had taken it upon himself to calm both Miss Lyon and the maid, who, once the responsibility of getting her mistress to come to was relieved from her shoulders, burst into tears.

There was dirt on Emerald's face, but no tell-tale red. He untied her bonnet and dislodged a few curls as he ran his fingers through her hair, searching for cuts or the sticky dampness of blood. He found none, and with his immediate fright at bay, he took a moment to study her peaceful face.

He ran a thumb over her smooth cheek with a touch so light it was as if he feared she might break under the pressure of it.

'Emerald.' Her name came out as a sigh, a plea, a wish. In his arms, he felt her chest expand with a full breath. Once more he said her name, the word hushed, only for her.

Her eyelids blinked open, and she looked up with a vague stare, her mind no doubt trying to work through a haze of confusion.

Relief surged through him. 'There she is.' He allowed himself one solitary second to enjoy the feeling before asking, 'Can you tell me your name?'

'Emerald Doubleday,' she replied with uncharacteristic weakness in her voice.

'And who am I?'

She closed her eyes, the movement slow, and took twice as long to open them, each second further shredding Beau's nerves.

'My adversary. Or my lord guardian, whichever you prefer.'

He expelled a loud, long breath of gratitude. Her wide, nebulous eyes held him in a trance, and Beau was busy thanking every god he could name when she tensed in his arms.

'Easy, easy. You've had an accident,' he said, helping her to her feet. Only then did he look around to discover the driver of the hackney long gone.

She, too, brushed her head from side to side, taking notice of their conspicuous position in the middle of Piccadilly. A little group still hung about on the fringes, their curious stares averted when met with a blast of pure ice as Beau looked their direction.

'Where is your maid? Ah, Gwen,' said Beau as Saunders came forward with the two ladies. 'Is the carriage near?'

'We came by foot, sir. The ladies wished to enjoy the temperate day.'

With a nod, Beau hailed a hackney. When one came to a stop, he turned back to say, 'Saunders will see you and Miss Lyon home,' before helping his ward into the vehicle and then climbing in himself. The lady's maid bobbed a curtsey and looked considerably relieved to leave her charge in her employer's care.

When the hired vehicle lurched forward, Beau ventured to ask Emerald how she felt.

Her gaze had been fixed forward, where it remained, and she took her time responding to his question. 'I cannot be sure I know. It seems certain I have been near death. Yet without broken bones or cuts or much beyond vague soreness, my body can convince itself the entire episode was a dream.'

Even next to him, he sensed she was far away. It was no

great surprise. With ease, he could remember the first time he'd been shot and how certain he'd been death was coming for him. He thought of all the things he'd wished he had done, all the things he could not change. When he had eventually regained consciousness to find himself abed, torso bandaged, Saunders reassuring him he'd see another sunrise, Beau hadn't amended his ways. He instead began to see death as an inevitability, especially in his profession, and taught himself not to fear it. He could die in five years or fifty, but that he would was certain.

'I imagine you may find yourself with a nasty bruise or two on the morrow. When we are returned to Avon House, I will call for the physician just to be certain you are well.'

'That hardly seems necessary.'

'Perhaps not, but all the same, it will ease my mind once the physician has had a good look at you.'

There was very little space between them in the hackney, hardly more than an arm's width. When she turned to look at him, her face read like a map of emotions. He could see every thought behind her eyes and anticipate, like any good spy, his quarry's next move.

'What were you doing in Piccadilly?'

'Walking home.'

Her eyes narrowed. 'What were you really doing in Piccadilly?'

Beau considered her, gave in to the affectionate smile curling his lips, and said, 'Following you.'

To his delight, she snorted. 'I can't decide which is worse: the action or you admitting to it.'

With the added task of seeing Miss Lyon home, Saunders and Gwen arrived at Avon House around the same time as the physician. A cheaper rug would not have withstood the rough wear caused by Beau's restless pacing the length of the corridor outside of Emerald's rooms. He was rewarded by the door opening a short half hour later. Gwen had been discharged to secure a restorative tea, and the physician had the pleasure of assuring Beau all was well, aside from the good shake-up the young lady had experienced.

'Thank you, sir. Let me see you out,' said Beau, not really wishing to do so but knowing it was right.

The spry, grey-haired man who had known Beau since he was a child shook his head, waved Beau off, and said he was perfectly able to make it down the stairs and to the door himself. Beau did not bother to wait. He nodded and turned towards Emerald's room. Her door was open, and his throat constricted when he looked in. An unusual fragile air hung about her where she was propped atop her bedcovers against a wall of pillows, eyes closed, chest rising slowly with shallow breaths. From his place in the doorway, he rapped his knuckles on the frame.

She glanced his way, observing him with a sweet, musing look. 'Oh, do you wish to come in?'

The words sent a shiver of wanting rippling through him, and he chided himself for how quickly his mind had gone from deep concern to deep desire.

'I brought something for you,' he said, approaching the side of her bed with a little jar of arnica jelly. 'A little bird told me it helps with pain and bruising.'

Her lips parted, and her whole countenance was the perfect picture of artless surprise. 'Well, my right shoulder is a little sore.'

Beau unscrewed the lid and set it on the bedside table. 'May I?'

She nodded, and with care, he pulled down the shoulder of

her dressing gown, exposing the reddened skin of her shoulder. He dipped two fingers into the cool jelly, and he heard her breath hitch when he began to apply it with light pressure. Goose bumps prickled out over her flesh as she watched his movements with heavy eyes.

It was impossible to ignore his growing awareness of her, and he teased his fingers from her shoulder further along than necessary to the delicious stretch of her collarbone. She whimpered, the quiet, involuntary noise intoxicating. Her nearness overwhelmed him, and the surge of blood through his body told him he needed to retreat to his own room. With reluctance, he pulled his hand back.

'I'll leave this for you,' he said, returning the lid to its place.

She nodded and reached out a hand to him. He took it, pressed her warm palm to his mouth, and curled her fingers around the kiss he'd left there as he set her hand back on her bed. With one last look into her probing, depthless eyes, he left before he did something as foolish as devour her whole.

31

*T*he following morning Emerald took a tray in her room for breakfast and remained in bed for most of the day, so it came as a surprise to Beau to find her donning a silk domino when he next saw her.

She was in the entryway of Avon House, preoccupied with securing the thing about her neck, but it was her dress that caught his attention. It was a deep blue affair embroidered with flowers, vines, and feathers in shades of green and gold winding up from the hem, over the curve of her hip, to the generously cut bodice that set off the tantalising swell of her breasts. Following the trail of creamy skin, he studied the gentle arc of her neck, imagined the sweet, clean taste of her skin against his lips. Sweat prickled between his shoulder blades; his arousal strained against his breeches.

Candlelight caught the shine of her obsidian eyes as she moved, and Beau had to force down the knot of yearning in his throat. She was a marvel to behold.

He was obscured by the darkness of the hall and made no

move to step into the light. Feeling selfish, he stood still and quiet, mesmerised by the sight of her.

'My lord?'

Beau jumped at the sound of the butler's voice. 'Wallace. Send Saunders up to me.' And because her head whipped up when Wallace spoke, Beau had little choice but to pretend he'd been moving in her direction all along.

'What ballroom will you dazzle tonight, my enchanting ward?'

'All of them.' Her reply was delivered with a wry smile. 'But I believe I'll start with Lady Amelia Norton's. Esther and her grandmama are taking me to the private masquerade there. I understand it is her ladyship's favourite party and one she throws each year.'

He was familiar, having attended the same party six or seven years ago. Except for a few sticklers, many among the *ton* loved private masquerades. A controlled guestlist gave the illusion of propriety, masks the guise of anonymity, and the expectation of meeting only people from one's same sphere encouraged guests to push the bounds of modesty and decorum.

'Are you sure you're well?'

She chewed her lip a moment before answering. 'Well enough. I've always wanted to attend a masquerade.'

He worked to keep the dismay from his voice when he asked, 'Is my mother not accompanying you?'

Emerald's expression grew serious. 'No. She dropped one of her wood jewellery cases on her foot. She's well, but in no mood to be moving about a crowded ballroom. Have you any engagements this evening? I thought you might also be attending. It seems as though everyone is.'

'I received an invitation, yes, but planned on a quiet evening at my club.'

'Oh.'

Beau thought there was disappointment in her one-syllable answer, but the sound of the bell prevented him from saying more.

'That will be Esther,' said Emerald, picking up her mask of blue and gold with peacock feathers billowing off the right side.

One of the footmen opened the door for her, and she bid Beau a good night. He waited for the door to close behind her before he took the stairs two at a time. He was tearing through the drawers in his dressing room, searching for the mask he'd used an eternity ago, when Saunders entered and gasped in dismay at the destruction unfolding.

'Sir, I beg of you, let me,' the valet said, manoeuvring Beau out of the way.

'Where's that mask? Surely we didn't toss it out with the rubbish?'

'What mask?' Saunders asked, already refolding the lengths of cotton and silk used for Beau's cravats, which had been haphazardly tossed to the floor.

'The one I had made in Venice ages ago. Gold. Conceals most of my face. How many masks do you know me to have?'

'Four.' Saunders reached into the back of a large wardrobe and retrieved something wrapped in white silk. He carefully unfolded the fabric, revealing a heavy gold mask. 'The remainder of the costume is in the attics, but there's a white shirt with more ruffles than I can count within easier reach just tucked behind some of your more staid pieces, as well as your white waistcoat, black satin knee breeches, and the aubergine coat.'

'Pirate it is. Saunders, you're worth your weight in gold, which I believe is what I pay you.'

It hadn't mattered where Emerald had said she was going. Beau had known the moment he'd seen her standing there that he would follow—because she was breathtaking, because in her company was when he felt most himself, because only the day before someone had tried to harm her.

There were at least five hundred people already arrived when he entered Lady Norton's home less than an hour later. Still, he was a needle in a compass and Emerald his north star. She was walking away from the last set on the arm of a gentleman dressed as a chimney sweep who was escorting her back to Miss Lyon's grandmother. He saw his opportunity and stepped into the path to block their way.

'I beg your pardon,' the chimney sweep said, attempting to steer them around Beau.

'It's for me to beg yours. This little bird has honoured me with her next dance.' Beau adopted an American accent and spoke in a deep, languorous way.

He knew, as well as she, of course, that she hadn't promised him anything. Emerald's gaze was penetrating as she weighed whether or not she wished to go along with his lie. He'd disguised himself in look and sound but wished only for the illusion of anonymity. What he craved was her aware-ness and understanding; there was freedom for them both behind their masks if she wished for it.

Her eyes looked even more mysterious and compelling against the sea blue of her mask, and the moment of prolonged anticipation was rapidly becoming unbearable. When she removed her hand from the other man's arm and stepped forward towards Beau, he had to steady the possessive gratifi-cation threatening to topple him.

'Are you always so bold?' she asked, slipping her hand through his arm as they moved towards the other dancers taking their places for a waltz.

'When I see something I want, like you, beautiful little bird.'

Her easy laugh awakened in him a sense of satisfaction.

'You may save your practised flattery; I've already agreed to the dance. By the by, I do hope the disgruntled chimney sweep hasn't a brush hiding somewhere.'

'I couldn't care less.' Beau pulled her close to him, closer than he would have had their identities not been secreted away. He felt her surprised intake of breath as her ribs expanded under his right arm. 'Have you waltzed before?'

'Not like this.'

'Good.' The word rumbled from deep inside him and came out rough, like the bark of an oak tree.

'Is this how it's done in America?'

'I'll take you one day, if you like, and you can find out for yourself.'

She was staring at his neck, the skin of it bare and free from the restraint of a cravat. The top of his shirt was open, the tie undone and falling loosely towards his chest. He knew there was a hint of his tattoo rising beyond the limp white collar.

'Tell me about this.'

Beau knew it was the tattoo she was asking about. 'What is it you wish to know?'

'Why did you get it? There must be some significance.'

'There was a man I met through work, an artist really, who could give life to something in black and white. When I went to him, I just wanted to distract myself, to feel a different kind of pain than that which had been eating me from the inside out.'

'Did it help as you'd hoped?'

'In the beginning. One of the hardest things we can ask of ourselves is to reconcile two halves of our own whole. This is the half of me I ignored for too long.' He felt the energy between them change as he spoke, their left arms coming up to meet overhead once more. Her delicate scent teased his nostrils, and he filled his chest with a greedy inhale. With each chord of the dance, he lost more of himself to her and wanted more of her in return.

They made the final turn; he felt almost feverish from their closeness, and she sounded a little breathless. The music died out, but they stood staring at one another. The candlelight reflecting in her eyes looked like stars glowing against the night sky.

'I'm feeling a trifle overheated,' said she as the other couples around them applauded the musicians and moved away to change partners.

Before she said another word, he looped her hand through his arm and turned them for the row of French doors leading to the terrace. Neither spoke as they wandered further from the stuffy rooms, the masked revellers enjoying themselves with impunity, the torches radiant in the garden.

When they came to the high stone wall at the back of the property, the noise of the fête buffered by the tall hedges, Beau brought them to a stop. 'We've gone too far.'

Emerald stepped in front of him. She raised a tentative hand, tracing the ink on his chest. The silk of her glove against his hot skin made him tremble.

'Impossible, when there is something keeping us contained.' She was staring up at him, but in the dark of night, it was difficult to make out what she was thinking.

Under her hand, his heart hammered, and he knew his

resolve was crumbling with every second they remained alone. He covered her hand with his own and wrapped his arm around her waist, pulling her against him.

'I like when you do that,' she confessed in a hushed voice.

'What?'

'Touch me.'

Beau groaned, dropping his head to nip the soft flesh of her neck as he ran a hand up the bodice of her dress. He cupped her supple breast, reeling at the pleasure of touching her. She arched into him, and he ran his thumb over the silk, cursing the layers of fabric between his skin and hers as he felt her soften for him.

'What do you want, little bird?'

'This. You. More. Everything,' she half said, half begged, her voice huskier, more arousing than he'd ever heard before. He licked his lips. Until he could put his ring on her finger, Beau would deny himself the taste of her. He must, if there was any hope of preserving her virtue, but his need to touch her had become dire, vital even.

In one quick movement, he turned her, bringing her back against his chest, the latent strength in his arm pinning her close. The evidence of his arousal pressed along the base of her spine, and when she shifted ever so slightly, grazing his hard length, he groaned. His warm lips brushed against the exposed skin of her neck. She quivered.

'This?' He took her earlobe between his teeth in a light grip, his tongue teasing the soft hollow at its base, before skimming his mouth along the delicate curve of her jaw.

'Yes,' she whispered on a gasp.

He dipped his hand below the neckline of her dress, circling her nipple with his middle finger and lightly pinching the rosy point when it hardened. 'This?'

She shuddered in agreement.

His other hand slid down her waist, along the rolling swell of her hip, to the heavenly juncture of her legs. Beau cupped the mound of her sex, her needy heat palpable through layers of satin. His cock twitched. 'This?'

Her voice shook with desire, and her 'Yes' came out little more than an airy moan. She layered her hand over his, pressing his fingers more firmly to her as she rocked against him.

Beau trailed slow, thoughtful kisses across the back of her elegant neck. She shivered in his arms when he blew softly in the little crevice behind her ear. He increased the tempo of his hand. His caress was a command. Her breaths came faster, sharper, and her body quaked against him.

'Let go, little bird,' he urged, in a low, glowing voice.

She moaned again and again, each one louder than the last, and Beau covered her mouth with a hand just before she cried out. Her pleasure spilled over, and the vibrations from her wild cry travelled straight down to his throbbing cock.

He could feel her legs trembling against him and wrapped his arm more securely around her. Emerald's hips jerked, and she released a whimper. He forced himself to slow his fingers to a tender caress, despite wanting nothing more than to bury himself under her skirts to lick, suck, and tease her to a second climax.

She sagged against his chest, and he turned her to face him. Her body melted into his, and he wrapped her up tight against him, placing a gentle kiss on the top of her head. Her heavy breathing and his heartbeat rang loud in his ears.

With her face still buried in his waistcoat, she said, 'I've never—' and broke off as if unsure how to finish her sentence.

He rubbed slow, calming circles over her back. 'I would never have assumed so.'

'It's just—'

He put enough distance between them to easily take her chin between his thumb and forefinger, tilting her head up to look at him. 'Pleasure is for women too.'

She nodded, but Beau could see the crease of uncertainty between her brows, and he ached for her to understand. His fingers had slipped into the glossy hair at the nape of her neck, and he wound a loose curl around his finger. The silky slip of her strands tickled his bare skin, and gooseflesh pebbled his arms.

'I would stay wrapped up with you like this always if such a thing were possible, but we ought to return to the ballroom.' She stirred his basest instincts and most tender impulses. Had they been married, or even engaged, he would've bent her over, put her hands to the wall, and taken her from behind right there in Lady Norton's garden. It was for her own safety he saw her back to the house immediately.

He re-pinned her hair and helped her adjust the bodice of her dress, then turned her in a small circle to make sure she looked as tidy as when she first entered Lady Norton's. Once Emerald was ready, they turned back to the house, but their steps were languid, and at the small of her back his hand hovered with a possessive touch. When they reached the terrace, he urged her forward first, giving her hand a reassuring squeeze. He went to the other door, watching as she made her way towards the edge of the floor where she offered a little wave for Miss Lyon, who was dancing with a man in a turban.

For the rest of the evening, he kept his distance, although more than once their eyes met across the crowded room. He remained at Lady Norton's until Emerald was safely ensconced in the carriage, and even then, followed it on foot the four blocks to Avon House, hanging back in the shadows till he was certain she'd been admitted through the front doors. Instead of going in after, he sat in the little park across the street. The London townhouse had always felt more like home to him than Oakmoss. He felt more at ease, his two halves more at peace. Maybe such accounted for the madness that had possessed him to act as he had. In London, he wasn't a man divided by duty and desire. He was a singular force unto himself, undeterred in his pursuit of that which roused his soul and resolved to attain it with unyielding determination.

32

*E*merald had watched the man prowl towards her, something familiar in his movement sending a thrill through her body. At her side had been a friend of Mr Lyon's who was dressed as a chimney sweep and saying something about a horse he'd seen at Tattersall's, but her attention had all been on the man in the aubergine coat, his shirt open at the collar. She hadn't been sure if it was the words or the silken way he'd said them that had caused her skin, all of it, from her hairline to the tips of her toes snug in her satin dancing sippers, to burn.

He'd spoken with an American accent, but his eyes—he could disguise himself as much as he pleased, but she would always know those winter-blue eyes. She'd been certain it was Beau, and her consciousness had told her that he'd come just for her even if her heart had been reluctant to let her believe it was so. She'd listened to the familiar assured tone of his voice, focused on the full softness of his lips and how they formed words when he spoke. Under the guise of anonymity, she'd felt free—and after her scare in Piccadilly, a little reckless too.

When he'd drawn her to him during the waltz, he'd engulfed her in his desire, and a wave of awakening had coursed through her. A little voice inside had warned her of the dangerous game they were playing, but she'd blocked it out, determined to be bold and follow the path of her own choosing.

It had been a mistake to let him attend her outside. Not because she would ever regret a night spent in his company, but because she didn't wish to deny herself his touch and no longer had to. Alone in near darkness, surrounded by nothing but the sound of her excited heart thrumming and his heady, earthy smell, she could ask for what she wanted: him.

He pinned her back against his chest, the rigid sign of his arousal momentarily startling her. Then he groaned, the sound acting as a match lighting every nerve ending in her body. She'd done that to him, and the realisation thrilled her.

Emerald reeled when he massaged her breast through the silky fabric of her dress, but when his fingers slipped below the neckline and found her tender nipple, she knew she was lost. After weeks, months, years agonising for such a moment, if he wished for everything, she would give it to him, even if it meant ruining herself.

He found the juncture between her legs, the pressure of his fingers against her most sensitive part strange at first and exhilarating. The more he stroked her there, the more her limbs shook, as if trying to contain all the energy and heat trapped in her body. Little beads of sweat glistened at her hairline. His touch was gentle but demanding. He was kindling a fire inside her and wouldn't stop until she burned brighter than the sun.

She rolled against his hand, panting through the low, feral noises to bear the exquisite torture. Her core coiled. Emerald didn't know what release she was chasing, only that she was spiralling with desire and growing lightheaded as sensation claimed her.

'Let go, little bird,' he whispered against the bare, damp skin of her neck. The words sent a shivering command down her back and to her centre, and her pleasure came, pure and explosive. His warm hand covered her mouth, catching her frenzied cry of delight, and he held her tighter as her body jerked. As she came back to herself, his fingers continued to rub her sensitive sex at a slower pace, each gentle caress sending a tiny tremor of delight through her.

Her body went limp, useless in his arms. The intensity of the moment had made her skin tingle and her body throb, but in the silence after, an entire lifetime of being taught desire was reserved for shameless, unprincipled women made her feel like an explanation for her wanton behaviour was necessary. When she failed to find the right words, he offered his own. He forced her eyes to meet his so she could see there was no rebuke or disgust, only support, reassurance, and acceptance.

There would never be a world where Emerald could fall asleep after such a night, not least because as she lay in her own bed, her ears strained, catching every little noise that might possibly be him walking to his room. She'd found his eyes on her, or he'd caught hers on him, several times after they'd returned to the ballroom, but she had no idea when he'd left, if he'd been home for hours, or if he had gone out to one of his clubs.

The greater hindrance to restful sleep, however, was how every time she closed her eyes, she could see him, hear him, smell him, *feel* him. The memory, burned in her mind, set her ablaze. Emerald kicked off her bedcovers, certain fire, not blood, ran through her veins. She rolled to one side and then the other before returning to her back and suppressing a groan. She reached up both hands to adjust the pillow under her head in a feeble attempt to ignore the way her body ached for him, her breasts tingling under the soft cotton of her night-dress, the pulse of desire at her core.

Emerald held her breath as she brought her index finger to her nipple. She made slow, small circles, mesmerised by the way it peaked at her touch. Her whole stomach clenched, forcing her breath out in one harsh, ragged gasp. Once more she closed her eyes, folded her hands over her middle, and attempted to think of anything calming: the sound of the creek at Oakmoss, the first snow of winter, being crushed against the hard planes of Beau's chest. He had told her the pleasure churning inside her was nothing to be ashamed of.

With her eyes still closed, Emerald dared to trail a hand down her taut abdomen until her fingers rested at the juncture of her legs, hovering over the patch of springy curls. She shifted, parting her legs a little. She imagined his arms wrapped around her, his hand where hers was now, and pressed her fingers against her mound as he had. A sharp intake of breath broke the quiet of her room, and she began rocking her hips in long, slow motions.

Emerald swallowed tightly, the bud at her centre growing more sensitive with every movement. As if by instinct, her fingers started to stroke, increasing the friction created by the thin fabric of her nightdress. She brought her other hand up, taking turns to circle and caress each hardened nipple as she had minutes earlier. A little moan escaped her parted lips, and she writhed against herself as her pleasure built. In the dark behind her eyes, images of Beau undressing for her. She imag-ined the lean muscles of his body flexing under her touch as she traced the lines of his tattoo. A finger at her neck mimicked the tickle of his breath, the teasing graze of his kisses. Her hips lifted, her body worked into a frenzy, and she cracked like lightning before the thunder. Vibrant delight, intense and incandescent, surged through her, and she bit her lip to keep from moaning. Emerald's thoughts fragmented as she panted with contentment, her consciousness slowly returning to her own body.

Eyes still closed, she tried to steady her breath, not realising she'd fallen asleep until Gwen opened the drapes to let the sunshine in hours later.

Beau was not in the breakfast parlour when Emerald came down. Half an hour later, eggs untouched, toast only nibbled, she was so deep in a debate with herself as to whether it was relief or disappointment she felt that she didn't notice him stroll into the room until the dowager asked if he'd enjoyed himself the night prior.

Emerald choked on her coffee, and as the hot liquid burned her throat, she settled on wishing he'd stayed away. He looked composed. There were no dark circles ringing his eyes after a sleepless night, no downward bend of his mouth. He didn't avert his eyes to avoid her stare, tug his sleeves, or clear his throat. It was impossible to discern if he felt guilt and shame or bliss and contentment.

He didn't so much as flinch, and his answer, 'Very well, thank you,' caused her to flush through a scowl. Even though she knew it was impossible for him to say *I had a lovely time compromising my ward*, she wished for some sign, some acknowledgement, some confirmation she'd been right in assuming he'd come to the party for her, knew it was her. Without it, a niggling doubt crept into her mind. He'd seen her before she left, but other women had worn blue dresses and *everyone* had worn a mask.

She excused herself and went to the music room, playing notes as they came to her mind, until interrupted by a footman sometime later who told her his lordship was asking to see her in the sunroom. The words made her quake with anticipation and uncertainty. The walk along one corridor, down the stairs, and along another, took as long as crossing from one side of Oakmoss to the other, or so it felt to Emerald, who completed the journey on legs made of jelly.

The door was open, but she paused several feet from it, put a hand to her chest and a hand to her abdomen, and forced herself to take three deep breaths before stepping into the room.

'You wished to see me?' Emerald was pleased with the steadiness of her voice.

Beau turned from where he stood looking out the window. The sunlight at his back cast him in an ethereal glow, and his eyes impaled her where she stood. A rush of pink stained her cheeks, and she couldn't stop the blush from blooming for all the money in England.

'This is one of my favourite places in the whole house.'

Emerald blinked. Whatever she'd been expecting, it hadn't been that. Taking her time, she crossed to him, coming to a stop by his side and letting her eyes rest on the garden beyond the enclosure, showing signs of life as winter faded and spring pushed in.

'There is so much to be said.' There were raw edges in his voice and eloquence in the silence that followed.

Her breath caught when she felt him graze the hand at her side. He traced each finger and the lines crisscrossing her palm. Emerald found the space between his fingers and folded them in her own, marvelling at what it was like to hold a piece

of him, the magnificent sensation transforming her into a creature of need.

'Emerald?'

She spun around, although Beau did not, at the sound of
Louisa's voice, the girl herself arriving a second behind it.
There was a quiet pause during which Louisa looked at her
brother and Emerald, still standing shoulder to shoulder, and
creases formed at the corner of her eyes, narrowing briefly in
suspicion.

'Perhaps you've forgotten our plans to visit Bond Street this
morning?' Lou asked, arching one eyebrow in a way Emerald
never could manage.

'Not at all.' Her hands were curled in the folds of her dress,
and she forced herself not to jump when Beau's hand found
hers once more. She flicked him, trying not to draw attention to
them, but he caught her fingers and gave them a squeeze.
'Allow me a quarter hour to change, and we can be on our way.'

Louisa held her in a look so full of incredulity Emerald
almost laughed. 'All right.'

When Louisa retreated, Emerald whirled on Beau, whose
shoulders shook with mirth.

'Insufferable man. We're not done here,' she said, feeling
back on familiar ground.

'I do hope that's a promise you mean to keep,' replied he,
with a boyish, mischievous smile she'd never seen him wear
before.

Emerald left him, her own lips curling unconsciously
upwards.

She couldn't remember anything she and Louisa discussed
while they strolled in Bond Street, the younger girl recalling
Emerald's attention to their conversation more than once with

humour lurking in her eyes. The shops they visited and the items she purchased would remain a mystery till Emerald sorted through the packages the footman carried home.

Later, she paid no mind to which gown Gwen selected for the theatre and found herself taking her seat in the Avon box without the slightest idea of how she'd arrived there. It was a shame she was so distracted; the play was new and much anticipated on Drury Lane, featuring Edmund Kean and a new fellow—William something—Emerald had never heard of, and depicting Napoleon's defeat by the English.

At the first interval, her ladyship went across to pay her respects to the Marchioness of Bath, while Emerald begged off, savouring a few moments of peace. When the curtain of their box pushed open not long after the dowager left, she said, 'Have you forgot something, ma'am?' and jumped out of her skin when a very male voice answered.

'Not at all. My apologies for startling you. I wished to say hello, and to discover if you had any interest in seeing what goes on behind the curtain.' Mr Babin was grinning, but there was a hardness about his features and in his eyes.

'That's kind, but I wouldn't wish to worry her ladyship with a protracted absence.'

He came into the box, and Emerald stood to counter her urge to shrink back a little. Mr Babin placed a hand on her arm, and when she tried to yank it away, he said, 'I'm sorry, I really must insist.'

'Unhand me.' As she issued her demand, she felt something small, hard, and deadly at her side.

'You see why I cannot.'

Emerald stood motionless, frozen in fear. 'If I scream?'

'I shoot.'

'You'd never get away.' Emerald willed someone, anyone to enter the box at that moment.

'You wouldn't be here to know one way or the other.'

The casual way he spoke such callous words sent a shiver of fear down her spine, and when he nudged her, she squared her shoulders, raised her chin, and began to walk.

---

33

*B*eau needed to speak with Emerald, wished to, but when she'd come to stand next to him, he could only think about how very lovely she was, how brave, how bold, how perfect.

He'd never wished his sister at Bedlam till she interrupted that morning. He'd been forced to let Emerald go, and she'd floated from the sunroom on his heavy sigh. Although with her birthday still some days away, perhaps it had been for the best.

He ran a hand through his hair and glanced at the clock over the mantel in his study. He could still make it to the theatre for the second interval. Saunders had gone to the Palace of Westminster, *Something in the gut,* he'd said as he left; Allard was at the theatre in Beau's stead to keep an eye on Emerald; and Beau sat in his study, agonising over everything they knew about Babin and what they were missing.

'My lord,' Wallace said, approaching the desk. 'A Mr Lyon.'

Beau nodded, and a minute later the young man stood in the doorway looking uneasy. Instinct raised the hairs on Beau's neck. 'Come in, Lyon. I'm surprised you're not at the theatre with the rest of the *ton*.'

'Yes.' Lyon swallowed, cleared his throat, and swallowed again. 'That's what I'm here about, my lord.'

Beau's stare was opaque, but his heart rate quickened, his thoughts turning immediately to Emerald.

Lyon stepped further into the study, coming to stand in front of the desk, but he didn't sit. In his hands, he spun his hat round and round by its brim.

'I had thought to go, planned to, with my sister—even the Prince Regent will be there—but then Babin—' Lyon broke off when Beau pushed back his chair with such force it toppled to the ground behind him. His hands pressed firm into the desk, the tips of his fingers going white from the pressure.

'Babin, what?'

'We—we—were playing hazard, erm, playing last night.' Lyon tripped over the words as he spoke. 'He asked if I planned to attend. I said yes. Then he threw the dice and suggested I ought to keep away. I asked why, and he just said it was a feeling. I didn't think much of it, but I haven't felt quite right all day. Something in his demeanour— I can't describe it. It struck me as particularly odd given he knows, erm, one of the actresses,' he said with a meaningful look. 'A Charis or Charlotte Newling or some such. I suppose it's of no import.'

'Newling?' The word came out with the bite of a snake, and Lyon shrank back.

'Y-yes.'

Three things happened all at once. Beau slammed a fist to his desk, rattling the inkpot, Saunders ran into the study saying, 'It's all gone.' And a panting footman in Allard livery put a hand up in the doorway and choked out the following message between breaths: 'You. Theatre. Immediately.'

Beau was out the back of the house and into the mews without a thought or care for anyone or anything but Emerald. Lyon's words were ringing in his ears: *even the Prince Regent will be there*. Of course. Beau had been a fool. Babin wasn't going to blow up the House of Lords. He was going to blow up the theatre, assassinate the prince, and take almost all of the aristocracy with him. He didn't wish only to avenge his father; he wished to avenge France, and what better time and place than on the opening night of a play celebrating Napoleon's defeat?

'Tell Duffy,' he commanded, mounting the horse still saddled from Saunders's return. He didn't wait for a reply—none was necessary—and he kicked the horse into motion, spurring it into a gallop behind the long row of townhouses. The roads were empty, all of Mayfair already at the theatre, and Beau covered the mile and a half to the entrance on Brydges Street in mere minutes. With a coin for a boy to watch his horse, Beau ran through the grand saloon and up the stairs to his box, throwing open the curtain to find Allard waiting for him.

'The dowager is already in a carriage back to Avon House, confused but compliant. Your ward, however—' He nodded towards the hall. Away from curious stares that had begun to turn in their direction, he said, 'I saw Babin enter. She went with him, reluctantly from my vantage point. I sent out three men. One went for you, one for the front entrance, one for the back. If he'd left the theatre, we would know.'

'He hasn't.' Beau raked a hand through his hair and told Allard what he'd learned from Lyon.

'Ah. A *Miss* Charlie Newling.'

Beau had begun to pace, his mind whirling. 'There must be a cellar, somewhere he moved the barrels, but easily accessed for his own escape.'

'A trap room where they can store heavy equipment, large pieces of scenery. There's a theatre in Paris not unlike this one with something similar. You go. I'll wait for Duffy and Saunders.'

Beau nodded. He went downstairs and slipped through a side door that carried him down a long, dark hall and into the labyrinth backstage. Instantly, he was absorbed by the chaos of a live production on its opening night.

It seemed at first as if there were infinite ways to go, but when Beau got his bearings, he counted four passageways and stairways shooting off in different directions. He stopped, closed his eyes. Intuition told him to move towards the back of the theatre. He hadn't a clue what he was looking for as he passed open doors leading to rooms full of costumes, wigs, actors in various states of undress. Although time passed at a crawl, it couldn't have been more than five minutes before he came to the end of a long hall with only a left turn possible.

He paused at the corner, pressing himself flush against the wall. Slowly, carefully, he peeked around the corner. The passageway was empty, except for a bored-looking man sitting in front of a door—the smuggler from Kent who had twice tried to accost the one most dear to him. Beau was going to enjoy this more than he had any right to.

He would only have one chance to get it right, and when he pulled out his gold snuff box, he imagined how Saunders's eyebrows would rise.

Beau lowered himself to his knees. He set the snuff box on the ground before reaching into another pocket and pulling out a little case. From the case he removed a slim pair of tweezers then returned it to its proper place. A pocket ran across the back of his breeches. He slipped a hand in and pulled out a quill.

Beau plucked a handkerchief from his pocket, folded it, and held it in place at the tip of the quill with a finger. With his other hand, he used the tweezers to extract a needle-thin dart from the snuff box open beside him and dropped it point down into the quill. The whole sequence was much easier completed with two persons, but with Emerald in danger he could not wait. Using one hand, he closed the snuff box, returned it to his coat, and simply tucked the tweezers where the quill had been.

With such a short barrel, the closer he could get the better. He slipped his shoes off and crept along the wall. The rest of the theatre benefited from gaslights, but several of the back-stage corridors were still lit by candles in wall sconces. The dimness was to his benefit, but the sconce that prevented him from getting any closer without moving fully into the hall wasn't. Ten feet from the man, Beau stopped and raised the quill. The man turned. Beau dropped the handkerchief and blew hard. The smuggler hardly had time to open his mouth before he grasped for his throat. Beau shot forward, easing the man down to the ground and moving him a little ways from the door.

Beau strained to hear anything inside the trap room through the cacophony of the theatre noise on the stage above. When he could make out Emerald's voice, the dulcet tone if not the words, he ached with relief. He tried the handle. It gave way, and Beau slipped in without catching either his ward's or Babin's notice.

Babin had his back to the door, his frame blocking most of

Emerald from Beau's sight. Behind them were dozens of barrels of explosives.

'I'm disappointed with myself for only giving you credit as a mere smuggler. Revolutionary is so much grander, do not you think?' remarked Beau into the dimly lit room.

Babin wheeled around, and Emerald cried out, 'Beau!' Her wrists were knotted in rope, and as she stepped towards him, Babin wrenched her backward by the shoulder as he squared himself against Beau, who did nothing more than spare her a cursory glance, knowing what distraction could cost. He depressed the violent fury quivering inside him and ignored the sharp pang knocking around his chest.

'I appreciate how a man might lose focus,' Babin said, leering at Emerald.

Beau's muscles tensed with strangled fury. 'And yet you would see her dead?'

Babin shrugged. 'In truth, the idea of punishing you for your father's crime only presented itself to me once you returned—you'd been gone so long, I'd never thought much of you at all. Then there you were. Putting yourself where you didn't belong. Just like your father.'

Beau felt bile rise in his throat. He'd been gone from Oakmoss too long, but his return had made her an object of Babin's revenge.

'I found that afternoon tea at Oakmoss inspiring. I thought perhaps you just wished to bed her, but it's so much more than that, isn't it?' Babin ran the tip of the gun along her jaw, and Beau could feel his insides begin to tremble with seething rage. 'I could kill you, yes, but how much more delicious to take something you love, like your father did to my family?'

'Your father was a criminal.'

'Are your hands clean?'

Beau remained silent.

'No, I did not think they were.'

'There's a chasm between killing an entire theatre of inno-cent people and killing the man planning to do so. Or, say, killing an innocent woman because your father chose the wrong inlet for his boatful of brandy or tobacco or whatever else.'

Babin scoffed. 'It wasn't *what* was in the boat. It was *who*.'

For a stretch of time too small to be measured, Beau was stunned.

'Spoiled Englishmen and their desire to possess what someone told them they cannot have. You understand.' Babin's laugh was ugly, his smile jeering. 'Brandy brings a tidy amount, but the real money is in people. The younger ones in particular fetch an eye-watering sum.'

Of all the experiences Beau had lived through, none had brought him as close to casting up his accounts as the one unfolding before him. Out of the corner of his eye, he noticed the convulsive bob in Emerald's throat.

'Well, this has already gone on too long and the curtain call is nearing. You will not walk out of here, although she will. Only I cannot but think it a shame she must live with more sadness while you escape it,' said Babin, raising his pistol and cocking it. 'But I promise she'll love France.'

s soon as the words *But I promise she'll love France* left Mr Babin's mouth, the sick Emerald had been working to keep in came out. Her white soup and lamb, the fish with the wine sauce—every bite had been a delight—vegetable pie, and lemon cheesecake. She folded over, and everything she'd eaten sprayed all down the front of that awful man's breeches and shoes.

Whether it was learning Mr Babin had been smuggling people or the idea of a forced sojourn in his company that sent Emerald's dinner tumbling out of her, she could not be sure, and everything happened too fast for her to give her contemplations due reflection.

Beau called her name. Mr Babin cried out in disgust, yanking his handkerchief from his pocket and trying to wipe away the sick while keeping the gun trained on Beau. And Emerald, knowing what wish was foremost in her heart, made a bold choice.

She flung herself upwards, bringing her knotted hands around like a mace and striking Mr Babin on the underside of his chin. The blow staggered him, and he stumbled backward. Without sparing a second look behind her, Emerald raced towards Beau. He grabbed the rope around her wrists and practically dragged her down the dim corridor at a gruelling pace. They neared the corner, and Beau pushed her ahead. The sound of a gunshot reverberated off the tight walls. He wrapped her up from behind, taking them both down as a second shot was fired.

Emerald was falling in slow motion. Her mind had enough time to register the gunfire, and her heart enough time to freeze with fear. Beau suffering a gunshot—or worse—in his bold rescue of her was unfathomable. His homecoming had roused her from a sleep so deep even dreams couldn't survive. Their time together had been unhurried, and she felt them drifting to eternity, one touch, one look at a time. The awful bang threatened to take from her what she wished for most before it was even truly hers.

Landing on the hard ground sent a wave of shock through her. She felt hot all over, and bearing Beau's full weight was making it hard to breathe. Next to her head, a flurry of foot-steps ran past in the direction of the room where they'd just come from. Above her, his voice swimming, Saunders told Beau he was bleeding. Beau pushed up to his knees beside her, but Emerald still couldn't get enough air.

'A flesh wound,' Beau said. 'I don't even feel—'

Emerald found his hand with hers, but the effort to close her fingers and hold his warmth as cold began to creep in was too great. The last thing she remembered was the odd tone of her voice and how distant it sounded as she said, 'Beau—Beau, I can't—' and the terror-stricken blue eyes that met hers before they closed.

BEAU CRIED OUT. The anguish with which he said Emerald's name brought the dozens of armed men around him to a standstill. For one moment everyone stared in shocked silence before the chaos. Lord Duffy was yelling for a carriage. Allard sent someone for the physician and the surgeon. Saunders was already tying together handkerchiefs from the men.

A flower of red bloomed on her side, and blood was pooling under her. Beau tore his cravat from his throat, folded it over itself, and gently pressed it to the wound. With care, Saunders lifted her just enough so Beau could wrap the handkerchiefs around her and secure his cravat in place. She whimpered, and Beau's eyes burned with tears.

'I'm sorry. I'm so sorry.' He kept saying those words, but he didn't think he was hoping for her forgiveness so much as his own. 'It's all right, my love, everything will be all right. I've got to lift you.' Beau knew she was unconscious, but if she could hear anything, he wanted her to know he was there, tethering her to her earthly body, to him, to the life they would live together.

One of Lord Duffy's men appeared at his side with a thin, flat panel of scenery painted like a hat shop. Saunders took her legs, Beau her upper body, and together, they shifted her onto the wooden board and carried her out to the carriage.

The ride to Avon House took years off his life. He sat back in the corner of the carriage, cradling her close to him and doing his best to protect her from the jostling movements as they rode over the cobblestones. Her pallor paled with every minute, a sure sign of the life leaving her, even though the flow of blood had slowed.

Saunders sat across from him, face grim, and bounded out of the equipage as it rolled to a stop in front of the house.

Beau, with quick, careful movements, carried Emerald out of the carriage and cleared the steps of his townhouse in one long stride, sailing through the door flung open by Saunders and shouting orders that woke the entire house: hot water, clean linens, Gwen.

His mother and sister were racing from their rooms as he approached Emerald's door, their shock and worry finding footing in overlapping exclamations, none of which he heard. He laid her on her bed as Gwen rushed in, her bleary eyes clearing as she took in the scene before her.

Beau was already cutting the bodice of Emerald's dress.

'My lord, I can— You ought not—'

'No!'

Gwen nodded and turned her attention to shooing his mother and sister from the room as the surgeon entered. At Beau's elbow, the maid placed a bowl of hot water and a stack of clean rags. He washed his hands, and a new bowl appeared directly after.

Beau stared at the torn, bloody flesh of Emerald's side, and bit his own tongue till he tasted a metallic tang to prevent further tears. With tender caution, he cleaned her wound before soaking a rag in brandy and dabbing it against her angry skin.

'My lord,' said the surgeon, ready to remove the bullet lodged in the curve where her waist met her hip.

He nodded and moved to the other side of the bed. Perched on the edge, he possessed himself of her hand and made gentle, soothing circles on the back of it.

'It will only hurt a moment, my love,' he said quietly. 'Remember, we feel pain and gain strength in equal measure.

I'm right here.' Beau exhaled a tremulous sigh. 'I'm right here.' He inclined his head once more, a sign of silent permission, and the surgeon dug into her with his pincers.

Emerald whined, but the sob he heard belonged to Gwen.

'Oh, miss.' The maid had come to the foot of the bed and stood with her hands clasped tight over her heart.

'She's lucky,' remarked the surgeon, dropping the bullet into a little dish on the table. 'Missed her ribs and her organs. Her greatest risk is infection.' He opened a jar and used a small spatula to scoop out something golden and viscous. With a delicate hand, he applied it to the open wound. 'Honey. Helps prevent contamination, swelling.'

Beau's stomach turned when the surgeon picked up a needle, and he winced when it pierced her soft flesh.

When the surgeon finished the sutures, he left Beau with instructions for her ongoing care, a promise to return in the morning, and a directive to send for him should she develop a fitful fever.

'If you please, sir.'

Beau wasn't surprised to hear Saunders's voice rising from the corner of the room. The valet thanked the surgeon, and Beau heard the door open, their retreating footsteps followed by two tentative, worried feminine voices. He finally looked over his shoulder to see his mother and sister clinging to one another in the doorway.

'What happened? Will she be all right?'

He turned back to Emerald. 'She needs a fresh nightdress.'

'I've got one here, my lord,' replied Gwen.

'Beauden.' His mother articulated his name as a warning.

He wanted to rail, to refuse to leave her side, to threaten violence if anyone tried to force him. No one would be so tender, take such careful care of her as he. But he had already taken liberties, tearing into her chemise. When he saw her in a state of undress, it would be because she'd chosen to share herself with him.

There was a soft touch to his shoulder. 'Go, brother. Clean yourself up. I'll help Gwen.'

With a heavy sigh, he acquiesced, placing a kiss on Emerald's palm and curling her fingers around it before he left her side.

---

35

*B*eau left Emerald long enough to wipe himself clean of the blood and grime that covered him from head to toe, and he threw every piece of clothing he'd been wearing into the stoked fire burning in his room. Allard appeared with further information from the theatre and a genuine desire to know how Emerald fared.

'Once I learned not to fear death, I hadn't thought anything could scare me.'

'You are fallible, as are we all.'

The tell-tale sting bit the back of his eyes. 'Knowing how close I was to losing her— Hell, Theo, I still could.' Beau choked on his cracking voice.

Allard studied Beau with a thoughtful expression. 'You know what must be done. You've had a long, lucky run, friend.'

Beau considered the words with a wayward frown while he dressed. 'Yes.'

From the mantel, where Saunders tutted as he poked at the

superfine ablaze in the grate, came a low whistle, filling the quiet with meaning.

Asperity tinged Beau's voice when he asked, 'What would you have me do, Saunders?'

'Exactly as Allard suggests, only I never thought you'd agree without a struggle.'

'I never thought anyone would mean more to me than my work.'

One corner of Allard's mouth slipped into a faint smile. 'You will find plenty to occupy your time in retirement.'

'And we know the Home Office won't let you go as easy as that,' added Saunders. 'Very likely they'll want you codebreaking, translating, pilfering correspondence from some lord's study.'

'You think you'll miss it—the rush of danger—and sometimes you will, but how quickly we grow comfortable, fill with joy, when our roots are allowed to take hold.'

Beau knew Allard spoke from his own experience leaving espionage behind, at least in an official capacity. A knock drew their attention. Louisa's wan face appeared around the edge of the door, and Beau tensed.

'She's dressed. She looks so peaceful.'

He could hear the worry in her statement and noticed how she clamped her lips tight to hold back her sobs. Stepping away from the other men, he went to his sister, opened the door wide, and wrapped his arms around her.

'Go to bed,' he stated in such a way as to prevent opposition. 'I'll send your maid up with a sleeping draught.'

Once Lou had walked away, he turned back to Allard and Saunders. 'You'll excuse me.' He said nothing else—he did not need to—as he left his room for Emerald's.

Beau pulled one of the bergère chairs to the bedside,

clasped her hand between his own, and let silence envelop him, content to memorise every inch of her proud, beautiful face as he kept watch over her.

'Is now or now a good time to explain yourself?' Beau's mother asked from where she stood over his shoulder.

He'd heard her enter a quarter of an hour after him but found it impossible to look away from the woman who held his whole heart.

Without preamble, he said, 'After Cambridge, I went to work for the Home Office. My easy fluency in French, Italian, German, and Spanish made me an attractive prospect, but they were most interested in my access to drawing rooms, ball-rooms, and back rooms as an eligible heir.'

'Beau?' His name pitched up as his mother said it.

'I'm a spy, Mama, or I will be only until I tender my resignation.' Beau waited as his mother worked through the shock of his confession.

'Your father—' Out of the corner of his eye, he could see her shaking her head, trying to clear her confusion. 'You said he knew. The day you arrived in London, you said that to me.'

Beau twined a lock of Emerald's hair around his finger. 'I told him before I left for the last time. He didn't approve. We had a terrible row about it.'

'I can well imagine. Our name, the estate, they meant everything to him. He worked his whole life to ensure the productivity and prosperity of Oakmoss for you and each generation after, just like every generation which came before.'

'And there isn't a Calverleigh who will ever do it better than he. Work kept me away. For a stretch of time, I allowed it to keep me longer than necessary. I've regrets, but discovering I am more than a name is not one of them. I'm not asking you to understand.'

His mother had made her way to the other side of the bed and sat upon it. 'What's all that to do with this?'

As concisely as he could and excepting certain details, he explained Babin's illegal business and foiled scheme to redress the injustices suffered by France as he saw them. By the end his mother was reliant on her handkerchief to stifle her sniffles.

'This poor dear. After everything she's been through, my only wish is to see her happy.'

'In this, we are aligned.'

His mother glanced up at him but he didn't look over. 'I had wondered.'

'And stayed silent, surprisingly so.'

'She has been thrust into things her whole life,' said the dowager as she brushed back a stray hair from Emerald's forehead. 'I'm plagued by my own culpability to that end. After your father died, it was easier to let grief consume me than to leave my rooms knowing wherever I went, he wouldn't be there.'

Beau shoved a hand through his curls, leaving them ruffled.

'I loved my husband. You deserve to know the same in your own marriage.' After a wistful pause, she added, 'Little else would delight me so much as seeing you two make a match. She challenges you at every turn, and you are her shelter, succour, a rampart outside herself. Nevertheless, I refuse to put undue pressure on a girl to whom I—*we*—already owe so much.'

Beau finally bent his attention in his mother's direction. He tried to push down the lump lingering in his throat, but his voice still broke when he spoke. 'I owe her everything, and yet everything I have to give isn't enough.'

'Oh, Beauden. For so long Emerald has drawn only from

her own well.' The dowager stayed another few minutes and gave his shoulder a reassuring squeeze before she left, ensuring the door remained open behind her.

Beau would not abandon his vigil for rest, not when his own life lingered somewhere halfway from what was and what might be. Perhaps his body would remain behind if Emerald never woke again, but all the rest—what use had he of his heart, his lungs, his mind if he spent the remainder of his days living in a dream where he could walk among the dead? He closed his eyes and searched the dark till he could see. Between guilt and grief, an oak tree. From its branches, leaves falling free. Lifting her hand, he slipped it just inside the loose collar of his nightshirt and held her slender fingers to the black boughs reaching over his heart.

'I took the long way round, but how I love you now.'

36

*E*merald was cold all over. Chills raced down her body and raised the fine hairs on her arms. She wanted to pull her bedcovers higher, tighter, but her body was so heavy she couldn't even lift an arm. There was a quiet whine of defeat—her own, she surmised—followed by someone saying her name.

The voice was familiar—calm, rhythmic, the same bristle as a dry brush. A voice she knew would always reach her through time and space. *Beau.* Her lips wouldn't cooperate when she tried to form his name. All that came out was a low, ineffectual groan from somewhere deep in her throat. On her forehead, she felt his hand, firm, searching, heating her through like the July sun.

'Christ.' He sounded displeased, and Emerald wondered if his brow had wrinkled like a crushed sheet of hot-pressed paper. If she could lift her arm, she could smooth the unhappy lines on his face, hold his hard angles between her palms. 'Gwen, Allard left ice in the kitchen. Put some in a bowl, fill the bowl with water, and bring it up.'

'Right away, my lord.'

Minutes later, Emerald was still struggling to sort out what her maid was doing in her dream, or what the odd dream was all about, when something as frigid as one of Beau's imperious looks landed across her brow.

'It's all right, my love. I'm here. I'm here.'

Who was his love? The cool cloth was a horrid surprise. Emerald no longer cared for this dream and commanded herself to wake up several times, only to be disappointed when she remained in the same ethereal state.

'Shall I tell you a story, dear one, about a foolish man and a brave woman?'

Yes. She would listen to him read Fordyce just to hear him speak. Near her hip, an opaque kind of pain, fuzzy at the edges, burgeoned. Beau was close, but she wished him closer still, close enough to curl herself into him as she'd done in the portrait gallery.

His fingertips began to trace light patterns on her wrist, the back of her hand, over her knuckles, and she cursed her sleep-laden body for preventing her from reaching out. If it was her dream, she ought to be able to do as she pleased.

He was talking, his words rolling into one another as her mind crawled along the fringes of consciousness. How fine he sounded. How soft and gentle. She was drifting away on the soothing undulation of his voice, the wisp of a memory, the whisper of a promise if only she could wake herself up.

'BEAU.' Louisa's voice was hushed in the dim room. 'Go rest. Let me stay with her.'

He shook his head. He'd been at Emerald's bedside for three days.

'Then may I sit with you?' She waited for him to nod his consent before placing a chair on the opposite side of the bed. 'Mama told me everything.' When he didn't offer so much as a nod in response, she tried again. 'It sounds like a very exciting way to live. I see why your work kept you from us.'

'Do you?'

'If you have forgotten our conversation in my gig, I have not. You are a man considerate of the language he uses. There is much to glean in what you don't say, what you don't contradict. You ought to have returned home sooner, but how is it possible to find fault when you were protecting King and country? When you dared to do something as rebellious as design your own future?'

'I apologised to Mama and to Emerald. I owe you one as well.'

Louisa shrugged dismissively. 'There's something cosy, peaceful even, about a household comprised only of women. It's not easy for me to explain.'

'Would you like it if I went away again?'

'You are being flippant, but no—and neither would Emerald. She'll be all right, brother.'

Beau squeezed his fatigued eyes shut. He was so disconsolate even his veins throbbed. 'You can't be sure.'

'When has she ever let you down?'

Whether his sister's words were meant as a mild chastise or not he didn't ask. She rose from the chair and asked if he wished for Saunders or Gwen so he might rest for an hour or two. He had not slept, could not, while his love tarried between two worlds.

'No. The house has gone to sleep, and besides, there's nothing to be done.'

'I'll check on you both in the morning.'

Louisa slipped out. When she was gone, he folded himself over the edge of the bed, bowing his head on his hand where it rested over hers. He'd seen too much, done too much, to continue as a steward of religion, but he could pray to her, to her courage, her kindness, her spirit and fortitude. With incantations on his tongue and tears hanging from the crooks of his eyes, Beau fell asleep.

37

*I*t was late. Only darkness could be seen among the cracks in the heavy velvet drapes, and the few candles in the room guttered as they fought to stay alive.

Emerald's whole body was sore from disuse. The side where she'd been shot pulsed. A tangle of soft, earth-brown curls tickled her wrist where it lay limp next to her hip. She watched the steady rise and fall of Beau's back, a little enthralled with the controlled power she knew was coiled in the peaceful body in front of her, the etched muscles of his form, the scars telling their own stories—two halves of a whole.

Her right arm shook as she brought it across her body. The movement of her finger was slow and uncertain, and with breaths uneven from exertion or excitement, she touched one of the thick, mussed locks. It was silky against her skin and coiled around her like it had been waiting for the moment as long as she.

She slid her fingers into his hair, making a slow combing motion and luxuriating in the feel of her hand nestled there.

Against the hand upon which he lay, she could feel his low moan of contentment. Back and forth, she raked her fingertips, and when his head tipped, she brushed aside a tendril that had fallen forward. Even in the near-dark, his long curling lashes could not hide the pronounced hallows under his eyes. Her own drifted closed for a faraway second as she imagined a life not yet hers.

When she opened them again, he was watching her. His clear eyes, sober and uncertain, seemed to ask her a question.

'Are you aware you drool while sleeping?' Her voice sounded like two sticks rubbing together, but he smiled, pure and bright and so full of happiness she felt her own lips curling upwards.

He retrieved a water glass from the table, tipping it against her lips until she turned her head. 'How do you feel?'

She tried to lift a shoulder. 'How long have I been asleep?'

'About three days.'

Emerald started, overcome by the sudden awareness she could see every part of him. She knew the answer before she asked the question. 'How long have you been here?'

'About three days.'

He was a dear, dear man. 'You have not gone to bed?'

'And miss this opportunity?'

Sudden weariness enveloped her, and tears welled in her eyes. 'I could've got you killed.'

'I almost did get you killed, so on that score you may rest easy,' he replied, dabbing her cheeks with a piece of clean linen.

'If I hadn't gone with him. If I hadn't run.'

'If I hadn't come home. If I hadn't upset his plans. If I had simply shot him where he stood. No one wins in this game, so let us agree not to play it. You are alive, as am I. What more can matter?'

'What happened? I don't recall—' She sucked in a breath, wishing her tired arms could lift her hands and cover her mouth.

The laughing look in his eyes suggested he knew which memory had just come rushing back, much as her dinner had at the theatre. He asked, his voice vibrating with mirth, 'Would you rather we go on as if it never happened?'

'I was sick.' Had Emerald the energy to pull the covers over her head, she would have.

'Indeed.'

She groaned and closed her eyes against this beautiful man who had watched her experience her dinner for a second time.

'Let it be some consolation that you made his arrest even more uncomfortable. He'll be sitting in those dirty clothes awhile. Maybe even until he's hanged for treason. And really, it was quite mild compared to much of what I've seen in my line of work.'

'Oh! Yes. Your work. I've gathered you're a spy for the government.'

'A specialist in espionage, yes. I mentioned something of it at Gunter's—' He was running the length of linen through his fingers.

'You alluded. Called it complicated.'

'It is. Was.'

What was it he had said? 'Your hands are not clean.'

There was a long pause, and one of the candles finally died out.

'No. It is impossible they should be so. I understand if that's—if that's unacceptable to you.'

Never before had Emerald considered Beau may feel

nervous about how she would perceive his work. She felt she *should* be bothered but could not manage to be anything more than curious.

'A lot of men?'

There was no hesitation in his answer. 'Enough.'

'Any—any—women?'

She heard the breath in his chest hitch.

'Inconvenienced?' he asked, using her word from the day she applied arnica to his eye. 'Or—*or*.'

Emerald frowned, confused at first by his own apparent confusion. And then, because she couldn't resist teasing him, she said, 'Oh. I was thinking only of the former, but you mentioning the latter I think indicates you've flirted, flattered, and seduced to get your way. And now I know from my own experience how capable you are of such things.'

Beau veritably flung himself away from her, his countenance a mix of horror and panic. 'You cannot think— I would have you know— I never— You are so much more to me—'

She had done it, fully unravelled the man, but she pocketed her amusement for another time. Taking pity on him, she reached her hand out, accompanied by a cheeky smile.

'You tease me?'

'Shocking, I know. What was it you said? What else would you have me do? Cut up at you? Faint away out of maidenly horror? A trifle excessive, do not you think?'

His lips pinched into a tight line, but he couldn't hide his amusement. She knew him too well for that.

'There is so much I want to say to you,' he said, gliding his fingers back and forth over the top of her hand where it rested on the bed covers. 'Something I so badly wish to ask.'

'And yet?'

'And yet tonight, you are still my ward.'

'But tomorrow?'

He lifted her hand and pressed her fingers to his lips. 'Your birthday.'

'I'll reach my majority.'

'You'll reach your majority. Take over control. It seems only fair you should. I've held your future in my hands. Tomorrow, you will hold mine.'

38

*B*eau had remained with her until her eyelids had grown heavy, although they were mostly silent after his near declaration, with Emerald too mired in her own thoughts and excitement to string together a coherent thought, and Beau content to just sit and stare at her. But when she fell asleep, it was with a small smile on her lips and her hand in his.

When she woke, her body was fatigued, but not her spirits, and she was determined to go down for breakfast, readying with extra care. She checked her appearance not once or twice but three times before leaving her room, wishing each time for some colour on her pale countenance and darting a critical glance at Gwen, who tried and failed to hide her giddy amusement.

Once outside the breakfast parlour, Emerald ran a hand over her skirts before nodding to the footman to open the door. The breath she sucked in quivered, and the smallest knot tied itself in her stomach as she stepped over the threshold.

'Good morning, Em. How pretty you look! Not at all like someone so recently injured.'

Louisa's sweet, flippant compliment did nothing to stem the dismay welling in Emerald's chest upon seeing Lou, and only Lou, down for breakfast. She made a plate, but did little more than push the ham round the china and stare at her buttered toast piled with jam.

'I wasn't certain you'd be down, but in case you were...' Louisa reached over to the empty chair next to her and, from under the table, pulled a little box with a fine bow tied round it. 'It was impossible for me to choose between two things, so you may have one now and one later,' added Louisa in mock strictness as she rose to hand Emerald the gift. 'Happy birthday, Emerald. I am not happy for the circumstances that brought you to us, but I am certain I am happier with you in my life.' Louisa punctuated her sentiment with a kiss on Emerald's cheek and a demand that she open her gift.

Emerald was quite moved and felt the pricking of tears at the backs of her eyes, blinking rapidly to clear them away. 'You are too kind to me and too sweet for this world,' she said, tugging the tail of the bow. The box was small, no bigger than her hand, and had very little weight to it. Rather than speculate, Emerald pulled the top from the bottom and gasped in genuine surprise. Inside, nestled in a little bed of silk, was a delicate strand of pearls.

'Louisa, what have you done? This is much too fine a gift for me to accept.'

'Pah. It's what I'd get a sister, and what are you if not that?'

Emerald shook her head and pressed her palms to her eyes.

'Oh goodness, what have I said?' cried Louisa, wrapping her in an embrace.

'You've only been the most outrageously dear creature,'

replied Emerald, regaining her composure. 'Whatever else you purchased, I hope you can return it. This is already too much. I cannot believe your mama let you be so extravagant.'

'Of course you can,' Louisa replied with a little giggle. 'But it wasn't her who took me shopping. It was Beau. We went one day last week while you paid calls with Mama.'

Emerald blinked at this information, not quite sure she had heard correctly. 'Your brother?'

'You know more than one Beau?'

'Of course not. I—I am just surprised, that's all.'

Louisa had returned to her own seat and was busy cutting her slice of ham when she spoke. 'He's got quite the refined eye. When I was struggling to choose between this necklace and the bracelet, it was his idea to simply get both, reasoning both would flatter you in equal measure, and to leave one behind would be a crime to your beauty.'

She blushed. 'He never said as much.'

'You're right,' replied Louisa, lifting a forkful of eggs. 'He was far more eloquent.'

'I thought perhaps we might see him this morning.'

At this, Louisa lifted her gaze, her mouth going still like she'd forgotten about the food she was chewing. 'Hm.' It was the most she could say without being able to speak. But her sparkling eyes, and the smile she fought to control lest she reveal her mouthful of breakfast, said plenty.

Emerald had thought to ask where he was but reconsidered under Louisa's assessing stare. She sipped her coffee, pushed her eggs from one side of the plate to the other, and finally excused herself from the table.

She took the long way to her room, passing the library, the music room, the study, the billiards room. If Beau was at home, the only place remaining in which she might find him was his bedchamber. The door, however, was closed. Even if it had been open, it was not as if she would push in and demand a proposal.

It had been silly to think he would waste no time in securing her hand. If that were even what he wished to do. The night before, she'd felt so sure of it, but the longer the day drew on without sight or sound of his person, the more confused Emerald became.

Emerald walked into the music room but couldn't sit on the bench without thinking of the evening before, and so left to take a turn in the garden. The air was cool, and she hadn't brought her gloves outside. She looked to the windows of the library, feeling for a moment as though someone was watching her. No one was there, and she retreated inside once more, passing the library once again on her way to her chambers.

She couldn't continue to haunt the corridors like some spectre, so took a seat at the little writing table in her room and stared at the window until Gwen came in to help her ready for dinner.

The maid had set out Emerald's new dress, a champagne-coloured silk gown overlayed with an ivory gauze intricately embroidered with spangles and pearls and tiny crystals, which caught the light at every angle. Emerald wore her new necklace from Louisa, and Gwen used diamond pins to keep Emerald's black curls in place.

The lady's maid sighed when she stepped back. 'Oh, miss. I've never seen such a sight. You look like an angel.'

'Thank you, Gwen. But I must give you all the credit.'

Gwen waved this comment away and retreated to the dressing room to hang Emerald's day dress, leaving Emerald to study herself in the mirror. This was what she had always dreamed of as a little girl: the beautiful gowns and jewels and an elegant townhouse in the fashionable part of London. And yet, she still felt something was missing. Knew it to be so.

Lady Avon had organised a small family affair with all of Emerald's favourites for her birthday. They would no longer cross the square after dinner for a ball at the Duke and Duchess of Hazelhurst's home, but Emerald had assured the dowager she was robust enough to dine as planned. She was the only one present in the drawing room when Emerald entered before dinner. Lady Avon complimented Emerald on her appearance and gave her a beautiful leatherbound copy of her favourite book and a pair of stunning diamond and pearl drop earrings.

'Your husband will buy you all the jewels you could wish for, but I am happy to help you begin your collection,' the dowager stated with a pat of Emerald's hand and satisfied inspection of the earrings that Emerald had just donned.

Louisa entered a moment later, and the dowager rose. 'It's just us for dinner. Beau wrote of some business keeping him.'

Emerald swallowed the lump forming in her throat. She had attained her majority and was free to do as she pleased, as was he. To her mind, there was no other explanation for his absence: He regretted his noble speech, his actions at the masquerade, and everything he'd done after.

Every course had been planned with Emerald in mind, and she made a credible show of savouring her favourites and keeping up with the discussion happening around her, or so she hoped. Each time the door opened, Emerald held her breath, only to release a disappointed sigh when it was a footman there to carry a new dish in or a dirty plate out.

The table was cleared of the main dishes and the tablecloth, and Wallace set out the dessert service along with elegant crystal flutes he filled with champagne. At the head of the table, a footman set a fourth plate, and Emerald stared at it so hard it might have shattered from the force of her gaze. The door opened, and the wild beat of her heart told her it was him.

Beau stood at the threshold, outfitted in the aubergine coat he'd worn the night of the masquerade, and her heart jumped from her chest to her stomach and back again. He greeted them, then went to stand behind his chair at the head of the table and raised the champagne glass the butler had handed to him.

'To Emerald.'

'To you, dearest,' echoed the dowager.

'You look beautiful tonight.' One corner of his mouth tipped with a sensuous lilt, and his vivid eyes were full of appreciation, adoration, assurance.

Emerald sucked in a bottomless breath, awed by his candour. The words made her feel pulled open, like he could see through her pale dress and straight down to the muscle, sinew, and marrow that was sewn together to make her who she was.

Her cheeks flamed, and her head dropped, the only safe place to look being the empty plate set before her. When she once more felt in control of herself, she lifted her face. In the centre of the table sat a large white cake topped with wild strawberries. She knew that when she took a bite, a hint of rhubarb would prickle her tongue. Her lip quivered, and she was terrified to look at Beau, to come undone at the table.

'Happy birthday, Emerald.'

His voice, so soft, so earnest, was more than Emerald could bear. She brought her napkin up to cover her face, insensible to Lady Avon ushering Louisa out of the room, insensible to Beau coming to her side, insensible to everything except this one little gesture that broke her in two.

'What's all this, my brave love?'

She felt the napkin being pried from her hands and her hands from her face. When she opened her eyes, the only thing she saw was Beau kneeling in front of her, looking at her with such concern she swallowed convulsively to avoid another outburst.

'I don't understand. After last night, I thought— But then today, you've avoided me all day—and, and now the cake, the coat. You haven't said a word about the masquerade.' She sniffled and stammered through her incoherent speech, all the while unsure if she wanted to pull her hands from his or fling herself into his embrace.

'You didn't think I'd called you into the sunroom simply to tell you it was one of my favourites, did you? The moment I saw you in the foyer, resplendent in that blue dress, I couldn't keep away. Only my plans to speak with you were interrupted. And I have not been avoiding you. It took me until about an hour ago to come up with enough wild strawberries to cover the top of your cake. No little feat, that, in the city in early spring. There was another little errand as well,' he said, removing a small box from his coat pocket. He opened it, revealing the most magnificent emerald ring she'd ever seen. The stone was the deep green of oakmoss and set between two glittering diamonds.

She slipped from her chair and onto the ground in front of him, her knees touching his. Her lips parted in surprise, but she said nothing. His eyes caught hers, dropping for a moment to her lips. Beau reached up, taking her cheek in his palm, sweeping his thumb along her smooth skin in slow, appreciative strokes.

She pressed herself into the warm comfort of his hand. He threaded his fingers into her hair, his gentle touch sending chills cascading down her body. Emerald studied him, his uncompromising jaw, generous lips, and sharp blue eyes mellowed with desire.

'Are you going to kiss me?' Her words came out whispered, as if stuck in the thick breaths getting caught in her lungs.

'Do you wish me to?'

She trembled as her body burned with the memory of the masquerade. For so long, she'd hungered to feel his mouth on her. Emerald had wanted to know what it would be like to be kissed by him since she'd first thought about being kissed by anyone. In her imagination he tasted cool and crisp, like the early morning air of a late December day.

'Desperately.'

He dropped the ring box and rose to his knees, taking her with him. A possessive arm gently pinned her to him, careful of the bandages hidden under layers of cream silk. Against her, she felt his body quake with restraint. Her breathing was laboured as his lips descended slowly but with purpose to meet her own. Emerald had lived with wonder for so long, she feared she might swoon with anticipation before she tasted him.

He claimed her mouth in a kiss, warm, tender, lingering. His tongue traced the soft shape of her lips, coaxing her to open for him, and he swallowed her gasp with a hungry moan. Her body melted from the heady sensation of passion. She yielded to the light pressure, to the dizzying tremors thrumming through her body. The tip of his tongue found hers, encouraging it in gentle demand. She responded by drawing his lower lip between her teeth with a teasing graze.

On a groan, he pulled back, letting his forehead rest against hers, as breathless from the kiss as she. When she licked her lips, she could taste his subtle, surprising sweetness of vanilla and oak. He took her hand in his own and placed it upon his chest. Against her palm, she felt the eager beat of his heart calling to her like an echo in time, as if she'd lived the moment a hundred different ways in a hundred different lives.

'This is yours, if you'll have me. If you'll marry me and let me love you forever, even when we're long-forgotten dust in the crypt.'

She pulled the ring from the box and slipped it over her finger.

'You promise to love me forever, but I have loved you that long already.' Her voice hitched, and she felt the violent sting of tears behind her eyes.

Beau's cheeks creased with a smile. 'Is that a yes?' he asked, taking her hands in his own and gathering her to everything he was in the living world and beyond.

She was overcome and nodded her acceptance through a burst of emotion. 'Beau.' Emerald breathed his name, releasing years of loneliness and longing.

Her fragile voice seemed to fracture his restraint, and he crushed her to him. His mouth consumed her, claiming her as his to love and cherish, to ignite with wonder and joy. She shivered and let her hands find their way into his dusky, thick hair, her fingers curling round the tendrils on passionate instinct. His hand dropped to her backside, and he pulled her to him as if he could fold their two bodies into one. Pressed to her belly, the hard length of his arousal. She reached for him, desperate to feel more of his body. He moaned her name when her hands caressed him through the silk of his knee breeches.

There was a pulsing ache at the juncture of her legs. She begged him for release.

'Emerald,' he cautioned in a husky voice.

'Please.'

He seared a path of kisses down her neck to the hollow of her collarbone, lifting her skirts as he did so. His thumb rolled over the swollen bud of her pleasure. Her belly swooped and a sudden rush of warmth spread outward from her core. He caressed her in long, even strokes, stoking the ecstasy building within her.

'More,' she panted, clutching at Beau's shoulders to stabilise herself against the mounting pleasure.

Emerald mewled when he responded by tracing a deft finger along her folds, slick with moisture. She wriggled as he teased her entrance and shuddered when he finally slipped the tip of his finger inside, working a little more in each time he withdrew. His mouth reclaimed her lips, and she kissed him back with all the aching need coiling in her body. Her hips rocked by instinct, her mound pressing into the fleshy heel of his palm with every move. Little tremors shook her whole body. A sob of desperation broke their kiss. Just as she reached the crest of pleasure, he removed his hand entirely.

Emerald cried out, on the brink of demanding he finish what he'd started, when she felt two fingers instead of one trailing her wet centre. He traced her from her core to her sensitive bud, his fingers gliding over it again and again, the action short and quick. She rode hard against him and gasped as every muscle began to seize, her nerves stroked to a frenzy. His fingers came away a second time, but she had hardly registered their absence before he eased them both into her needy core. Her body tensed at the intrusion, the momentary discomfort as her untried passage adjusted. But the fullness was delicious. She writhed against him in a silent plea. He began to pump his fingers in an agonising rhythm. When he brought his thumb to hover over her bud, she came apart at the seams, burying her face in the soft fabric taut over his shoulder to stifle her cry of delight. His hands continued to play her, and she bit down, her body convulsing with every touch. The unbearable pressure of pleasure coursed through her veins, and Emerald was left undone in his arms.

Beau wrapped himself around her, his heart beating as hard as hers, and dropped kisses into her mussed hair. Emerald didn't know how long they stayed that way, only that being held by him was her most favourite thing in the world.

'Let us agree on a short betrothal,' remarked Beau, tidying the curls he'd loosened and smoothing her skirts.

Emerald straightened his cravat and brushed his wayward strands off his forehead. She hoped she only looked as dishev-elled as a woman newly engaged who had been kissed merci-lessly and not a woman who would have allowed her betrothed to take her right there on the floor had he been less of a gentleman. Then, she took his sculpted cheeks between her palms and kissed him before rising on unsteady legs. The surprise of her sudden movements was evident on her love's face.

'Where are you going?'

'To arrange the chessboard. If you win, we may set the date. If I win, you teach me how to do that thing you did to the dreadful man in the alleyway that day in Ramsgate.'

EPILOGUE

*E*merald sailed into the study at Oakmoss, her lips set firm with determination. The dowager and Louisa were out paying calls, and her husband wasn't due home for some hours still. He'd been gone a sennight at the Duke of Cudworth's, where he was collecting some sort of intelligence for Lord Duffy under the guise of attending a hunting party.

In the weeks following the debacle at the theatre, her husband had resigned from his role within the Home Office, or rather he had attempted to. Beau was resolved in his decision —said it was past time he stepped away—but Emerald knew he was doing it for her and couldn't bear to watch melancholy tug at his handsome features as he reconciled himself to life as a country gentleman.

Between her firm encouragement and Lord Duffy's reluctance to part with one of his best men, Beau gladly agreed to work domestically, spying on the gentry in a capacity which would keep him safer and much closer to home.

Home. The word had taken on new meaning since her marriage. For so long Emerald had lived in the in-between.

She ran her hand over the polished wood of the desk, *her* desk as much as it ever was Beau's. As she came around to take a seat, her stare drifted to the wax stamper he gave to her on their wedding day. On it, an oak tree with *E.C.* tangled in its roots. Emerald pressed a finger against the little hollow under her eyes to stop the tears that formed every time she dwelled too long in her happiness, in the unfamiliar security of knowing she was forever a part of the family she'd loved for so many years already.

Settling herself, Emerald plucked a clean sheet of paper from a drawer and tucked the top edge a little under the book open that sat on the desk to hold the sheet steady. She splayed one hand across the pages to keep the volume open and cast a quick glance over the recipe, licking her lips as she did so. The rose and thyme drops were one of her favourite sweet treats, and she had promised to share the recipe with a friend. Dipping her pen in the inkpot to her right, she began to copy the list of ingredients.

As she wrote, she ran through a list of everything else she hoped to get done before everyone returned and the house bustled with life once more. On a breath, she caught hints of oak and spiced vanilla in the still air around her.

'How long have you been watching me?' she called out without looking up, the smile on her face warming her voice.

'Long enough to be pleased with myself,' answered her husband with a chuckle.

Her eyes came away from her elegant, even lines when she heard the hush of the door closing and the click of the lock. Beau sauntered towards her, still dressed in his riding clothes, his glacial blue eyes warm and mischievous.

'Are you this very moment returned?' Emerald couldn't keep the surprise from her question, even though whenever he returned from a trip he always found her for a kiss before retreating to wash the travel off. She wasn't sure the novelty of him belonging to her would ever wear away, nor did she wish it to. 'You must've spent the last four or five hours on horseback.'

'Just over three. Arion would be offended to know how little you think of him.

'Which would you like first, a bath or refreshment?' she asked, setting her pen down.

'Neither. You're my first order of business.'

He came round the desk and pulled her chair out.

'I'm in the middle of copying a recipe for the Duchess of Hazelhurst, and after that, I've got a list of improvements to the attics from Mrs Marshall to review, and then an article on selective breeding Sims left for me to read,' she replied, doing her best to imitate the haughty manner her husband was known for but hearing the huskiness creep in as she undressed him with her eyes.

'How about a little wager, my love?' Beau slipped between Emerald and the desk and knelt down in front of her, squeezing her hips in his hands and pulling her forward till her bottom nearly came off the seat. 'If you can finish copying your recipe before I make you call out my name, I will take myself off forthwith and leave you to your lists and articles.'

Her eyes narrowed, but she smiled. 'I won't ask what you get if I win. The recipe is quite short—it would be a feat even for a man of your skill.' Although as she said so, the thought of her husband touching her quickened her pulse.

Beau slid his hands under her skirts, grazing the back of her calves with his fingertips and trailing them up to draw circles on the underside of her knees. The light touch prickled her skin.

'When I win,' he began, his hands finding their way to her thighs and opening them. 'You are mine the rest of the day, work be dammed.' He smoothed his hands up to the creases of her legs, pushing her dress up in the process.

Emerald opened her mouth to reply, but the only sound that came out was a quivering whimper as Beau glided a thumb over the bud at her centre.

'Am I to take that as your agreement?'

'Certainly. Only, I can't—' The gentle heat of his tongue on her sex made it impossible for her to concentrate on what she was saying. Her head tipped back against the smooth leather of the chair, and her eyes drifted close. She tried to shut her mouth, but found it impossible to keep up with her increasingly rapid breaths.

He paused only long enough to ask, 'Can't what, my love?' Beau caressed her in slow, firm strokes, cupping her backside and drawing her more fully to his mouth.

Emerald felt the aching anticipation building with every sweep of his tongue, every flick of its tip. 'Can't—can't reach the paper—' Beau moaned against her, the vibrations cascading over her in little tremors of pleasure. She dropped her pen, mindless of the ink still in it, and glided a hand along the flesh of her collarbone before her fingers dipped under the edge of her bodice to tease her own painfully taut nipple. He skimmed the pad of his finger along her entrance, and when he dipped only the very tip into her, her thighs trembled on either side of him.

'Beau, please.'

'Please, what, beautiful bird?' he asked, the tip of his finger still teasing her.

Emerald writhed, trying to take more than he was willing to give. 'Please. You. Inside me.'

On a throaty groan, he rose and lifted her, knocking over the ink pot as he settled her on the desk and positioned himself between her legs. Her eyes lingered a moment on the hardness constrained by his breeches before her hands took over, undoing the buttons with frantic efficiency while his own tugged the bodice of her dress down to free her breasts. He bent to take the rosy peak of her nipple into his mouth, and she moaned when he swirled his tongue around one and then marched across the valley of her breast to the other before working his way up the sensitive bare skin of her neck. The action had forced her back onto her elbows, and when her husband came away, she watched him release the last button of his breeches and push the fabric down his hips with hungry eyes. He let his length rest on the springy curls between her legs, gliding it back and forth and stoking the heat building within her.

She wanted to push up into him, but had no leverage with her legs dangling from the edge of the desk, and was on the verge of begging for more when Beau wrapped her leg around his waist and took himself in hand, tracing her entrance with the warm, soft head of his cock.

'Bring your other leg up,' he whispered, and she followed his command, encircling him with her long limbs.

He pushed the tip in. She whimpered with desire just as he withdrew, dragging the head along her seam before slipping into her once more. Emerald dug her heels into his backside, urging him to fill her completely, but he resisted, and his lips quirked in a sensual smile. She reached for the lapels of the coat he was still wearing and drew him to her until his soft lips met hers, and he was parting them with his tongue to taste her. Another inch of his hardness pressed in, and she mewled on his bottom lip caught between her teeth. With wicked slow-ness, he let the rest of his length fill her.

'Is this what you want, my love?' he asked, hot breath tick-ling the shell of her ear and making her shudder beneath him.

Emerald panted something like *Yes* and moved her hips in little circles, desperate for more sensation while her husband remained still inside her. Just as she thought she might go mad with anticipation, he pulled out as slowly as he'd entered her, maintaining his deliberate, unhurried manner while stroking the wild need growing inside her.

Her hands snaked around his neck, and Beau bent his fore-head to rest on hers. Her legs twitched and shook where they were hooked around him. She let out desperate little cries each time he withdrew, and she welcomed him deep within.

'So close,' she panted. 'More, Beau. I need more.'

Beau smothered his own growl as he kissed her again, hard and probing, and brought her to her peak with quick, demanding thrusts. Emerald cried out. Her whole body weightless and humming with exquisite bliss. A moment later, her husband called out her name in a blistering moan. She felt his cock swell and the warm release inside her. His thrusts slowed before stopping, but they remained joined as he folded over her, nuzzling her neck and kissing whatever skin he could reach.

'Did you find what you were looking for at the Duke of Cudworth's?' Emerald asked, loving the uneven feel of her husband's chest against hers as they both worked to catch their breath. She could hear the smile in his voice when he spoke.

'I did. I'll tell you all about it after a bath.'

Emerald played with the soft curls at the base of his neck.

'I'll ring the bell just as soon as I can move and have the footmen fill your tub.'

'You mistake me, my love,' said Beau, pushing off the desk and pulling his wife up with him. 'I believe I won the wager. They might bring the water, but it's you who will fill the tub.'

Her eyes went as round as two saucers.

'I'm disappointed in myself for not acting on such an idea sooner,' he said, shaking out her skirts and beginning to right the bodice of her dress.

'Sooner? When did it first occur to you?'

He glanced up from efforts, a wolfish smile on his handsome face. 'The day you snuck into my room and hid under my bed.'

Emerald's mouth made a little 'o', and Beau laughed as he tucked himself back into his breeches, took her hand, and led her from the study.

ALSO BY GEORGINA NORTH

ACKNOWLEDGMENTS

This book has lived many lives—one where the reader met Emerald as a young girl, one where Beau was engaged to someone else, none where he was a spy until this one.

During each step in every iteration, there were people helping me discover a little piece of something missing: Joanna Hinsey, Beth Stedman, my Auntie Reen. My editors—Sarah Pesce, Amy Scott, Lee Tipton. The woman who crafted this stunning cover, Jennifer Therieau.

A special thanks to my friends and family, to the strangers at grocery stores, restaurants, airports, who have to repeat themselves because I can't hear what they're saying over the characters speaking in my head.

As always, a special thanks to my husband, Keola, who ignores me when I'm working unless it's to tell me breakfast, lunch, or dinner is ready, which is the greatest gift a writer can ask for.

The biggest thank you of all goes to you, my dear readers. With so many books in the world to choose from, I'm humbled you picked mine to spend some time with.

ABOUT THE AUTHOR

Georgina North lives in Southern California with her husband and their two cats. When she's not curled up with her laptop and a cup of coffee, you can find her daydreaming in her favourite chair, eating fish tacos, or adding more books to her to-read pile.

Be the first to know!
Sign up for Georgina's newsletter
to receive updates
on new releases and more.

www.georginanorth.com

Printed in Great Britain
by Amazon